Praise for *Wife With Knife*

Molly Giles' stories have always been among my favorites since I first read her work thirty-seven years ago. This collection is her best ever. What an irreverent original voice! I found myself gasping in shock and laughter, feeling at the end of each tale that I had garnered strange wisdom on the human heart and its unerring sense for finding trouble.
Amy Tan, author of *The Joy Luck Club*

The reader experiences an immediate immersion into the story and characters' lives . . . This partially comes about through masterful first lines.
Cris Mazza, 2020 Leapfrog Global Fiction Prize Judge, author of *How to Leave a Country*

With insightful prose and a sharp sense of humor, Molly Giles once again reminds us why she is one of the best short story writers writing today. Whether it is the tale of the beleaguered artist's wife angered by being overlooked or the quick sketch of two teenage girls offering a silent protest in the middle of a busy road, Giles' fantastic use of voice will have you clearly recognizing these characters and their frustrations. Smart and original, these stories capture the wild interior lives of people on the verge.
Luisa Smith, Buying Director, Book Passage Bookstore

THE HOME FOR UNWED HUSBANDS

MOLLY GILES

Also by the author

Wife With Knife
Winner of the Leapfrog Global Fiction Prize for Fiction
Rough Translations
Winner of the Flannery O'Connor Award for Short Fiction
Creek Walk And Other Stories
Iron Shoes, A Novel
Bothered
All the Wrong Places
Winner of the Spokane Prize for Short Fiction

THE HOME FOR UNWED HUSBANDS

MOLLY GILES

Leapfrog Press
New York and London

First published in paperback in the United States by Leapfrog Press, 2023
Leapfrog Press Inc.

www.leapfrogpress.com

Cover design: James Shannon
Author portrait © Stephanie Mohan

Typesetting: Prepress Plus

ISBN: 978-1-948585-55-1 (paperback)
ISBN: 978-1-911673-56-9 (eBook)

987654321

Printed and bound in the United Kingdom

The Forest Stewardship Council® is an international
non-governmental organisation that promotes environmentally
appropriate, socially beneficial, and economically viable management of
the world's forests. To learn more visit www.fsc.org

To Ellen

I got a right in this crazy world
To live my life like anyone else...

Neil Young

WEEK ONE

Rat-a-tat. Rat-a-tat. RAT-A-TAT-TAT-TAT.

Kay reached for a pillow and pulled it back over her head. Someone at her door at 6:30 a.m.? Her rent was paid, she had no debts; she wasn't married to Neal anymore and didn't have to fear collectors. Maybe Nicky had come home early from his overnight? But Nicky had a key. Was the building on fire? Had there been a shoot-out in the neighborhood? As she shrugged into her robe she remembered: Charles! Charles always dropped by early. Breakfast was his favorite meal and he liked to sit and eat toast with her and Nicky and tell them about the paintings he'd been working on all night in his studio. He must be back from Bangkok! Kay pushed a hand through her tangled hair and, smiling, ran barefoot to the door.

"Uh-oh," she said, the minute she opened it. "What's wrong?"

"Now why," her father asked, "would anything be wrong?" He adjusted his gold-rimmed glasses, leaned down to peer at her, and frowned. Kay knew what he was seeing: a forty-four-year-old divorced single mother with bad breath and smudged mascara in a torn flannel bathrobe with choo-choo trains across it. Thank God he can't see my tattoo, she thought. Not that it would matter. Her father's opinion of her couldn't get much lower. He had never liked her. Which was too bad, because, Kay couldn't help it, she had always sort of liked him. She closed in for an awkward bump against his shoulder, and stepped aside to let him into the apartment.

"It's just that I've scarcely seen you since your marriage," she said. She paused. "What are you doing here?"

Francis didn't answer, merely tipped his head and cupped one hand around his ear.

"You're raising chickens now, are you?"

"Oh, you mean because of the rooster? That's just Diablo. He crows all day long. But he's not staying. The Sanchezes next door are taking care of him until their son gets back from ... " better not say *prison* ... "this place he's staying."

"And your son? My only grandson? Nicholas? Where is he?"

"Nicky spent the night with his friend Tico."

"Ah," Francis said and Kay knew what he was thinking. Her father was an unapologetic racist. She could not understand why he had not been shot dead through the heart long ago. She shifted her weight and dropped her eyes to his polished loafers.

"Tico is the chess champion of the middle school," she said stiffly. She hurried to make coffee and sweep the unpaid bills, half-finished sketches, and tangled wad of knitting off the kitchen table while Francis scrutinized the apartment. She saw his eyes move from the cheap aluminum-framed windows to the dimpled ceiling with its flecks of glitter to the cupboard doors scarred by a previous tenant's pitbull. An architect, her father made no attempt to hide his contempt for her place. He rapped the kitchen walls for studs, kicked the molding, tapped a loose light fixture. He took no notice of the herbs and bright flowers she'd planted on the windowsill, ignored Charles's oil paintings on the walls, glanced only briefly at Nicky's straight-A report card on the refrigerator. He clearly did not care that this was the best place she could afford on her salary, and she was not surprised when he turned from scraping loose grout out of the kitchen tiles with his pocketknife to say, "I want you to move." What did surprise her was the one word he added: "Back."

"Back where?"

"To the castle."

Kay shivered. She would never return to the huge house on the mountain where she and her brother Victor had grown up. Just thinking about it made her blood run cold. She watched her father light a cigarette, smiled politely, and said, "No thanks."

Francis nodded. Perhaps he had not heard her. Francis often didn't hear the things she said. It wasn't that he was deaf. His ears, small and elegant, worked just fine. He heard other people. She tucked her hands under her armpits so she wouldn't start to pick at her cuticles and raised her chin to look into his eyes, appalled to find herself staring at his cigarette instead. She jerked her head away and shut her eyes quickly. She had thrown her last pack away seventeen days ago.

"I thought you quit," he said. "Look, the castle's sitting empty. I've been paying a small fortune for security guards but that's hardly a satisfactory arrangement. The place needs to go on the market soon and the realtor thinks it would sell faster if a family lived in it. Glo won't live there. Ever since she saw the 'ghost,' my child bride won't even step inside. So now that we've decided to stay in Carmel ... "

"You hate Carmel."

"Well, that may be as that may be but we have nonetheless bought a place there and I need to sell the castle. We only drove up to Marin this morning to meet the realtor and authorize a few repairs. I'd like you and Nicky to care-take the place until it sells. It will be a chance for you to save money and it might even keep Nicky from joining *Nuestra Familia*, at least until he's twelve."

"No," Kay repeated, a bit louder. "Coffee?" she added, handing him a cup.

"I'm offering you a free place to live, completely furnished, as you will recall, with a swimming pool, garage, satellite TV, internet, pool table, rose garden, security alarm, all utilities paid, your own old Chickering piano, and—" his eyes fell pointedly on a pile of laundry she had tried to kick out of sight into a corner, "a washer/dryer. Plus, the advantage of the best school district in the county, which has to be a marked improvement on Ghetto Grammatico or wherever it is that you've enrolled Nicky. What's not to like?"

"Memories?"

"Memories are what you make them, Kay."

Kay shook her head. She'd spent the first eighteen years of her life trying to get out of the castle—those cold rooms, marble floors, creaking stairs. Why go back now, in her forties? Why subject her son to it? She'd made a home for them here. So what if the apartment was small and shabby and cheaply built? It was theirs; they had made it theirs.

"Did you ask Victor?" She offered her brother's name, but without hope.

"Of course not. Victor's useless."

And I'm not? Kay thought.

"Not yet," her father answered. "But," he stubbed his cigarette out in his saucer, "if you don't want to."

"I don't want to." Looking up at the row of cookbooks on the kitchen shelf, Kay saw *Ninety-Nine Ways to Say No* and gasped with relief—so that's where it was, safely tucked between *Mindfulness for Beginners* and *Fitness for Dummies*. She hadn't lost it! She wouldn't have to order a replacement copy for the library and pay for it out of her own pocket. Now if only she could remember some of the things the book said …

"I don't feel comfortable moving back to the castle," she began. "I feel returning to live there at this point in time will compromise my life goals and chances for successful individuation."

"Oh my," Francis said.

Kay flushed but plowed on. "I have to think of my own needs right now, Dad, and right now I need to focus on my ... " she stalled. Career? Her job at the West Valley branch library was being threatened by county cutbacks. Her music? The only place she played the piano these days was at the department store on Sundays. Her personal life? Her boyfriend—if that's what Fenton was—had not phoned all week. Her son? Nicky was in his last few months of sixth grade, playing soccer, learning guitar, doing fine. Her mental health, emotional stability, inner growth, spiritual development? Francis would hoot. She swallowed and hurried on. "It's not about the castle. The castle is great. I mean, you designed it! It's a beautiful building! It's won awards! This is about me. No. Not really." She stopped, took a gamble. "It's about Mom."

"She'd be glad to hear that," Francis said. "She died, you know."

"I know. But she died in the castle."

"Don't tell me you're afraid of ghosts, too."

"Of course not," Kay lied.

"Because we've all got to die somewhere. You want to die here?"

"Nicky and I are happy here."

"Nonsense. Nicky's happy everywhere and you've never been happy a day of your life."

"That's not true!" Kay flared.

"What?"

"Nothing."

"I wish you'd learn to speak up, Kay."

"I said I've been happy in lots of places."

"As well you should be. It's a big, wide, wonderful world. Correct?"

"I don't know."

15

"What?"

"I said I don't know. I've never been anywhere."

"Mutter mutter." Francis set down his untouched cup, turned and walked toward the door. With one hand on the knob, he paused. "When was the last time I asked you to do something for me?"

"You asked me not to come to Christmas dinner," Kay reminded him. "You asked me not to come to Easter brunch."

Francis made a dismissive wave. "That was Glo. No one does what Glo says. Glo was just mad because you divorced Neal. Why *did* you divorce Neal? Never mind, I never knew what you saw in Neal in the first place. But the point is, you *do* know the castle. You've always taken good care of the castle."

Was that a compliment? Apparently not, for he continued, "And who knows? Once you start taking care of the castle, you might start taking care of yourself."

"I am taking care of myself, Dad."

"By living in a chicken coop? By reading Dale Carnegie books? This is not the way I want you to live. It is not the way I want my grandson to live." He clucked his tongue and then, alarmingly, did the strangest thing she had ever seen him do. He opened his arms and held them out. Was he offering a hug? Her father didn't hug. Yet there he stood, head cocked, waiting, his lips lifted below his short military mustache in what could, possibly, pass for a smile.

"Stop," Kay warned. "You're scaring me."

"I'm scaring myself. Look. I'm in a bind here. And I need you to help me out." He paused, and then, and it could not have been an act, he began to cough, a long sick cough that that drew his thin shoulders inward. Without thinking, Kay moved swiftly to his side. She did not embrace him, she knew better than that, but she stood close with a warm, steady hand on his arm until the cough at last subsided. The familiar smells of lemon soap and tobacco filled her lungs and her love for this mean old man brought tears to her eyes, even as she dropped her hand. She watched as Francis, pale but with scarlet cheeks, pressed a monogrammed handkerchief to his throat. He was working her, she knew. But what could she do? She had never been able to say no to anyone who claimed they needed her. She would just have to stall.

"So," she began, "you're saying you want Nicky and me to caretake the castle until it sells?"

"That's right."

"What then?"

"Then," Francis said, looking a little surprised, "I'll cut you into a percentage of the sale. You'll be able to buy your own house. That's what you want, isn't it?"

"Yes." It was her turn to be surprised. "Yes, that's exactly what I want." She paused. "How much?"

"How much what?"

"Percentage."

"I don't know. We'll figure that out later."

"No. Now."

"Have I never not been fair?" Francis said. Before she could counter, he said "Good-o," and extended one cold, white, freckled hand, adorned with the golden owl ring Glo had given him as a wedding present. Kay had no choice but to take it. They shook. Then he turned her hand over. "Still cannibalizing your cuticles, I see."

"It keeps my weight down."

"Apparently it does nothing of the sort." In two quick motions, her father produced a heavy set of house keys, pressed them into her palm and turned to leave.

"Hey," she said, "I didn't agree."

"You didn't disagree."

"I need to know more! At least let me know how long you think it will be?" He didn't answer, so she raised her voice. "How long will it take for the castle to sell?"

"Who knows? Six weeks? Six years? That dump isn't for everyone, is it?"

"Six *years*?" Kay watched his nimble exit down the front stairs toward the black Jaguar in the parking lot. Someone was waiting inside it. Glo? Her evil stepmother refusing to come in and say hello? She kicked the door closed. She was not going to do this. No one should have to go home again. That was the bottom line. No one should have to go back to a place where they had been miserable. She hugged herself. If only Charles was here. He would understand. *I was a slave in that castle*, she would tell him. *I had to vacuum and dust and scrub the floors, I had to wash the windows and do the laundry and make the beds, I had to cook all the meals, iron all the clothes, do all the dishes. And if I go back? I will be a slave again!*

But Charles had heard all this, a hundred times, and Charles was gone. She hadn't heard from him in months. And anyway, she knew what he'd say: He'd remind her that she was not a child anymore. Confront your father, he'd say. Tell him the deal is off.

She plopped down in a kitchen chair, retrieved the mail she had cleared off the table, and looked at it dully—a bill from Nicky's orthodontist for another two thousand dollars, two creditors wanting to know how to reach Neal, an advertisement for some symphony tickets she craved and could not afford. She had never asked Francis for a loan—and never would—she had seen all too clearly how indebtedness to their father had damaged Victor—and she had been proud of being able to support Nicky on her own. But she hadn't been able to plan for his future and she had not even come close to saving enough for a down payment on a house. Reaching for a pen, she tried to figure out how much she could put away if they lived rent free for a few months— quite a bit—and then, when the castle sold ... and it was in an exclusive neighborhood on the mountain and must be worth a lot ... and Francis had, yes, always been "fair," financially at least, so she would surely get at least twenty percent of the profits ... then she might indeed have enough to buy a small house. And how terrible would returning to the castle actually be? Wasn't she being overdramatic? Her mother was gone—hopefully—so there should be no more tantrums in the morning or rants in the afternoon or sobs at night; Kay would not have to push Ida's wheelchair or wash her hair or sing her to sleep. Nicky would be in an excellent school, with a real music department and a champion softball team. She would have a slightly longer commute to the West Valley Library, but she would be going against the traffic ...

She examined the set of keys on the table. Front door, back door, pool house, garden shed. She had always loved the garden shed, cool and dim, light falling through the leaded windows in colored shafts. She had hidden there for hours as a child. And the pool—perfect for Nicky, good exercise for her sore shoulder, a wonderful place to swim at night, naked, looking up at the stars. The tiered decks bordered with tea roses in their terra cotta pots would be a joy to care for. The grove of ancient redwood trees was shady and fragrant. Her turret bedroom opened onto a view of the mountain and her secret perch on the slanted slate roof was perfect for moon gazing. Her beloved Chickering piano was still in the music room! She could bang out Bach as loudly as she wanted, bothering no one. But the winds that came at night. The cold smell of stone. The ghosts ... .

She picked Francis's half-smoked cigarette out of the saucer, rose to light it at the stove, took a deep drag, immediately felt dizzy, and inhaled again. The castle had five bedrooms, a maid's room, a butler's pantry, a dungeon, a keep. The kitchen had granite counters and a Wolf range and every bathroom had a bidet. The doors had been widened to accommodate her mother's wheelchair and there were railings in the showers. As for "ghosts"—that was ridiculous. And anyway, she could sage the place. Hire an exorcist. Rent a karaoke machine. Invite her friends Zabeth and Dana over to belt out "I Will Survive" and shimmy to Zumba until every vestige of her first eighteen years was eradicated. She could lure Fenton into having hot sex to sanctify every room. Nicky's friends could rattle dust from the rafters with their raucous boy energy. She could cook fabulous meals, host great parties. This was an opportunity to bury her past and be reborn, like her righteous brother Victor, the militant Christian. Rise from the ashes, like this, her final cigarette.

She extinguished it under the faucet, coughed, and recited an impromptu affirmation: *I am an intelligent adult. I am the respected and efficient director of a fine public library. I am the lucky mother of a beautiful boy. I worked full-time while putting myself through college and graduate school. I got out of a disastrous marriage in one piece. I have not had a drink for twenty-eight months and I have just quit smoking. I am not dominated by my addictions. I have the ability to make my own decisions. I have decided to return to the castle not because I am a weak stupid helpless idiot with a lifelong history of trying and failing to please my father, but because ...* She paused, shook her head to clear it and finished up: *but because I am a smart, savvy, and sensible woman who wants to buy her own home and is willing to take risks to get it.*

She sat down and reached for the sketches scattered across the kitchen table—drawing after drawing of the dream houses that she and Nicky had designed together. She picked one of them up—an old-fashioned bungalow with a red roof and green shutters, a garden full of flowers, a basketball hoop over the garage door, a piano in the parlor, a puppy on the porch, an apple pie cooling on the window ledge, cheesy as hell and hokey as heaven. She smiled as she set it aside and reached down to retrieve the yarn basket she had shoved under a chair. She was knitting three rows a day on an alpaca scarf for Charles, hoping to have it finished by the time he returned. She'd chosen a rich amber colored wool, perfect for Charles' brown eyes and black curls, but the pattern was complicated and she'd already made mistake after mistake. In this morning's clear light, she saw a dropped stitch, a coffee stain, a drop of taco sauce—all things she hadn't seen yesterday, but all fixable, she told herself. She'd simply rip back and start over. You could always start over. She knew because she was a pro at it, had been starting over her whole life.

Diablo crowed, as he did all too often, and she glanced longingly at the cupboard under the sink where she used to keep her breakfast wine, sighed with nostalgia, and rose to shower, dress, and be seized by the day.

Moving day came too soon, but Zabeth and Dana came over to help her pack, and the Sanchezes and the Hoas helped carry the heavier boxes down to the car. "Just so you know," Kay said to Nicky as they drove off with the final load, "tonight we'll be sleeping in the richest neighborhood in the richest county in California."

"So that makes us rich," Nicky said, contented. He gazed out the window, balancing his soccer ball on his lap. "Brilliant."

"What would you do if we really did have a ton of money?"

"I don't know. Save the world or something. Can we stop at McDonald's?"

"Honey. No. You know I hate McDonald's."

"*Hate?*" He grinned at her. "Mom? Did you say *hate?*" He extricated a canister labeled MOM'S HATE JAR from the overflowing box of kitchen goods at his feet and rattled it at her.

"Get a dollar out of my purse," Kay sighed.

"Almost enough for a new skateboard," Nicky crooned, dropping the money in.

Kay reached over and rumpled his hair before he could twist away. He was short for his age, a sturdy boy with hazel eyes like

Neal's, quick fingers like Francis's, and pink cheeks like Victor's. Kay loved all the parts of him she could not stand in his relatives and was frankly relieved to find so few traces of herself in him— he had her unruly hair and her love of music, but he had inherited none of her major character defects and he'd been as calm about this move as he had been about the two others they'd had to make since the divorce. He had no bad memories about his grandmother—Ida had doted on him, as she had on all males— and he had already chosen his room—the downstairs guestroom overlooking the garden. He had set up his computer and hung his Jimi Hendrix posters on the wall. He did not have to change schools until the fall, and Kay had made arrangements for Tico to spend the night the following weekend, so hopefully—she crossed her fingers on top of the steering wheel—this transition, for her son at least, would be painless. To make it even more painless, she pulled into a McDonald's, ordered hamburgers and fries for both of them and, eating as they drove, they slowly continued up the mountain toward their new home.

The castle was only six miles from the apartment but those six miles covered a lot of territory. Leaving the freeway, the road wound through a stretch of wooded hills, straightened as it passed through the garden community where her friend Zabeth lived with her pharmacist husband and adopted twin daughters, circled around the stylish industrial complex where her friend Dana had her design studio, plodded past high schools, churches and shopping centers, then zigzagged up the side of the mansion-studded mountain. Hedged with oleander and evergreens, and lined with enormous hybrid Spanish/Japanese/Tudor/Italianate homes, some of which Francis had designed, the road opened to vista after vista of the valley below. Kay felt she had been traveling this road all her life, trudging up it with her backpack when neither parent had remembered to pick her up after school, running down it at night to secretly meet a boyfriend.

She remembered learning to drive with Ida beside her, drunk and laughing, insisting she release the brake and "just take off," and she remembered later teaching Victor how to maneuver the curves in his first car. *Home*, she thought, as the castle appeared at the top. *Where you hang your head.*

"Hooray," Nicky said, as they pulled in, adding, with an anxious sideways glance, "Dad's here."

Kay tried not to groan at the sight of her ex-husband's battered green van at the end of the driveway.

"Came to help, babe," Neal called. He held his thin arms out for a hug and Kay stepped in and out gingerly, glad when Nicky replaced her. Neal, funereal in black jeans and hoodie, his gray ponytail limp over one shoulder, his eyes blurred behind his tinted glasses, looked as unable to "help" as ever, and today, for some reason, he even smelled bad. Hadn't he bathed recently? His voice was so hoarse Kay guessed he hadn't spoken to anyone for days and despite herself she wondered when he had last eaten. The child support payments he had managed to make before he declared bankruptcy had long disappeared. He had lost his frame shop, his plans to develop property in downtown Rancho Valdez had backfired, he had neither patents nor backers for any of his inventions. He had never been a dynamic man but she had never imagined he'd be this defeated. The odd thing was, he didn't seem to mind. He seemed perfectly comfortable with himself, unaware that no one else was.

"Fine," she said, in the bright voice she hated but found herself using with him now, "you could carry in the kitchen things."

She hefted her own suitcase and left Neal and Nicky to unload the other bags from the trunk. The castle, leaded windows glinting, rose tall and gray above her, familiar and formidable. She crossed the cobblestone courtyard and pushed open the massive front door. A wave of stale air, still, she swore, carrying a trace of her mother's *L'heure Bleue*, met her as she stepped inside. Perhaps

23

it came from the oil portrait of Ida that hung crookedly over the baronial fireplace or perhaps from the brocade fainting couch where she used to curl in a Japanese kimono to greet her guests. Glo insisted she had seen Ida's ghost mocking her from the hall mirror, and there was no reason to disbelieve her. Ida had staying power. Kay set her suitcase down and glanced into the hall mirror to reassure herself. Round, rabbity, creased with worry lines and topped by a tangle of brown curls, hers was not a face to haunt anyone. Her hazel eyes and long lashes were okay, she supposed, and so was her rosy skin, but her nose was too small, her mouth too big, her legs too straight, her breasts too heavy, her ankles too thick. *"You're* Ida McLeod's daughter?" she mouthed, repeating the question she had heard so many times. She wound her hair up to show off her long neck and yanked her tee-shirt down to show some good healthy cleavage, began to stick out her tongue, remembered the advice from *Six Steps to Self Esteem,* blew an impatient kiss to her image instead, retrieved her suitcase and crossed through the Great Room to go into the kitchen.

It was clear that Glo had never used it—she and Francis must have gone to restaurants every night of their short tenure here. There was dust on the granite counters, the cupboard doors were sprung, the orchid plants in the alcove were long dead. Kay turned on the faucet to a gush of rusty water and went to help Neal with a box of food she had packed, surprised by its lightness.

"I had to get rid of a few things," Neal explained.

Kay waited.

"Just the white stuff. Your flour. Sugar. Salt. Some of your canned soups had preservatives in them. A lot of your produce wasn't organic. And all those paper products? Babe, you use far too many paper products. And the chemicals in your cleaning supplies?" Neal shuddered.

Kay glanced in the box and saw it contained nothing but a box of Ivory flakes, a few spices and a half empty jar of unsulphured molasses she'd used for gingerbread three Christmases ago. She closed her eyes.

"Where'd you put the rest of my stuff, Neal?"

"Nicky's already genetically predisposed for diabetes, cancer, atherosclerosis, alcoholism and mental illness on your side of the family. You can't continue to feed him junk, Kay. You can't let him eat Happy Meals. You are corrupting his immune system with carcinogens."

"Where did you put the rest of my stuff, Neal?"

"Don't shout. Do you want him to end up like your mother?"

"Did you put them in the garbage bin?"

"I said don't shout."

"Did you?"

"No," Neal said, hurt. "I recycled them."

"Well go cycle them right back in again. Neal? Now! I mean it."

"What were you shouting about?" Nicky asked, coming in with his guitar case.

"Nothing, honey. I dropped something."

"Oh. Good. I thought it was because of Dad's vegetable garden."

Kay, gripping the jar of molasses, froze. "What vegetable garden?"

"It's okay. I talked to Glo," Neal said. "She said it was fine."

"Glo isn't living in the castle. I am. It's my responsibility to take care of it. And I don't want you digging holes all over the place …" Aware of Nicky turning from parent to parent, she stopped, rubbed her forehead. What was Neal doing here anyway? Why could you only divorce the same person once? Divorce should be renewable at every encounter. Her ex-husband still stood in the doorway, round shouldered, slack lipped, slyly smiling. Oh, the wiles of the passive aggressive!

"I've already cleared the space," he said.

"What space?"

"You know that area below the pool area where you used to wheel your mother out to watch the sunset?"

"Neal, you can't plant anything there. That's where Mom's ashes are scattered."

"Huh. Well. I didn't see any. I've already turned the earth and put two bags of horse manure in for you. By summer you and Nicky will be eating fresh vegetables from your own back yard."

"Jesus Christ!" Kay said, her voice rising again. "That's not a *back* yard. That's a *grave*yard!"

"Hey hey! Watch it! No taking the Lord's name in vain. Especially not here, in our family home." Another, deeper, voice came from the hallway and Kay turned to see her brother's handsome face, set in its familiar lines of censure.

"You'd swear too if you heard what Neal just did," she said.

"I would not," Victor corrected her. "I do not," he added to Neal, "tolerate blasphemy."

"He dug Mom up."

Victor turned his frown toward his ex-brother-in-law. What a pair they made: Victor tall, blonde, as clear-eyed and rosy-cheeked at forty as he'd been at four, dressed for his job at the European Used Car Dealership in a light spring suit and pink shirt; Neal dark and frail in his black hoodie and sandals. They had nothing in common and yet, Kay remembered, they had always gotten along. They were getting along now.

"What is she talking about?" Victor said to Neal.

"Come outside," Neal said. "I'll show you." Kay watched them leave, heads together, trailed by Nicky, who turned to mouth: *Really, Mom? Grand-Mere's buried out there?*

"Part of her," she answered. Other parts had been deposited other places. She and Charles had sprinkled some of Ida's ashes in the garden, it was true, and some on the mountain top, but the rest of her mother was safely encrypted in a vault in the cemetery.

"Beets," Neal was saying earnestly to Victor when they came back in. "Pole beans. Corn. Carrots."

"Ida-ho potatoes," Kay offered, grimly.

Nicky gagged and her brother and ex-husband stared at her. "That isn't funny," they both said.

"It sort of is," Kay said.

The twitch in Victor's forehead showed Kay that he was having trouble processing all this. She knew he wanted to take a stand. But Victor, who spent his days making deals and juggling figures, hated personal confrontations. He was comfortable only with money. She watched him struggle now to figure out the right thing to say. He'd probably fall back, as he had these last few years, on The Bible. He did. "'The body that is sown is perishable,'" he finally said, "'it is raised imperishable.' Corinthians."

"Meaning?" Kay asked.

"Meaning Mom's soul is in heaven and everything else is fine." Relieved, Victor began walking around the kitchen, opening cupboards and peering inside. "You going to use this old Waterford? Stacy was just saying we need some nice crystal for 7-up sherbet punch when her church group comes over. And whew, look at this, Dad's electric knife sharpener. Can't believe he left it here. Anyone could come in and take it. I could really use a good knife sharpener."

"It's still Dad's," Kay said, taking the knife sharpener from her brother's hands and setting it back down on the counter. "Did you come up to pillage and loot or did you come to say hi and see if Nicky and I need help moving in?"

"I thought your hippie boyfriend was going to help you move in."

"Fenton has been busy," Kay said, aware she flushed at the sound of Fenton's name.

"And he's not her boyfriend," Nicky said.

Victor turned. "You mean he doesn't sleep over?"

"Hey!" Kay snapped. "That is none of your business."

"Sometimes Mr. Redpath spends the night on the couch," Nicky answered, unconcerned. "When it's too late for him to drive home."

"What couch? Our old, flowered chintz couch?" Neal roused himself from reading the label on the molasses jar and gave Kay a hurt look. "You let a stranger sleep on our old couch? I loved that couch." He looked around. "Where is it? Did you bring it with you?"

"It was forty years old, Neal. It had no springs. It went to the dump. Nicky, why don't you take your father and uncle down the hall to your room and introduce them to Orville?"

"Who's Orville?" Victor asked, opening the silver drawer and peering in.

"The class python. It's Nicky's turn to snakesit."

"And if he likes it here," Nicky said, "I get to keep him all summer. He's brilliant, Dad," he said, turning to Neal. "I'm teaching him tricks."

"I'll look at him when I come back with the next load of manure," Neal promised, turning to go.

"Manure?" Kay cried. "No! Come back with my groceries!"

"Maybe we can use him to catch gophers," Neal mused as he left.

"Count me out too, Nicky." Perhaps aware that he sounded abrupt, Victor cleared his throat. "Your Aunt Stacy might enjoy meeting a serpent but she's at Pastor Paulsen's Prayer Practice this afternoon."

Because Victor's born-again wife had once explained that the purpose of prayer was "to get things," Kay was curious. "What's Stacy praying for?" Kay asked.

Victor didn't answer. "Want to see my car?" he said instead.

"Sure." She followed Victor out to the driveway, admired his new used Audi or whatever it was, and after his expensive engine headed back down the mountain, she went to the garbage bins and began to fish her gluten, lactose, sucrose, and genetically modified salad greens out before the raccoons got to them. Returning to the kitchen she was not surprised to see that the knife sharpener was gone.

With its casement windows and canopied bed, her own room at the top of the castle was as cloyingly fairy-tale as it had been when she left for college, but she had already replaced the pink bedspread with an Indian silk shawl, thrown out the shag rug, and hung Charles's paintings on the walls. They were from his "Ch-Ch-Ch-Changes" show at the Blue Mountain Gallery and she wasn't sure she liked them as much as his earlier abstracts, but the images of men's faces and torsos morphing into dragonfly forms were oddly companionable and reminded her of Charles himself. She remembered sitting in his studio for hours last year, watching the paintings take shape, listening to David Bowie's old albums on his turntable, a cup of tea cooling on the table beside her. She hadn't talked much, hadn't needed to. Charles had known she was struggling to stay sober, concerned about the cutbacks at the library, and insecure in her relationship with Fenton. His warm smile as he looked up from his canvases was all the comfort she needed—which was good, she had complained once, as it was the only comfort she was going to get.

"Boo hoo," Charles had agreed, and then, with a hand on her shoulder, "You don't need comforting, lambkin. You need a better job, your own piano, a car that starts in the morning, and a man who thinks you're the best thing that ever happened to him."

"Thanks, darling." Kay had kissed his hand and twisted away before he could see the longing in her face. Charles, with his butterscotch skin and peach fuzz cheeks and chocolate drop eyes,

was not only delicious to look at, but kind, intelligent, good na-
tured, and fun to be with. He would make a perfect husband. For
some lucky man. Perhaps he had found a lover in Thailand by
now, though selfishly she hoped not.

She opened her suitcase and began to unpack as the afternoon
darkened around her. She could hear sounds from the neighborhood she'd forgotten: the creak of redwoods, the call of crows, a
snatch of television news from the elderly neighbors' house below. If she listened hard enough, she might even hear the tinkle
of her mother's highball glass as she rattled the ice for a refill, the
rumble of her father's latest sports car as he disappeared down the
driveway. But instead, thank goodness, all she heard was Nicky
downstairs, practicing his guitar, and even though the song he
was playing was "Heartbreak Hotel," the shaky notes made her
smile. Nicky's childhood in this house, she realized, could be an
antidote to hers: maybe he could do what she had never been able
to do—maybe he could be happy here. She went to the window
and looked out at the mountain, grateful. She had been given a
second chance. She would do things right this time.

WEEK TWO

The castle had been listed privately, Francis said, which sounded impressive but made Kay wonder if any one besides Glo's socialite friends even knew it was for sale. To be honest, it wasn't ready for buyers; it was, as Francis had said, a dump. The tall windows were clouded with gassy rainbow whorls, the skylights were littered with bird droppings, the slate roof leaked, the plumbing still spurted rusty water or none at all, and the marble floor was cracked. The chandelier in the Great Room had lost a tier of crystals after the last earthquake and the baronial fireplace, flanked by stone griffins, no longer drew. The tapestries were faded, the Persian rugs were threadbare, the velvet curtains hung stiff with age. Her father's red leather armchair had tufts of stuffing coming out and the lion skin rug Ida used to kiss and fondle had lost both yellow glass eyes. Nicky had put a pair of motorcycle goggles on its nose as a joke.

The entire castle, Kay thought, as she scrubbed and dusted, had been designed as a joke. Francis had chuckled over the blueprints, never dreaming that Ida would adore his comic book creation, would insist on moving in, would want to raise their children in its chill majesty. There had been rewards for Francis—the place had been photographed on the cover of two major design magazines and his reputation as an architect for the wealthy and eccentric had been established. There were little castle clones up and down the coast now, selling for millions. This one too, Victor had announced, rubbing his hands together, was probably worth "a lot"—his vagueness about the precise amount so uncharacteristic that Kay guessed Francis hadn't told Victor any more than he had told her. Expecting to see a realtor pop in at any moment, she continued to keep the floors swept, the beds made, the vases filled with fresh flowers, the kitchen fragrant with baking banana bread, and, before and after her hours at the library, she also continued to look for places where she and Nicky—and maybe Charles, when he came back from Thailand, if he ever came back from Thailand—could live once the castle was sold.

"Are there any nice houses for sale in your neighborhood?" she asked Fenton now. Francis, to her surprise, had agreed to hire her "carpenter friend," sight unseen, to repair the kitchen cabinets, and Fenton's presence in the castle had kept Kay in high spirits and black lace underwear ever since. She had not expected to see him this afternoon when she drove in, so the sight of his truck in the driveway had thrilled her, and she had spent the last few minutes in her car, combing her hair, refreshing her lipstick, and mashing a breath mint between her teeth before coming inside. Fenton grinned as she hugged him but continued measuring the kitchen cabinets. "I don't exactly live in a 'neighborhood,'" he said.

"Where do you live?"

"In a nest."

"A lovenest?"

Fenton didn't answer and Kay, embarrassed, began to fill the coffee maker with cold water. She knew that Fenton lived alone. What was she doing—testing? He was a self-described hermit, and seemed to be proud of it. "I'd rather sit on a pumpkin," he had said once, quoting Thoreau, "than be crowded on a velvet cushion," and the image had enchanted her, at least at first, before she understood that Fenton's pumpkin-sitting precluded seeing movies or going to parties or joining her friends for dinner; he was not, he explained, "very social," and if she wanted to be with him, she would have to be with him on his terms—terms which only recently had begun to seem unreasonable.

"I need to find a new self-help book titled *How to Love a Loner*," Kay had complained once to her friends.

"Find it? You could write it," Zabeth said. "All your men have been loners."

"All my men? What do you mean? You've only ever known Neal."

"Point taken."

"And Neal's not so much a loner as a loaner, with an a. He was living with his ninety-year-old mother when I met him and if she hadn't died, he'd be living there still. I like the sound of that, though, 'all my men.' Makes me feel worldly."

"Is Fenton really a loner?" asked Dana. "What a shame. He's so good looking."

Fenton was good looking. Six-foot-four, broad shouldered, slim hipped, long legged, Fenton Redpath was—next to Charles—the most beautiful man Kay had ever known. Copper colored curls tumbled over his forehead and copper-colored freckles flecked his skin. With his golden eyes set close together, his broad nose and loping walk, he reminded Kay of a long lean honey bear, almost, but not quite adorable, an animal essentially wild. He had wooed her, as he had probably wooed countless women before her, with his shyness, his Native American heritage, and his tale of sailing alone for six months through the Pacific, an improbable pick-up line that improbably worked, though she wasn't sure why. He chuckled quietly now as she stood on tiptoe to kiss his neck and patted her head as if tapping down the bubble in a level.

"I didn't expect to see you today," she began. "It's Friday. You never work on Friday."

"I left my tools here," Fenton explained.

"Can you stay for dinner?"

"What is it?"

"It's Nicky's favorite: macaroni and cheese. But it's really good macaroni. I use pancetta. Cream. Caramelized onions. Farmhouse cheddar. Buttered breadcrumbs." She dropped her eyes, dreamily fixing on a swirl of copper hair in the cleft of his plaster splattered work shirt. "Nicky's going to a school dance later. We'll have the house to ourselves."

Fenton nodded and wrote some figures down on the notepad he carried with him. Kay had snuck enough glimpses into that notepad to know that it contained phone numbers and names—women's names—clients, she hoped, but so many? And had none of them husbands?

"So can you?" she asked as he continued to write.

"Actually, I just stopped by to get these measurements and pick up my tools."

"So … no?"

Silence.

"How about some coffee then before you go?"

"I thought you couldn't drink coffee."

"That was last week. This week … " Kay stopped. *The Miraculous Mindfulness Makeover*, which she still had not returned to the library, prohibited sugar, fat, salt, sodas, red meat, white bread, pasta, rice, and dairy products but the authors had apparently forgotten caffeine. "This week I can drink as much coffee as I want."

Fenton smiled but again did not answer. Kay tried not to watch as he rewound his measuring tape and pocketed the squared off wooden pencil in his blue work shirt. She was not going to let him hurt her feelings. He had hurt her feelings before, but the *MMM* book said that was her choice. Today she could choose not to make that choice. She could choose to accept that his plans for the evening did not include her. She could choose not to take it personally. Fenton had never been cruel or dismissive, he had never done anything worse than seem to not see her, and since he himself did not mind not being seen, she could not accuse him of being deliberately rude. If she sometimes felt invisible, well, that was her problem. One of her problems.

"Hey," he said now, "I was wondering, did you get a chance to look at that bill I left?"

"The one for five hundred dollars?"

"Seems like a lot, doesn't it."

"Sure does. I mailed it to my father. You haven't heard back?"

"No, and I was hoping you could pay it today. My truck payment's due tomorrow."

Kay caught her breath. Hadn't Fenton's verbal estimate been for three hundred dollars? Didn't he know (she had told him) that Francis would only pay the estimate and not a cent more?

"Kay?" he prompted.

"I thought our agreement ... " she began.

" ... was that you would pay upon receipt of the bill," Fenton finished. He looked at her kindly. "And I gave you the bill a week ago."

No arguing that. But had he not understood that anything over his estimate would have to come from her own pocket? She looked up into his waiting gold-flecked eyes. Did he think she had money because her father had money?

"I found all that dry rot, if you'll recall," he began, "and then I had to reseal the ... "

"Okay," she interrupted. She tried to swallow the sour bubble rising hot and hard in her throat; she didn't want to feel like this, angry, bitter, she wanted this "relationship," if that's what it was, to work. She reached into her purse, pulled out her checkbook, wrote the check quickly and gave it to him without looking, just as Fenton, in one of his uncanny moves, reached out and started to massage her shoulder. "Tight," he murmured as her knees began to buckle. No one gave better massages than Fenton. A few muscular squeezes and swirls from his large square hands and her shoulder began to sing; after one of his backrubs every ache in her body vanished for days.

"Unfair," she murmured weakly.

"Thanks, little mama. Wish I could stay but I gotta waltz!" And with a smile and a wave, Fenton left. Left without regrets. Left without curiosity. Left without a single word about seeing her again. She swallowed back another sour burp of hurt as his truck pulled out of the driveway but whether she was madder at him or at herself she could not tell. Paying him just now was wrong. She knew it. Why had she done it? Why hadn't she stood up for herself? What was the matter with her? Just because Fenton smelled like apples and wood smoke, just because he was a gentle lover who whimpered when he came, just because he read Thoreau sitting on a tree stump by a trout stream, the book so small in his large, strong, calloused hands … ?

"Is he gone?" Nicky asked, peering around the corner, Orville draped around his neck.

"Oh man is he ever."

"Good."

"You don't like him."

"No, Mom, I do not like him."

"Why?"

She waited. Nicky was wise—perhaps he could clarify this mess for her. Maybe he could explain why, after almost a year, she still felt as if she didn't know Fenton and he did not know—or want to know—her.

Nicky opened the refrigerator and leaned inside. "It's not Mr. Redpath so much, Mom, it's you," Nicky said. "Whenever he's here, you're different."

"How am I different?"

"You're nuts. I'm hungry. Is there anything to eat?"

"Banana bread. Loaves and loaves of banana bread."

"Get real."

"I'm beginning to ha … dislike it intensely too. How about an orange?"

But Nicky had reached into the refrigerator and was heading down the hall with the remains of a carton of chocolate ice cream that *The Miraculous Mindfulness Makeover* had almost convinced her to throw away. "Take that snake off your neck and put him back in his cage," she called, "or I'm returning him to the school."

"Okay," Nicky called cheerfully.

"And decide what you want to wear to the dance tonight."

"Listen to my laughter," he answered, as he disappeared into his room. What did that mean? Some secret phrase from one of his video games? He'd be in his room until dinner, probably tapping out goofy messages to Tico on Twitter. At least he didn't do what she had done at his age—sneak up to the castle's roof and smoke.

Frowning, she mopped up the dirty footprints Fenton had left on the floor, and walked around picking up papers and plumping pillows for the approval of the invisible real estate agent. Ida's portrait, she saw, was still hanging crookedly above the fireplace and she reached up to straighten it, surprised as always by her mother's beauty. The painter too had seemed surprised, his short brush strokes quickly capturing the blonde hair cupping the heart-shaped face, the red lips pursed in a mischievous smile, the strong cleft chin, the dark blue eyes. He'd caught The Afternoon Ida, before the first cocktail, before the tears and accusations and thrown plates and suicide threats, before the fall that eventually left her in a wheelchair.

Ida, Kay knew, would never have paid Fenton. She might even have found a way to make Fenton pay *her*. Ida had always known how to get people to do things—not always subtly. She remembered her mother's voice: "Oh Kay darling, would you mind, would you just, would you please, would you now, I said NOW, dammit, I am talking to you, stupid, I need, I want, I have to have … " and shuddered.

Her phone rang and she pulled it out of her pocket gratefully, without checking to see who it was. Who knew? It might be from Fenton. *Hey good lookin'*, he'd say. *Can't believe I left without remembering to tell you how much I love, desire, cherish, esteem, revere, adore, honor, worship and really really dig you. I tore your check up and if you stand right there I'll be over in ten minutes to tear your clothes off too.*

"Kay?" Zabeth sounded worried. "Are you laughing or crying?"

"Both. It's a good thing I don't write romance novels."

"I have an idea for one if you decide to start. Didn't you used to go with a musician named Biff Kelly?"

"A hundred years ago," Kay answered, bending to pick up one of Nicky's magic cards. What *were* these things? Were they dangerous? The card pictured an obscenely over-muscled one-eyed giant brandishing a spike-studded mace. "The last I heard he was playing at a jazz club in Japan."

"Well now he's playing here. Garrett met him today."

Kay tried to think of Biff—dark, quick, ragged Biff—waiting in line at the counter of Zabeth's husband's pristine boutique pharmacy in downtown Rancho Valdez. What was he doing there? Biff, unless he'd changed, got his drugs off the street. "Is he sick?"

"No no. He just wanted to put some posters up in Gar's window. For his show. He's playing at the Rode House tonight. I thought you ought to know. Actually," her voice was wicked, "I think you ought to go. Check him out. There's nothing like reconnecting with your first love."

"Did you ever?" Kay asked, stalling.

Zabeth's rat-a-tat laugh, the clatter of her silver bracelets, the chatter of her four-year-old daughters in the background. "First, second, third, thirtieth love—I reconnected with all of them! But I'm done. I have Garrett. You're the one who's still out there."

"I'm not 'out there,'" Kay said stiffly. "I'm dating Fenton."

"Oh right, only Fenton's idea of a date is propping an extension ladder against your balcony and coming in for a quickie after Nicky's asleep."

"Why do I tell you things?"

"Because you need advice and firm direction."

Kay sat down on Ida's fainting couch, phone in hand. "Biff Kelly left me," she reminded her friend. "He ran off with a waitress. I haven't heard a word from him in over twenty years. I don't think there's anything to reconnect to."

"Really? I remember you telling Dana and me about him that time the three of us went out to the beach."

"I was drunk."

"Well yeah. So were we. But you were the one crying all night. And I must say," Zabeth added, "if this poster is any proof, your Biff looks good for an old boy. You know. Haggard. Depraved. Didn't you tell me he was a gypsy?"

"He's not 'my' Biff and it was my father who called him that. He grew up in a middle-class family in Cleveland, he had three older sisters, his father was a high school principal, and he was an altar boy until he was fourteen."

"See?"

"See what?"

"Ha ha ha," Zabeth said, and hung up. Kay sat on with the phone in her lap. *Ha ha ha yourself*, she thought. The last person she needed to "reconnect" with was Biff Kelly. Not that any woman could connect with him for long. *But oh boy*, Kay thought, suddenly remembering Biff's light-gray eyes, the way he threw his head back when he laughed, the way some part of his body was always tapping, snapping, dancing, *I tried. Harder than I should have.*

Her phone rang again. "Babe?" Neal's reedy voice. There were street sounds behind him, cars, a siren. He must be calling from one of the last phone booths left in the county—which was odd, as he usually phoned from the health food store where he worked. "Babe, do you remember Victor's wedding?"

"Victor's wedding a thousand years ago? Yes? Why?"

Silence. Neal lived in the past even more than she did. Only he never saw the humor in it. Maybe there wasn't any humor in it.

"I remember Mother pushed her wheelchair into the circle of bridesmaids so she could catch Stacy's bouquet herself," Kay said. "I remember Dad loudly described the Matron of Honor as having 'the eyes of a Madonna and the jaw of an ape.' I remember Victor didn't tip the caterers. I remember you wouldn't dance with me. Is that what you remember?"

"I remember you were pregnant with Nicky but drinking champagne anyway."

"Is that the point you want to make, Neal? If so, point taken. I drank too much, yes, at Victor's wedding. I am sorry. But I didn't hurt him. Nicky's fine."

"So far," Neal said darkly. "You feed him junk, you let him play video games, you refuse to give him a colonic ... ."

Kay gazed out the window; she could just see a corner of the area beyond the swimming pool where Neal had put in the vegetable garden; like so many of his projects, it was unfinished, buckets and wheelbarrows and tools standing in the tilled dirt like war relics. "Is that what you called about?"

"No ... " Neal's voice drifted away, then, "Is Nicky still going to that dance?"

"Yes. You promised to take him. He needs to be dropped off at the school gym at seven and picked up at ten. Neal? Are you there?"

A long silence and then, "Odd time for a dance."

"Not really. Are you going to take him?"

"I'll try."

Kay clicked the phone off, flooded with the usual slop of guilt, fury, pity, and exasperation. Neal Sorenson: her second love. Her second failure. "Let it go let it go let it go," she chanted under her breath, tearing at her cuticles. She glanced at the antique cabinet where her parents used to keep their liquor. Five in the afternoon. Ida's time. A few glasses of wine and she could kick off from shore and float free for a while. How good that would feel! She could forget Fenton and Biff and Neal and just drift.

Her breath caught with the old longing, but it was just another choice and it would pass, if she let it, and anyway she had poured everything from the liquor cabinet down the sink the first night they moved back here. She roused, walked up a short flight of stone steps and slipped into the tapestried alcove where the piano hulked. The late afternoon sun struck Ida's gold harp, propped in a corner. Wrapping the soft green cashmere shawl that Charles had given her around her shoulders, Kay pulled the piano bench out and sat down. She should work on the Mozart sonata she'd been struggling with for months but instead her fingers found familiar keys and began to pound out the fast movement of the easy Beethoven piece that she privately thought of as the Heart Healing Sonata; it cleaned her blood to play it, cleared her head, and if it didn't work the first time through, it usually did by the third.

Nicky, recognizing the storm, came to the door, and waited with the empty ice cream carton in his hand until it subsided.

"Did you talk to Dad?" he asked. "Is he going to take me?"

"That's not clear yet. He's going to *try* to take you. He didn't seem to understand about the time."

"The clock in his van doesn't work," Nicky said.

"How about the clock in his apartment? How about the clock at his job?"

Nicky's face closed down and she regretted her tone at once. "I'll start dinner," she said, rising. "And I'm sorry," she added. "It's just that … "

"I know." Nicky's shoulders slumped; for a second he looked as weary as Neal. She reached in her pocket and held out the magic card she had found on the floor.

"Tell me about this, honey. It looks like a Cyclops."

Nicky brightened. "It is. It's a gladiator Cyclops," he explained, and he sat on a stool in the kitchen while she cooked and chatted to her about dragons and sorcerers and even listened politely when she chimed in to tell him about the original Cyclops in Homer's *Odyssey*.

"You'd like that book," she said. "It's about a guy who can't get home. Sort of like Charles," she added, under her breath, "who I'm sure *could* get home if he wanted to—if he wasn't having such a good time."

"I know all about *The Odyssey*. It's a great game," Nicky said, nodding.

"Game?"

"Sure. Poseidon. Zeus. The Gorgon."

"*The Odyssey* is a video game? You've learned Greek myths from a video game?"

"Duh," said her son, ducking before she could rumple his hair. She sat down beside him, picking at a green salad and sipping her sixth glass of water while Nicky ate what she had, in truth, told Fenton was his favorite dinner—macaroni and cheese—only Nicky liked it from the Kraft box, and that's the way she always made it. "I can't believe you're actually going to this dance," she said. "You've boycotted every one this year. How come tonight?"

Nicky shrugged. How handsome he looked! "Getting his fur!" Zabeth had crowed recently, a frightening expression for a mother to hear, but apt. Kay admired the thick fringe of lashes on his downturned eyes and realized, surprised at her own slowness, that he was going to this dance because he was interested in a girl. Maybe several girls. Well: good for him.

"What are you going to do while I'm gone?" Nicky asked, finishing his milk.

"What I do every night. Take a short run. Followed by a long shower. Plop down into Grandpa Francis's armchair and read a self-help book."

Nicky nodded and she glanced at him, wondering how much he remembered about her last lapse, when he'd come home early from an overnight at Tico's and found her passed out on the bathroom floor of their apartment.

"You ought to go out," he said now.

"Friday night? Where would I go?" She paused. "I did hear about an old friend of mine who's in town. He's a musician who's playing at the Rode House tonight."

"Is that a bar?"

So Nicky did remember.

"No, they just have apple cider and coffee. And stale oatmeal cookies."

"Could be okay," Nicky said, and stood to clear his plate.

Could be. Maybe. She didn't have to decide yet. She walked Nicky up to the end of the driveway and waited with him until they heard the familiar wheeze of Neal's van climbing the mountain. Nicky said, "Bye Mom," and hurried to meet it and Kay waved goodbye and turned toward the house, trying to shake the image of Neal's slack face behind his filthy windshield. Was he depressed? Was he sick? When she had confessed to the divorce lawyer that Neal hadn't talked to her, looked at her, listened to her, or slept with her for the last two years of their marriage, the lawyer had been amazed she'd stayed with him at all. "Now you're free to make a better choice," she'd said when she'd handed Kay her decree.

Did Fenton count as a better choice?

Maybe some mistakes just had to be repeated until you perfected them?

She stooped to deadhead the petunias in the driveway, straightened the For Sale sign that she'd put up herself, and pushed back a few twigs of the poisonous oleander that guarded the castle entrance. Looking up, she could just see the tip of Fenton's extension ladder leaning against the leaded window of her tower room. She'd been crazy to share that particular detail with Zabeth—but it had been irresistible. Zabeth, who had had a thousand lovers a thousand different ways, had never had a handsome prince climb into her bed at midnight—and Kay had relished the envy in her friend's eyes, even as the envy faded to concern. "He needs to take better care of you," Zabeth had said. No. The person to take better care of her was herself. Starting with a run around the mountain.

There were probably more beautiful places in the world than the dirt trail that wound below the castle, but Kay hadn't seen any. The California lilac was in bloom, as was the Scotch broom, a plant Kay knew was invasive but had always thought lovely with its spiky sprays of bright yellow buds and nutty fragrance. Redwood trees grew in the deep valleys below and madrone and manzanita hedged the wide dirt path. She had been exploring this trail all her life, it seemed—there was the streambed where she and Victor had built forts, the curve where she'd once spied a bobcat, the base of the eroded cliff where wild pigs came to root. Although she had left the castle when she was eighteen to attend—and, soon after, flunk out of—the Conservatory, she had often driven back up the mountain alone to hike. She could remember walking here hand in hand with Neal when they first met, and she could definitely remember running here without feeling like she was going to pass out, which was how she felt now. She slowed, wiped her forehead with her sleeve, and bent over, wishing she'd brought water.

When she looked up, she saw the Nordrums, her parents' elderly neighbors, hatted, gloved, shod in hiking boots and armed with machetes, dragging burlap sacks of Scotch broom behind them. "Kay McLeod!" Hazel Nordrum cried gaily as they neared. "How good to see you! How are you?"

"I'm fine. How are you two?"

"Oh you know us," Hazel Nordrum said. "We're plugging along. Trying to rid the mountain of planta non grata. It's a losing battle but what isn't? You have to do what you have to do, don't you, dear?"

Kay smiled into their ruddy faces. What secret of health and happiness did this couple have? She wanted it! She remembered that the Nordrums were founding members of the Sierra Club and the Marine Mammal Center and that they had spearheaded a group that rescued seabirds whenever there was an oil spill in the bay. She also remembered that Ida and Francis had called them The HoHums.

"So you've moved back into the castle?" Hal Nordrum asked.

"Just until it sells."

"It will take a special kind of person to buy it," Hal Nordrum said.

"We've been thinking maybe a Hollywood person." Hazel Nordrum added. "We always thought your mother was a Hollywood person."

Kay, after an expectant silence, said what she had always said when someone mentioned Ida: "Thank you."

"I remember when Victor used to 'run away' to our house and you'd come over to find him," Hazel Nordrum continued. "We always let you kids stay as long as you wanted. Victor loved my Toll House cookies and you loved our Horowitz LPs; you played them over and over."

Kay smiled, remembering lying flat in front of the Nordrums' stereo, feeling her entire body fill with Rachmaninoff's storms and sunbursts, knowing her mother, alone in the castle, needed her, but not caring, feeling, for an hour, almost guilt free. "You saved my life," she confessed.

"Well," Hazel Nordrum said, patting her hand, "yours is a life well worth saving."

It is? Kay turned her face aside to hide the tears that suddenly sprang to her eyes. Pathetic! What was the matter with her?

"Come visit anytime, dear; you're always welcome." And dragging their sacks of hacked blooms the old couple strode on, back to their own house below, which Francis too had designed, but not as a joke, as an actual place to live, with a family room, not a Great Room, and with a regular basement, not a dungeon.

Kay waited until they had rounded the curve before wiping her face, taking a deep breath and setting off to run a little farther. If I can just make it to that rock, she told herself. And then to that hard place.

She was glowing with self-satisfaction as she jogged back. She should do what Zabeth said, and go to the concert. There was no reason to be afraid of seeing Biff Kelly; he was just an old boyfriend; he didn't mean anything to her anymore; she'd outgrown any hold he might have had on her. She wouldn't have to go up and talk to him afterward; he probably wouldn't recognize her anyway. She could sit in the back and slip out early. It would be interesting to see how he had turned out. And as for Fenton—it would do Fenton good to know she didn't spend all her Friday nights alone.

She stopped at the head of the driveway. A black Mercedes with a Jesus fish decal on the bumper was parked next to her Honda with its Darwin fish decal. One of Victor's cars? Victor and Stacy often dropped by at dinner time. Which was all right. She didn't see them often these days; she could take something out of the freezer. She whistled two long notes of Yoo-Hoo as she pushed open the heavy front door, but the only answer was a sharp yip from inside the house, which meant they'd brought their dog with them: Awful Ed, the wired terror, the only animal in the world that even Nicky didn't like.

"Hey Vic," she called as her brother, holding Ed in his arms, emerged from his old room down the hall. Victor, usually so proud and confident, looked shaken. He was still dressed for work, but his sleeves were rolled up and his tie was undone. The nervous little dog in his arms was ruffled and red-eyed as well. Puzzled, Kay glanced behind them, dismayed to see a suitcase open on the floor. "What's going on? Where's Stacy? Are you all right?"

"I'm fine. No worry. Just going to," Victor's voice broke, "stay here for a little while."

"Okay. Why?"

"Do you ever feel like you know someone really well and then they ... "

"Yes?"

" ... turn out to be in league with Satan?"

"No."

"Well, that's what's happened to Stacy."

Kay blinked. It was hard to think of Victor's sweet, curvy, dimpled little wife being "in league" with anything other than a Christian charity association. Stacy wore white cotton blouses with a silver pin of an embryo pinned to the collar; she smelled like magnolia blossoms; she sang in the church choir; she taught Sunday school. She had once told Kay that she thought of Victor—Victor!—as her "master." "Submitting to him," she'd once told a stunned Kay, "is my duty and my joy."

"You've had a fight?"

"A fight? No. We never fight. Stacy just told me what she has done to herself—to us—and I had no choice but to pack up and leave."

"What has she done?"

"Transgressed," Victor said, fixing Kay with bloodshot eyes.

"Is she having an affair?"

"Of course not!"

"Are you?"

"For land's sake, Kay. Get your mind out of the gutter."

"I'm just trying to figure this out."

"There's nothing to figure out. My wife has chosen the path to damnation and I have chosen to come home."

"Move back here, you mean?"

"Why not? It's my house too."

"No, really, it's not. It's Nicky's house now, and mine. Did you talk to Dad?"

"What does Dad care? Here. Hold the dog."

"I don't want to hold your dog, Victor. Don't push him at me! Ed's heavy! Damn it, now look, he scratched me!"

"Don't put him down! Ed has to be carried. He goes to pieces if you put him down. And don't say 'damn.' I hate it when you swear, Kay."

"Well don't cry about it."

"I am not crying."

But he was. Kay, holding Ed, steadied herself as Victor took two steps forward and collapsed heavily against her neck. His sobs were rough and unpracticed. Had her brother ever cried before? He hadn't cried when their parents had forgotten to pick him up after a Cub Scout cookout and he'd had to spend the night curled in a park latrine. He hadn't cried when he got cut from the high school football team. He hadn't cried when Ida died and he hadn't cried—as she had—when Francis married Glo. But he was crying now, raw and real. These weren't the pretty crystals their mother used to manufacture at a moment's notice, these were real tears, snotty and explosive, and she was worried. Victor was not supposed to break down. He was supposed to find solace in his church, his wife, his job, and his love of material comfort. She patted his shoulder and found herself rubbing it, as she used to do, when she put him to bed each night. Victor: the trembling child who came to her wide-eyed when Ida slapped him or Francis made some cutting remark, the lonely kid who lay on his back under the piano when she practiced, singing along in his clear sweet voice.

"Vic," she murmured, "Vic. Tell me what happened."

She could barely hear his words as he babbled into her neck—something about "issue," Stacy wanting "issue, ten years of marriage and no issue." Confused, the dog's nails sharp on her skin, Kay tried to recall what *Playing Well With Others* had advised in times like this—don't give advice, she remembered, or express pity, just repeat back what you're hearing. "So if Stacy doesn't have an issue with it," she began, "why do you ... "

"I am so sick of your sense of humor." Victor brushed at his eyes and pushed back from her. "You are exactly like Dad. You turn everything into a joke."

"No, I don't. I mean I don't mean to. What *is* this 'issue?' Do you mean children?" Kay followed him back to his bedroom as he flung himself down on the faded Star Wars quilt that still covered his bed. She perched on the edge of the mattress beside him, Ed curled upon her lap lightly as a cat, tense, quivering, but silent. "Stacy wants children?"

Victor lifted a corner of the pillowcase and blew his nose. "She always said that without issue there's no point in matrimony. Well maybe she's right. Maybe there is no point in matrimony."

"Isn't love the point?"

"Matrimony based on romantic love is an abomination."

"An abomin-what? That's crazy. Who are you quoting?"

"Leave Pastor Paulsen out of this, Kay. And if anyone's committed *abominations* …" Victor's voice rose to a tearful high then sank into its familiar rut of aggrieved righteousness. "You may be an adulteress and a divorcee, Kay, and I am not judging you for that, believe me, I'm just saying you've done one thing right in your life: you've conceived as Our Lord intended you to. You've had a natural child. You've manifested your womanhood. Stacy," his voice broke, "has been a hollow vessel who has filled herself from a poisoned well …"

"I have no idea what you're talking about. But if you're saying that by having Nicky I manifested my womanhood and saved my marriage …"

"Your marriage didn't need saving! Your marriage was fine."

Kay knew not to argue. She'd heard it all from Victor before. The sanctity of holy wedlock, the blah blah of immaculate matrimony. Both he and Francis had opposed her divorce from Neal; both had turned their backs on her while she struggled to get her graduate degree and raise Nicky on her own. Glo, for some reason, had been even more critical than the men. "You knew what Neal was like when you married him," Glo had snapped. "He's not a businessman. He has no head for money. You should have helped him before he went under."

"How? I didn't know he was going under," Kay had protested. "He never told me his problems. He never told me anything!"

"Then it was your job to find out. That's what wives do. They *help* their husbands." This bit of virtuous advice from Glo—whose first two husbands had killed themselves!—and yet Glo was right. Kay had not been a help to Neal. His depression—if that's what it was—had defeated her. She thought she had caused it. She had not known what to do. *And I still don't*, she admitted …

Victor sniffled to stillness at last and lay flat on the pillow while she held his hand. The walls of his old bedroom had been stripped of their Guns N' Roses posters years ago but the air still stank of his youth: musk and airplane glue and gym socks. Unread gift copies of *Huckleberry Finn* and *Treasure Island* still sat on the bookshelf and probably the same *Hustler* magazines were hidden under the loose floorboard where he used to stash his marijuana. Marijuana, Kay mused, was supposed to be linked to infertility—as was coke, meth, LSD, angel dust, psilocybin, heroin—all of Victor's and Stacy's daily staples—and all given up without a murmur when Jesus appeared to them in a vision one stoned morning and shocked them into abstinence. Still, early damage might have been done. Kay opened her mouth to ask Victor if he was sterile, thought better of it, and clamped her lips shut. But a moment later, she couldn't help asking a question she had wondered about for years. "If it's just about wanting children," she said, "couldn't you adopt?"

"Right. Go to China and get a couple of Ornamentals like your slutty friend Zabeth?" Ah. This was more like it. The old Victor, intolerant and intolerable. "No thanks. Anyway, it's not about *not* having children, Kay. It's about having them." Seeing her puzzled look, he said, "Forget it. I'm going to need clean sheets and towels in here and Ed hasn't been fed. And no offense but you smell terrible, have you been running? You need to take a shower. Don't bother making me dinner. I'm too upset. I can't eat." And with that he flopped back on his bed and closed his eyes.

Kay stood, dropped Ed on his chest, and left. She would phone Stacy and find out what was going on.

But the phone at Victor and Stacy's house rang unanswered and the syrupy voice message: "God loves you and we love you too!" was no help. Kay clicked the phone off and sat with her hand on it a minute longer. She could call Francis down in Carmel and tell him about Victor moving in, but Francis would probably just think it was funny. He had never taken anything Victor had done seriously. And, really, what good reason did she have for not wanting Victor to stay here? How could she explain that Victor somehow *weighed* on her? He'd been such a sweet, fearful, affectionate little boy. How had he turned into such a cold humorless man? Was it her fault? She had, after all, raised him. From birth he had been her charge, her responsibility, her baby. She turned back to the phone again. Her friend Dana wouldn't have any advice on Victor but she would know whether Kay should go see Biff or not.

"Is Biff rich?" Dana asked, in her surprisingly deep voice with its modulated British accent.

"No."

"Is he famous?"

"No."

"Is he good looking?"

"No."

"Were you happy with him?"

"Not for long."

"Well. Look. Your hair? Up. And that one pair of jeans you have that actually fits? Wear it with your black top. Remind me, how old were you when you met him?"

"Eighteen."

"And how old are you now?"

"Forty-four."

"Oh dear. Well don't be nervous. You're not nervous, are you?"

"No." Kay looked down at her hands, which were trembling. "I'm terrified."

The Rode House was a run-down Victorian mansion outside West Valley where the Rode brothers lived and gave concerts every third Friday of the month. It was set back behind a white picket fence in a garden of hollyhocks and fragrant stock. Looking up at the house, Kay wondered how much it would cost to buy and if the brothers would ever be willing to sell it. It needed work, was too big for her and Nicky, but she liked it, as she had, almost helplessly, liked all the other charming and inappropriate houses she had been looking at recently. "You're hopeless," Dana had said in wonder, after accompanying Kay to a tidy ranchette in a new tract and watching her wander straight out the back door to a little shack in the abandoned orchard behind it that had not yet been leveled. "I can't help it," Kay had explained. "Once I see the potential, I'm hooked."

"Well stop seeing the potential," Dana suggested, "and start seeing the practical."

"I will," Kay promised. "I'll know the right place when I see it."

The Rode House, despite its gables and gingerbread, was clearly not the right place. The street in front was lined with parked cars and the wrap-around porch had already filled with people waiting for the door to open. Kay saw Lois Hayes, her part-time assistant at the library, talking to Barry Morris, a cellist from a chamber group she used to play with, and joined them on one of the porch swings.

"I didn't think this many people would know about Biff Kelly," she said, surprised by the turnout.

"I heard him interviewed on the radio today," Lois said. "Apparently he plays everything from zydeco to mariachi to country to Irish to slack key. The radio also said he was with the Boston Philharmonic for a season."

"Two seasons," Kay corrected, without thinking.

Barry looked at her. "You know him?"

"I used to. A long time ago. We went to music school together."

"I wish I'd gone to a good music school," Barry said glumly. "It would have made all the difference."

"There's still time," Kay said.

"I'm fifty."

"That's nothing. Any age," Kay began, piously quoting from *Putting The You Into Youth,* "is the right age to do what you want." She stopped when she saw Barry's eyes follow a girl in a gauze dress and realized that Barry, doing what he wanted, would not be going back to school.

"Speaking of time," Lois said, "Has *The Miraculous Mindfulness Makeover* come in yet? I put a hold on it months ago. Think I'll have a chance to read it before the County shuts us down?"

"They are not going to shut us down."

"Oh? Have you formed a Friends of the Library group yet?"

"I'm working on it."

"You'll need to draft a petition and talk to the Board of Supervisors."

"Yes. I know that." Kay forced a smile. Three easy steps. Why hadn't she taken them yet? Why did she think someone else—some grownup—was going to step forward and take over the leadership for her? The Board of Supervisors had been threatening to shut down her branch for so many years that she'd begun to ignore them. She should not ignore them. She should fight them. She glanced up. Lois Hayes was a small, dogged woman who fought for everything.

"So you've known Biff Kelly since college?" Lois said.

"Yes. He was the best guitarist in our class." Kay nodded, relieved to see one of the lanky Rode brothers opening the front door and starting to take admission. "We all thought he'd be the next Segovia. Or," she amended, "Ry Cooder." She stood to take her place in line, gave Roy Rode her ten dollars, and went in, choosing a seat as far away from Lois as she could. Her hands were trembling and she wished she'd brought her knitting to work on. She bit at a cuticle instead. She should not have come. Biff wouldn't recognize her and even if he did, what would he have to say to her? Would he be disappointed that she'd stopped studying music? He'd always said that all she had to do to be an "excellent" pianist—he'd never said "great"—was work harder. When she thought of the few short months she had spent at the conservatory, she winced. Unlike Biff, who had been everyone's darling, the bad boy who played Wagner to a rock-and-roll beat, she would not be remembered by any of her fellow students or teachers now. She had gone to class and attended workshops dutifully but she had rarely spoken up or taken part; she had always been aware that her real place was at home, with her mother, who phoned almost every evening in tears to say she needed her. The one memorable recital she had gone to, of course, was the one where she had impressed Biff by falling out of the balcony at the end of his guitar solo and toppling into the violin professor's lap. Not a bad act, her roommate had hissed. The roommate, a Korean flautist who had since played Carnegie Hall, probably still believed it was an act, and not the accident of a clumsy teenager who had been drinking Kahlua all afternoon alone in her room.

Deep breath. *Live in the present, look to the future, let go of the past.*

She clasped her hands and looked around. The Rode brothers had converted their living room into a concert hall for folk singers and bluegrass players; they had built a sturdy corner stage, hung spotlights from the ceiling, insulated the walls and wired the place for sound. The house still had the feeling of a family home; it smelled of coffee and the honeysuckle that trellised the porch. Evening sunlight lit the long lace curtains and burnished the planks of the scuffed hardwood floors. Sitting straight up, Kay kept her eyes on the stage. It held enough instruments to stock a small orchestra. She thought she recognized the concertina from her days with Biff and surely that was the battered guitar case she had re-lined for him years ago—could it be? She remembered the vintage silk ties she'd bought from a peddler on Telegraph Avenue and sewn by hand into a rich patchwork to cover the padding that was falling apart. A black stool and a standing mic stood at stage center, waiting, but there was no sign of Biff yet. There was still time to escape. She half-rose from her seat, and then he walked on.

William Matthew Kelly, birthday February 29, sign Pisces (why did she have to remember all this), nicknamed Biff by his adoring sisters, adored by women all his life, child prodigy on piano and trumpet, got his first guitar at age eight, soloed at the Monterey Jazz Festival while still in high school. Preferred not to wear shoes, was allergic to peanuts, laughed in his sleep, photographic memory, knew the scores to entire symphonies, smelled like warm wheat bread, terrified by the sight of blood, believed in UFOs, jean size 31/32, first girlfriend's name Lucinda, favorite writer Milan Kundera, fluent in Spanish, two sugars, one cream, pack of American Spirit and a daily dash of her Tea Rose perfume slapped on his cheeks instead of aftershave. And here he was.

Barefoot. That was the first thing Kay noticed. Barefoot with a new (to her) Celtic tattoo twined around one brown ankle. The gold hoop earring that had once horrified her parents was gone and the straight bangs he shook back were grey now. Older, of course, and dissolute looking, like Zabeth had said, with hollowed cheeks and dark circles under his eyes. The eyes however were the same, light gray, fringed with black lashes, and so was the smile that lit his thin face and almost immediately lit the faces of his audience. He touched the back of his hair in a familiar gesture, then leapt onto the stage in a black tee-shirt, jeans, and a vintage leather jacket, pulled a harmonica out of his pocket and broke into such an exuberant rowdy melody that people began to sway in their chairs.

Kay had to clap with the others, there was no help for it, when Biff was on, he was on, and could not be resisted. He played every instrument on the stage in every genre he knew, and he was good at all of them, but it wasn't his music that enchanted the audience, it was him, and it was infuriating.

Kay hung back at the break. As others crowded into the kitchen to have Biff sign CDs, she went out on the porch swing to try and sort out her feelings. Her time with Biff had been brief—less than two years—and messy. He'd been having an affair with a cellist when he met her and an affair with a waitress when he left her. After they moved to the West Coast, they had lived in one cramped flat after another, and it seemed to her they were always cold, always hungry, and always laughing.

"So, what do you think?" The swing sank as Biff sat beside her. His head was bent; eyes downcast; he was intent on tuning a dulcimer. "Too high?" He plucked the bass string.

She swallowed before answering. "Way too."

"Can you fix it?" He handed the instrument to her. His pupils were dilated. Of course. Biff was always on something.

"I can't tune a dulcimer, Biff."

"Have you tried?"

"No."

"Well hell Karoony, how do you know until you've tried? Come on back in. I wrote a song for you and you never did hear it."

"When did you ever write me a song?"

"About forty minutes ago, when I saw you trying to hide back there in that corner. Now come on in and stop sulking."

The song, which he introduced as "Kay's Smile," was a light sweet danceable waltz and Kay had to struggle to remind herself that it had probably been featured in countless concerts as "Jenny's Smile," "Heather's Smile," "Georgia's Smile," etcetera. Biff played with his lips parted and his eyes fixed on her. Lois and Barry both swiveled to stare, and if Kay hadn't known that Biff was a mouth breather and that the spotlight meant he couldn't actually see her, she too would have been impressed. More impressed. Because there was no doubt about it: her heart was racing, her wrists were trembling, and a mad little butterfly had started to beat in her groin. Why did it seem as if no time had passed since she'd last seen him? *I've changed*, she warned herself. *Biff may be the same, but I've grown. I'm not the starry eyed Karoony who careened after him years ago.*

Who was this grown woman, then, who after staying to thank Biff for "her" song, found herself once again acting as his roadie, helping him pack his instruments and lugging them out to his car? Who was this wise, older woman and why was she sitting on the porch steps with him now? They sat without talking, listening, as they always had, to the sounds that offered themselves: crickets, frogs, night birds, a low rider's boombox, a baby's cry, the rumble of a neighbor's television. Kay refused the cigarette Biff offered and shook her head too at the beer he brought out. She wasn't asked for the kiss he gave, bringing her face up to his. The kiss was as light and sweet and practiced as the waltz he had played, flavored with tobacco and hops and something chemical, slightly bitter. Just a kiss, Kay thought. Nothing to it. Still, when he put his arm around her, she did not move away.

"So," he said, as he took another swig from his beer.

"So," she repeated. Then remembered: Biff always wanted a report card. He would want to know how he had done tonight. "You played exactly like I remembered," she said, which was true, as he had played neither better nor worse than he had years ago. "And you've learned so many new instruments. It was an amazing concert." He waited. "Really wonderful." She remembered Nicky's favorite word and threw it in. "Brilliant."

"Yeah," he nodded. "Good. And how about you? Still playing piano?"

"No. Not really. I crashed my car and injured my shoulder a few years ago; it hurts to practice so now I just give lessons. On Sundays I sometimes play show tunes in a department store." She paused, then, reminding him, said, "I was never ambitious."

"Your husband play anything?"

"I'm not married."

"Good."

"Did you say good?"

Biff chuckled. "And you still live around here?"

"Sort of. I'm camping out in my parents' old place."

"Don't tell me you still live with The Dragon?"

"No. Mom died four years ago."

"And The Ice King?"

"Dad married an heiress and moved to Carmel."

"So, you're all alone in that fortress?"

"My son's with me. Nicky's eleven. Oh, and as of tonight, my brother."

"Vic the Prick," Biff said lightly.

"You remember Victor?"

"I had to borrow a hundred dollars from him to get my guitar out of hock. He charged me ten percent interest."

"That sounds about right. Victor loves money. He's a bornagain now, but it hasn't affected his finances."

"Good. Maybe he'll forgive the debt."

"Debt? You never paid him back?"

"Hey! I'm coming back down this way after I finish up in Denver. May I call you?"

"Why?"

"Same old Karoony." He chuckled and pulled out his cell phone and Kay, after a short hesitation, gave him the landline at the castle.

"I'll call you next month on your birthday, okay?"

"You remember my birthday?"

"I remember everything about you," Biff said, and kissed her again.

They were just kisses, Kay told herself as she drove back up the mountain to the castle. Harmless. Sexless. She hadn't made a fool of herself, hadn't succumbed to nostalgia or nosiness, hadn't asked whom he was with now or what he'd been up to for the last twenty-three years. Of course he hadn't asked her any of those things either. She could see how he lived—he bummed from band to band, or worked solo gigs like tonight's, which could not have brought in more than a few hundred dollars, traveling in his over-packed car that some woman must have bought for him. It was a careless life, one she'd outgrown. Or had she? She remembered Dana's response when she'd told her about Fenton: "You seem," Dana had said to Kay, her beautiful voice puzzled, "to find poverty erotic."

Poverty, yes, and probably disability too. Kay had seen how Biff tipped his head toward her, favoring one ear when he listened. She guessed he was, as most musicians his age must be, at least partially deaf. And yet. Did anyone anywhere have more beautiful eyes? Alive and young, in that lean lined face, those light gray eyes.

She came to the top of the driveway and paused. Neal's van was parked next to Victor's Mercedes, which was odd. Neal didn't usually linger after letting Nicky off and she hoped this didn't mean that Nicky had gotten sick at the dance. She let herself in through the massive front door, dismayed to see Victor's golf clubs and another of his suitcases in the front hall. How long was he staying? Surely only a day or two; surely Stacy would take him back soon. Ed yipped from behind Victor's closed door but there was no sound from Victor himself and she guessed he was in the shower; she could hear water running. She went into the kitchen and, as they had done as kids, turned both faucets on full-force to get his attention. But it wasn't Victor who yelped from the bathroom—Victor would never cry *"Herregud!!"* It was Neal's voice she heard, swearing in his mother's Norwegian.

She turned the water off and walked into Nicky's room. He was in his pajamas, killing monsters on his computer, Orville draped around his shoulders. Kay stood in the doorway, arms crossed, well away from the python, who reared its flat head to gaze at her.

"Okay," she said. "What's going on?"

"What do you mean?" Nicky asked, not looking up.

"Why is your father taking a shower here?"

"How was the dance, son? Why it was brilliant, Mom. Did you dance, son? Yes I did, Mom. With a girl, son? No, by myself, Mom. Is that why your feet look stepped on, son? Yes it is, Mom."

"Nick."

"Dad always takes a shower here. He's usually finished before you come home."

"Why can't he take his own shower in his own apartment?"

Nicky didn't answer.

"Nicky, why can't your father use his own apartment?"

"Mom? He can't. Okay?"

Kay waited.

"He doesn't have an apartment. He had to leave. They're tearing the building down. Dad's homeless." Nicky looked up. There were un-childlike shadows below his eyes. "He's been living in his van for the last two weeks, okay? Sometimes he comes over here in the afternoons when you're at work to do laundry and watch TV. He said not to tell you. He said you'd be mad."

"I am mad," Kay said. "He was right. What happened to his job at the health food store?"

"I don't know." Nicky paused. "I think the store went out of business."

Kay got up, took a flashlight from Nicky's nightstand, and went back outside to peer into Neal's van. The fading beam of light picked out things she did not want to see: a mattress and sleeping bag, his mother's hand-stitched crazy quilt, a camp stove, a cooler, a crate of vitamins, an air purifier, piles of clothes, stacks of old *Prevention* magazines and medical pamphlets. When she had first met him, Neal had lived like this, a bachelor sleeping in the back room of his widowed mother's house. She clicked the flashlight off and walked slowly back.

"I want you to put that snake back in its container right now."

"I will."

"I don't want you sleeping with it."

"I won't."

She set the flashlight back down on the nightstand. "Does Victor know Neal's here?"

"Uncle Victor's been in his room all night. I think he's been crying."

"Well you've had quite an evening, haven't you? You know your father is a grown-up man. He can take care of himself. There's no reason why he can't find another job and a good place to live."

"He can have my bed," Nicky said.

"Oh no." Kay shook her head. "No. No."

"Don't worry, babe." Neal stood in the doorway, drying his hair. Draped in the ragged blue bathrobe she had made for him ten years ago, he looked blatantly pathetic. His chest sagged, his belly pouched, his white legs were knock-kneed beneath the uneven hem. His long gray hair hung around his face like a grandmother's as he toweled it and his eyes were red and damp. Neal was twelve years older than she—an age difference that had seemed manageable, even desirable when they met, but had annoyed both of them by the time they separated.

"Don't worry," he repeated. "I'm leaving. It's just good to be clean once in a while. You ought to get some new soap by the way. That stuff you have is loaded with BHA and BHTs. I'll be going now. Bye Nicky. Do what your mother tells you." He paused, his voice breaking. "Bye Orville." He picked up a bundle of clothes lying in a heap on the floor with one hand and his tattered Birkenstocks in the other and headed down the hall toward the front door, his pigeon-toed feet wet and silent on the stone floor. Nicky shot Kay a desperate look and she shot a cold look back. "If he's been living in his van for two weeks," she pointed out, "he can manage another few days until he finds a place to live. He can camp at the beach."

"He doesn't have enough gas to drive to the beach."

"So is he planning to sleep in our driveway?"

Silence.

"Did you give him money?"

"Mom! Come on! I don't have any money."

"There's the Hate Jar."

"Right. That's how I support my father. With the Hate Jar."

"You gave it to him, didn't you?" She didn't wait for an answer. "You know what he's doing right now, Nick? He's standing at the front door waiting for me to hurry down the hall and say it's all right, he can sleep here. You know that's how he operates. He is the world's most manipulat ... "

Nicky's face twisted. Kay stopped, rubbed her forehead. She hated herself for talking this way. It was demeaning and damaging and it wasn't even fair. Neal had been a disappointing husband but he had always been a devoted father. She heard the front doorknob down the hall twist and slip as his wet hand cleverly failed to turn it.

"All right," she called, "you can sleep here tonight."

"Oh, that's all right … " The little sigh. The little cough. "I'm fine."

"But you're not giving him your bed," Kay said, turning back to Nicky. "He can go down to the dungeon."

"Mom!"

"I'm not kidding. He'll love the dungeon."

She stalked down the hall. "One night," she said. Neal looked at her, eyes red, mouth slack, wary, not particularly grateful. "But you've got to promise you'll begin looking for a place tomorrow." She waited.

"I promise," he said at last.

"Come on then. I'll show you the guest suite."

She was right about the dungeon: Neal loved it. It was cool and dry, it had its own latrine and sink, six little windows looking out into the garden, lots of unused exercise equipment to hang his hoodies on. The futon was fine, especially with the fresh sheets and blankets Kay threw on top of it.

"Just for tonight," Kay repeated. "You'll have to find an apartment tomorrow." She crossed her arms. "Do you understand?"

Neal bowed his head, and she felt like screaming. Was his helplessness really her fault? If she had stayed in the marriage, if she'd supported his business plans, if her father had given him that loan he had asked for, if, if, if—if all that had happened, would Neal be strong, happy, and successful by now? Had that ever been possible?

"Don't worry, babe." With no warning Neal lurched forward, put his thin arms around her and said, "Thank you." Kay bit back another scream. His hair was damp and his breath was sour. She managed, "You're welcome," before moving away. Every encounter she had with Neal broke her heart in a brand-new way. She turned, and practically ran up the stairs to her own room in the tower.

She was in her nightgown before she remembered that she still had to meditate, drink another full glass of water, recite a round of affirmations, journal about her day, and knit three rows on Charles's scarf. She also still had to work on her lying, gossiping, criticizing, procrastinating, stealing, swearing, judging, raging, craving, fearing, and obsessing about the things she needed to stop doing.

Lois Hayes could have the damn *Mindfulness* book. It wasn't helping at all. Restless, she reached across the bed to her nightstand and picked up a copy of *The Odyssey* instead. She had brought it home from the library a few days ago, curious to see if it might connect her better to Nicky's beloved video games. "*Sing to me of the man, Muse, the man of twists and turns/driven time and again off course*"—the music of the translation caught her up at once, but the old story, which she thought she knew, surprised her. This first section was all about the son, the boy Telemachus, bossing the weepy Penelope around, delivering lines like "I hold the reins of power in this house," while deciding to find his father. He was a brave kid even if he did, Kay yawned, have to be tucked into bed in the last stanza by his nanny. All men, even as boys, she decided, are full of "twists and turns" and most of the ones she knew were definitely "off course."

Just before she fell asleep, she realized that she had been embraced by four such men that day—Fenton, Victor, Biff, and Neal—all men she had once, in one way or another, loved or tried to love. She thought of Fenton's spicy woodchip odor, Victor's helpless sobs, Biff's tobacco-warm breath, Neal's long strands of wet hair. *Four failures in one day*, she thought, *wow, that's a record. I must be doing something right.*

WEEK THREE

The brown-shingled church in Manzanita was depressing to approach; even on this warm morning, with a fragrance of redwoods and honeysuckle in the air, there was a Last Mile feel to the path leading up to the door. The cars parked badly up and down the street outside were late model BMWs, Audis and Mercedes with bumper stickers that said things like "Let Go and Let God," which seemed to Kay a particularly dangerous way to drive, and "Happy, Joyous, and Free" which simply begged to be rear-ended. Still, who was she, Slogan Sue, to criticize; she had written "no carbs" on the inside of her wrist that morning and she had a Just For Today bookmark tucked into her wallet.

The people smoking outside on the deck had their backs turned to her, as did the people milling around in the kitchen. The ones sitting inside, hands folded, emitted a cold cheer as they finished mouthing The Serenity Prayer. Kay slipped into a folding chair in the back row, adjusted her sunglasses, and was not surprised to see, looking down, that she had dribbled coffee down the front of her blouse. Not a lot a lot of coffee. Just enough to remind her that even though she hated being here, among the saddicts, she belonged. Quitting drinking had saved her life. It was ridiculous to sulk about it.

She crossed her arms over the stain and sat up straighter. Strangers she knew only by first names surrounded her. Lawrence, bald, tattooed, sucking on a lollipop, sat in front. Chloe, a grandmother in leopard skin tights and stilettos, and Miles, a youth counselor who wept when he spoke, sat on either side of Lawrence. Wendell came in with his Chihuahua peeking out of his jacket pocket, and Jennifer entered with her enormous baby, opened her shirt and started to breastfeed. That baby, Kay thought, trying not to listen to it slurp, was the one who needed a 12-step program; it had to be two years old at least. She wondered where everyone lived outside the meetings; she never saw them at the library, at the grocery store, at Nicky's soccer games, or standing in line for the SRO tickets at the Symphony. Perhaps they remained anonymous even outside these rooms, perhaps they moved, as she sometimes felt she did, ghostlike through their own lives. Or perhaps they just hung out in bars.

She offered "Kay, Alcoholic" at roll call and endured the chipper chorus of "Hi Kays" that followed. She tried to keep her expression blank as Lori, "grateful alcoholic," complained about finding a good trainer for her Arabian racehorse, and Carney, "recovering lush," talked about his recent DUI, which he "knew intellectually but not emotionally" had not been issued just because he was driving a pink convertible through rural Alabama with his boyfriend. Seth's half-sister was in jail because "the disease" had made her attack a member of her golf team with a nine iron and Traynor was having a hard time since his pot-bellied pig had died. Miles had "gone out" after his mother's sixth wedding but was "back in" and requested a twenty-four-hour chip, which he received with a fresh flood of tears.

Kay watched him press the plastic disk to his lips as he sat back down. She had several tiddlywinks just like his in a box under her bed—too many, actually. She had been coming to AA off and on for over two years but she still did not feel at home in these meetings the way the others seemed to. One of these days the program would surely "take;" until then she'd listen as politely as she could while Jason, the handsome young businessman, confessed he could not stop shoplifting in hardware stores, and Ruth, a bitter-faced woman in running shorts, bragged that she had poured an entire bottle of Nyquil down the drain without drinking it and Emily shared how she had given her fiancé his ring back after she smelled beer on his breath.

Kay looked down at her right hand. Her mother's sapphire ring glinted coldly back. She twisted the stone to the inside and pressed her palm over it. Ida would die all over again if she knew Kay came to AA. Real alcoholics lived in shelters and slept in gutters. Her mother, clawing at the moon as she lurched from her wheelchair, wasn't a "real" alcoholic. Her father, teeing off into the redwoods from the deck, wasn't one either. But Kay, passed out on the bathroom floor while Nicky, terrified, banged on the locked door, was. Or had been. And could be again.

"It would be nice," Lawrence was saying, pulling his lollipop out of his mouth, "to hear from someone new this morning. Anyone who hasn't shared for a while? Anyone who has never shared?"

Kay clamped her lips shut and held her breath. She could not imagine adding her woes to the ones in the room. What could she say? That living in the castle, with Neal and Victor still there, shuffling into breakfast every morning and shuffling into dinner every night, was driving her crazy? Burst into tears because Fenton hadn't showed up for work in three days? Confess that she still hadn't organized a Friends of the Library meeting, that she was worried sick about Nicky's slipping grades, that Charles hadn't written in weeks—that nobody loved her? Love wasn't part of the lexicon here. The word "love" wasn't even in the index of her book of *Daily Reflections*; she'd looked it up, the same way she used to look up "Crying" in the baby books she'd studied when Nicky was born. "Loneliness," the index went, with three entries, and then it skipped straight to "Maintenance," with one entry. The maintenance of loneliness was a skill she did have. Boohoo. Should she add her own self-pity to the atmosphere already dripping with it? Whatever for? She studied the ad for Charles Schwab Investments printed on the cardboard cuff of Jason's coffee cup. Jennifer's baby burped. Wendell's Chihuahua yawned. The silence went on.

Then the door banged open and Kay exhaled with relief as Chiana swung in, dressed today in what looked like chewed animal hides, tufted, braided, knotted, and tied, her fat feet in sandals that wound up her legs, her hair in blonde dreads. She predictably plunked down in the front row and stretched, exposing a smooth slice of pale belly. Chiana was a champion stretcher. She introduced herself in a firm pretty voice, and launched into the morning's melodious psychobabble; today's rant had something to do with evening primrose oil, which had stopped the heavy monthly bleeding which had plagued her since she was eleven years old. Intimate details followed. At the end she stretched again, swiveled cross-legged on her stool, her little Buddha belly poking out through the fancy rags, and graced the room with a practiced smile.

Kay did not smile back, but she was impressed. Chiana might be a professional waif but she sure knew how to ask for what she wanted. At the meeting's close, Chiana danced into the circle, grabbed Kay's resistant hand, and prayed louder than anyone, saying, "Our *mother* which art in heaven" and "Give us this day our daily *strength*," which was all right, no one here said "bread" anymore, even if it was gluten free, and "Deliver us from *ego*," which was probably asking too much. "Keep coming back," she finished, beaming at Kay as she pumped her hand up and down. "It works if you work it."

Week Three

As always, Kay was the first out the door. She stepped into the sunshine and walked head down toward her car. The worst part of the day was over. Now she could get to work.

The West Valley Library sat on a knoll surrounded by oak trees—the perfect location, the Board of Supervisors seemed to feel, for yet another housing development. The meadow behind it had been bulldozed years ago, and now boasted sixty mini-mansions on tiny parcels of land, and the acreage on either side was in the process of being torn up as well. The little library, with its brown shingles and shake roof, was as out of place in this new landscape as if it had been abandoned by a klutzy time machine, and Kay's heart always rose in a surge of protective affection as she neared it. She pulled into the empty lot and unlocked the front door, stooping to pick up the mail dropped on the floor through the slot. There, among all the magazines, bulletins, bills, and flyers: a postcard from Charles! After all this time! Charles was alive; he hadn't forgotten her! He seemed to have left Thailand, for this one had a Greek postmark. It was hand painted—an amethyst ocean seen from a balcony—but it didn't say anything. A few lines of poetry that she recognized from her nighttime reading of *The Odyssey* were printed on the back in his small clear script: " ... *out at sea on a wave-washed island* ... "

She examined the postmark more closely. Paros. Where was Paros and why, if he'd finished his art classes in Bangkok, hadn't he come back here? The card was exquisite—which made it art, she supposed, but did not make it Charles. Charles was chatty, catty, affectionate. Had he met someone? Had he fallen in love with some gorgeous foreigner and forgotten all his English?

Troubled, she slipped the postcard into her pocket. The least he could have said, she thought, was Wish You Were Here. Not that she'd ever get there. Airfare was expensive and if the library did indeed close, she'd be out of a job.

She hoped not. She loved this place. Loved the long oak tables and brass lamps and worn chairs and over-crowded shelves of books and movies. Librarians, she knew, were not supposed to be sentimental. They were supposed to be curious, energetic, aggressive and forward-thinking. They were supposed to embrace change and rapidly adapt to serve the public needs. She was a lousy librarian. Lois Hayes was right. She had to do something soon, organize some resistance to the Board of Supervisors. What she needed was a plan, a prod, a push.

I'll figure something out, she thought, as she had thought for months, and she went into the music room to straighten up.

The music room was her favorite place in the library, possibly her favorite place in the world. Soundproofed by Fenton last summer, it contained an upright piano, Victor's old drum set, and an assortment of donated flutes and recorders for kids to use. The CDs, cassette tapes and vinyl recordings ranged from Albinoni to Zappa and somewhere in there, Kay knew, there was even a tape of Hawaiian slack key guitar music with Biff Kelly's gaunt face on the cover, leering above a lei. She started to look for it, stopped herself. Why look for an image she had memorized anyway? Then again, why not? She flipped through the box of old cassettes until she found it: *Biff and the Beach Bro's*. It would be like all the others he'd made over the years—*Biff and the Blarney Stoners, Biff and the Bolsheviks*—cheaply made, competent, with every now and then an astonishing passage of invention. She slipped it into her shoulder bag and headed toward her office, puzzled to hear the sound of water running. A small lavatory had been installed behind her office years ago, but no one but herself ever used it. She pushed open the door to her office and jumped back in shock. Her ex-supervisor was sitting at her desk.

"Hello dear." Mrs. Holland seemed to be wearing a man's tartan plaid bathrobe, cotton socks, and nothing else. "I can't find my glasses." Her thatch of white hair stuck out in all directions and her black eyes, once so bright and quick, blinked in confusion; dementia had claimed her a short six months after she retired and her descent—Mrs. Holland always did everything efficiently—had been rapid. "I've gone through every drawer in the desk. But I can't find them anywhere."

"You probably left them back at the home." Kay glanced out the window for a taxi or a caretaker's car from the assisted living residence, but there was nothing there. Had Mrs. Holland walked here? Hitchhiked? How had she gotten inside the building? She saw the familiar gold key ring, heavy as an Edwardian housekeeper's, glittering in the keyhole of the opened back door; she pulled it out and slipped it in her pocket. "Let me drive you back to Laurel House. We'll look for your glasses there."

Mrs. Holland nodded, but continued to sit. She had emptied every drawer, Kay saw, and the floor was littered with papers, staples, clips, and pens. All the photographs of Nicky had been placed in a circle and the yellow roses Kay had brought in last week were dumped in the wastepaper basket; Mrs. Holland had hay fever and had never permitted flowers inside the library. The little sink in the bathroom, filled with coffee cups Mrs. Holland had apparently started to wash, was overflowing, the computer was blinking on and off, the land line hummed. Kay turned off the sink, replaced the receiver, called Laurel House, said, "I've got her," to a frantic nurse, and helped Mrs. Holland to her feet.

"I've missed you," she confessed, her arm around the older woman as she led her out to her car. "You always gave the best advice. You were the one who told me to go back to grad school, remember?" She steered Mrs. Holland around a pothole in the parking lot. "You had faith in me. You told me to divorce Neal, stop drinking, start dating, continue running, and apply for this job when you retired."

"Sometimes I leave my glasses on top of my head. Are they there?"

"No. You see the thing is," Kay continued, "the Board wants to close us down. I wish you could help me figure out what to do. I know there are steps I must take to organize a protest, but I don't know what they are. I don't know what to do or where to start. I haven't done a thing, frankly, to stop the Board from tearing this branch down."

"A branch is not a tree."

"A branch … ?"

"They are just silly reading glasses," Mrs. Holland said. "But I can't hear without them." She settled into the car and let Kay fasten the seat belt around her.

"I don't know," Kay repeated, half to herself, as she slipped behind the wheel and turned the key. "I'm afraid I'm going to fuck up."

"Probably," Mrs. Holland said. She reached over with a sudden radiant smile of recognition and patted Kay's hand. "But try not to say 'fuck up.'"

On her way back to the library, Kay drove past the dentist's office where Stacy worked as a hygienist and slowed, but Dr. Blum's office was closed on Saturdays and Stacy's car was not in the lot. Maybe Stacy was having an affair with Dr. Blum—no—Dr. Blum was a good-looking man but he was Jewish and Stacy would never sleep with a Jewish man. Or a Muslim. Or a Taoist. Or with anyone who wasn't going to heaven after The Rapture. Besides, Stacy loved Victor. That was something Kay would bet on. Whatever had happened to her brother's marriage had not—unlike her own—been caused by a failure of love.

She returned to the library, ashamed to see young mothers with their toddlers already waiting for Story Hour to start, but the women were chatting with each other in the sunshine and smiled forgivingly as she ducked by to let them in. Her Saturday assistant, a retired firefighter named Jolene, followed a minute later. She helped Jolene on with her Story Lady hat and cloak, reminded her not to scare everyone with true accounts of local tragedies, and went to the front desk just in time to apologize to Mr. McAdams, who had not yet received the book of Civil War photographs he had ordered and to hear from one of the mothers that her son had dropped his toy truck down the toilet in The Ladies.

At noon, the van from the Senior Center disgorged a load of alarmingly fragile octogenarians, see-through people who wandered up and down the aisles like orphans in a forest, never touching a book. High school kids gouged unoriginal obscenities into the study desks, retired businessmen studied *Motorcycle World*, and housewives and the homeless slumped side by side in the stained easy chairs reading glossy magazines filled with photographs of movie stars they had never heard of. The two computers had long waiting lists and the copy machine jammed again and again.

"Have you announced the first Friends of the Library meeting?" Lois Hayes asked, watching Kay as she pretended to check the list of holds on the *Miracle* book, which she had forgotten, after all, to bring back.

"Not yet," Kay admitted. She had an idea. "It needs a chairperson. Would you be willing to take charge?"

"I could do that," Lois agreed. "I'll start calling around. I know a lot of people. How's about meeting here on Thursday, at seven. Have you drafted the petition yet?"

"Yes," Kay lied. "It just needs to be printed."

"Bring it to the meeting." Lois gave her a level look. "Some concert last week, wasn't it? *You* had fun," she added as she stepped into the music room.

Well, there goes my reputation, Kay thought. Again. The library had always been West Valley's equivalent of the village well. Births, deaths, and scandals were discussed here, and this week she would be the hot topic: the tramp who slept with the carpenter, kissed the musician, and lived with the ex-husband. She reached for her desk calendar, found Thursday and scrawled "Friends' Meeting, 7pm." She'd see if Zabeth or Dana could come with her and she'd go online to find out how to draft a petition. She looked up as an angry mother marched toward her out of the Story Hour corner. What had Jolene done now?

"I do not think young children need to hear about a house on fire with a parrot inside screaming 'Poor Polly, Poor Polly' as it burns to death, do you?"

"Ouch."

"Ouch is right. You better talk to your Story Lady. She shouldn't be allowed around kids."

"She saved several."

"What?"

"Lives. She's a firefighter. She saved four children in that burning house."

"That's fine. Tell you what. Let her save them somewhere else. And in the meantime: Get a new Story Lady."

Stacy would make a good Story Lady. As long as she stayed away from *The Book of Revelations*. Kay tried to reach Stacy several times during the day, but all she got was the phone message. After the library closed, Kay decided to drive out to Rancho Valdez and see if she could talk to Stacy in person.

Victor and Stacy had bought a 3,000-square-foot house on what looked like a 1,000-square-foot lot in a bleak new subdivision called Tuscany Terrace. The front lawn was sodded in green squares like bathroom tile and though there were no real plants in front there was an artificial ficus tree on the porch and an enormous wreath of dried sunflowers on the door. Kay had brought a bag of the pastel dinner mints she knew Stacy liked and she was just about to leave it on the door handle, with a note saying CALL ME! when, on her third ring, the door opened, and Stacy said, "Wow, look at you, cutie, what a nice surprise!"

"You didn't get my phone messages?"

Stacy dimpled, shrugged, looked into the bag of candy, cooed appreciatively, and waved Kay inside. It was not really an answer but then Stacy never really answered anything. The house was immaculate, as always, with its white leather couches and chairs, its gilt lamps, beige carpet, and banks of artificial flowers. Stacy, barefoot, looking curvy even in a long shapeless dress, led Kay to a couch and settled down across from her, one leg tucked under her.

"It seems I never get to see you anymore," Stacy said in her soft voice. "You're so busy with your job and all. Cute," she added, pointing to the chipped blue polish on Kay's bitten nails. "Do you want a soda?"

"No, I just wanted to see how you were doing."

Stacy nodded, eyes bright, hands folded in her lap. "Good," she chirped. Her makeup as always was immaculate and although there were diamonds in her earlobes, her hands were bare; she was not wearing her wedding rings.

"Really?" Kay said. "Because Victor's having a hard time. In fact, he's really torn up. He's moved back into his old room and he just lies in bed and cries. He cries all the time."

Stacy gave a sympathetic sigh but said nothing else. Kay's eyes drifted around the room, settling on a scrolled silver frame containing a photo of Victor with his glossy salesman's smile, and Stacy beside him, all curls and curves. Their pastor stood behind them, round faced and red haired, one hand on Stacy's shoulder. It seemed to Kay that his hand looked a little too possessive.

"How is your prayer practice going?"

"Good."

"Victor says he's not allowed to attend."

Stacy, smiling, eyes downcast, stroked the couch. "It's just girls."

"Girls who want to get pregnant?"

"Our purpose," Stacy chided in a gentle monotone, "is to glorify Jesus as the Designer and Creator of Issue."

"Jesus? Not your husband?"

Stacy giggled. It occurred to Kay that she might still be taking drugs.

"I don't know The Bible very well," Kay began, cautiously, "but I don't recall anything in it about marriages ending because of lack of," she paused, "issue. There are so many happy couples in the Bible," she floundered—David and Bathsheba? Samson and Delilah?—"with no children." She paused. "It *is* about children? Not just because Victor's selfish and immature and materialistic and you hate him?"

"I don't use the word 'hate,'" Stacy said.

"I don't either," Kay said hastily. "I mean, I do. But it costs me." She took a quick breath. Although she had not been able to find anything about "issue" or "empty vessel" in the Bartlett's she had consulted at the library that afternoon, she had found a Martin Luther quote she hoped would work. "'There is no more lovely, friendly, and charming relationship, communion, or company than a good marriage,'" she recited.

Stacy dimpled in recognition. "Isn't that the truth," she agreed, her voice light and sweet. Then she leaned forward, lips parted. "How's Ed?"

"Ed? He's awful. He barks all the time."

"He has to be held. I miss Ed," Stacy sighed.

Kay suddenly remembered that Ed was Stacy's dog. Victor must have kidnapped him. Victor would do that: he had a mean streak. But Stacy knew that about Victor, accepted it, and had even, for a while, tamed it. What on earth had happened to change her? Why did she care more about her dog now than her husband? "Why don't you come up to the castle and take Ed back?" she suggested.

Stacy cooed, but didn't answer; sometimes talking to her was like talking to a pigeon, but it was peaceful too; Kay could see why Victor depended on her; there was something about the way she stonewalled every question that was almost comforting. "So you won't take Victor back either?" Kay asked as she rose to leave.

"It's not up to me," Stacy said. After a few seconds of silence, Kay sighed, accepted Stacy's fragrant hug, and took the basket of dog toys that Victor had forgotten to steal.

On the drive back to the castle she thought about her brother's marriage. Like Kay, Victor had had his share of romantic false starts. His first girlfriend, Sasha, dreadlocked, braless, and tie dyed, had broken his heart when she left him for another woman. Martine, the elegant Asian girl he dated a few years later, married his best friend's father. Neither Sasha nor Martine had been kind to him and there had been a time when Kay worried that her brother might turn into a woman hater. She remembered seeing him fold a dollar bill into an arrow and jab it into the soft flesh above a belly dancer's girdle at a Middle Eastern restaurant, and she'd all too often heard his favorite joke, "How can you trust something that bleeds for a week and doesn't die"—a joke that, for some reason, had delighted Ida, who always clapped her hands and said, "I give up: how?" But everything changed when Victor met Stacy. She was with another salesman at a dealership picnic; he was with a stripper he'd paid to accompany him. Stacy caught his eye, winked, and slowly, holding his gaze, lifted her skirt with two dainty fingers and did the splits. "She got me with that one," Victor was fond of saying, both hands on his heart.

Stacy still did the splits, in a way, Kay thought. Her vocabulary consisted of giggles and sighs but her body language was eloquent. She was a gifted dental hygienist, with a light, intuitive touch. Her patients loved her, Nicky adored her, and even Francis liked her. Ida, disapproving, did not accept her until after The Conversion.

The Conversion: Kay did not pretend to understand it. But one morning Jesus appeared to Victor and Stacy. He looked exactly like his picture, they said: tall, bearded, and beautiful, dressed in a robe and sandals, his long hair curling on his shoulders. He didn't talk, just smiled at them as they huddled together in their waterbed, the sheets to their naked chests, their mouths open, tears of astonishment streaming from their eyes. After He vanished, they got up, got dressed, dumped the China White and Mexican Brown down the toilet, paid off their dealers, cancelled their contracts, dropped their old friends. Together they sent an open letter to the newspaper renouncing their past, a letter with so many grammatical errors that Francis edited it in red and sent it back to the paper corrected. Their conversation, which had never been sparkling, no longer centered on concerts and clubs but on Scripture, as interpreted by their newfound Pastor Paulsen. Serenely cheerful, they no longer laughed. College educated, they no longer read. They were impossible to be around, but they were good to each other and Kay had loved watching them sit side by side, hand in hand. She felt her brother had found a safe haven at last and only wondered why, having also found Jesus, he was still such a jerk.

She came home to find Neal's filthy van parked companionably next to Victor's shining Lexus. Both men were still here? Why? Aside from pointing out apartment ads, she had stopped talking to either of them and she no longer cooked for them, which meant the kitchen sink was always clogged with Neal's thick green smoothies and the kitchen stove was always littered with Victor's greasy frying pans. She entered to see Victor's scuba equipment and free weights dumped in the entry hall. Ed was barking non-stop at the television in the Great Room, which was on full blast. She turned it off, scooped the dog up and took advantage of the blessed quiet to rap on Victor's door. "Stacy wants her dog back," she said.

"You talked to Stacy?" Victor opened the door a crack and stared at her red eyed as she thrust the dog at him. Reluctantly he took it. *He doesn't like Ed either*, Kay realized.

"Yes, and I think if you apologized you two could … "

Victor closed the door in her face.

She tried the handle. It was locked. "Come on, Victor. I mean it. Ed's homesick and you are too. Do you want me to have to tell Dad you kidnapped your wife's dog?"

"Dad doesn't care."

Kay could see Francis saying exactly that as he bent over his putting iron, practicing on a Persian rug as Glo swept in with her daily haul from Carmel's most expensive boutiques. She'd have to try something else.

"What about the real estate agents?"

"What real estate agents?"

"The ones who are going to show the castle to prospective buyers. Ed will scare them away and then the castle won't sell and then you'll never get your share of the money and you won't be able to tithe at church and when the Rapture comes they won't let you evaporate with everyone else because you've been such a cheapskate."

"Go away, Kay."

"No," Kay said. "You go away. I live here. You said you were only going to stay a little while. It's been a little while. You need to leave."

There was no answer. She didn't think there would be. She walked slowly down the hall, heard rapid clicks behind her, and stiffened as Ed, yipping, trotted past her to the kitchen. She glared as he arrowed toward his food bowl. "I hate terriers," she said.

Nicky, sitting at the counter practicing his guitar, held his hand out for the Hate Jar.

She dug in her purse, saw her wallet was empty, and scrawled an IOU. "They're bullies and killers."

Nicky looked up. "What do they kill?"

"I don't know. Cats, rats, foxes, badgers."

"Snakes?"

"One can but wish."

"Rabbits?"

"Sure. They're actually bred to hunt rabbits."

"Uh oh. I better warn Dad."

"Why?"

"Dad has this sort of pet? Goldie? She used to live in back of his building? And when we went back to the demolition site this morning, we saw her hiding in the rubble. So we brought her here."

"Here? You're telling me there's a rabbit in the dungeon?"

Neal, always silent, materialized behind her. Kay leapt around, smothering a gasp as he in turn suppressed a chuckle. "Not in the dungeon," Neal said. "My allergies."

"So where did you put her?"

Neal's heavy sigh. Neal's heavy silence.

"We put her in your room," Nicky said.

"You put a rodent in my room?"

"Rabbits aren't rodents, Mom. They're lagomorphs."

"I don't care what they are. They don't go in my bedroom."

"This one does," Neal said.

"She's having babies, Mom."

Kay, disbelieving, went up the tower stairs. But it was true. Neal had turned her bedroom into a hutch. He had actually dumped a pile of alfalfa in the corner, and there were three carrots on the floor. She heard a growl and saw a buff-colored bunny panting in a bloody nest of good towels under her vanity table.

The bunny looked up at Kay with unblinking round eyes, bared her two teeth, gave another growl and ejected a small packet of gray slime. "God damn it!" Kay yelled.

"Watch your language!" Victor yelled back from below.

"Neal! Get up here this minute! I want these animals moved out of my room right now. Put them outside or lock them in the drum tower. And if there is one single goddamn piece of straw left on my goddamn floor, I swear to God ... "

"Language!"

"I will shove it down your goddamn throat."

Kay grabbed her purse, fished out her car keys, and stomped downstairs. Neal sidled by her, eyes downcast but lips twitching—he thought this was funny? A screaming woman was funny?—and it was all she could do not to push him over the railing. All day she had admired the way that Story Hour mother had snapped, *Tell you what.* She copied it now. "Tell you what," she said to Nicky, waiting for her at the foot of the stairs. "We're getting out of here. Grab your tennis racket."

She drove to the high school and she and Nicky hit balls against the backboard until they had both sweated the worst of the day out. Then they stopped to gorge on grease at McDonald's. Then, listening to *Biff and the Beach Bro's* playing "Little Grass Shack," on her old tape deck, they drove around neighborhood after neighborhood, looking at the outside of houses for sale, imagining what it would be like to live somewhere else, in peace and comfort, just the two of them.

"And Orville," Nicky added.

The next day was Sunday, Kay's day to fill the department store in the mall with motivational music. The piano there was a piece of junk but it was an enormous, glossy piece of junk and Kay enjoyed playing it on the crowded ground floor by the escalators; it was like steering a ship through a choppy sea. The stage fright she had felt all her life while performing was not a problem here; knowing no one was listening gave her the freedom to forgive herself the missed notes. She set her tip jar on the piano bench, sat down, and started out as the store manager had told her to, with catchy show tunes, rippling through standards from *Gypsy* and *Oklahoma!* and slipping in a few of her own favorites from darker musicals like *Into the Woods* and *Candide* when she thought she could get away with it. While plowing through the repertoire from *Hello Dolly* she felt two little tugs on either side of her jacket and heard a familiar ha ha ha at her back.

Zabeth. Zeng. Zai.

"Break time," Zabeth said. "Time for coffee. I promised the girls a cookie."

"Coming." Kay tinkled out a series of elaborate flourishes, reached into the tip jar to retrieve the five dollars she'd put in for herself earlier, grabbed a child by each hand, and followed Zabeth's slim hips as they twitched briskly through the cosmetic aisles to the café in the far corner of the store. With the four-year-olds poking holes in their cookies and peering at each other through them, she smiled at her friend and said, "Catch up time. You first." Zabeth's news was good: She'd won her last court case, Garret's pharmacy had received an award from the Chamber of Commerce, the girls were doing well in their tumbling class, and the antique Turkish rug she'd bought on e-Bay had arrived and she and Garret had made love on it last night.

"You're doing everything right," Kay whistled. "Admirable."

Zabeth grinned. Motherhood, career, and marriage suited her but hadn't softened her; she was still the tense, trim, untidy glamour girl Kay had met years ago at her first AA meeting. Zabeth, unlike Kay, still drank, but it had been years since Kay had had to drive her home from a bar or bail her out of jail. She still lined her eyes with kohl and encircled her thin muscled arms with heavy silver bracelets. She still wore a diamond in her nose and a hoop, Kay guessed, in her clitoris, and her designer clothes reeked of tobacco, Bordeaux, and her own musky scent. She had finished law school in one and a half years and was one of the best prosecutors in the county, with a gift for cross-examination that Kay wished she'd reserve for the courtroom. "Did you," Zabeth said now, "or did you not see Biff Kelly the other night?"

"Yes. It was fine. Don't look at me like that. Nothing happened."

"Nothing?"

"Just a kiss."

"What kind of kiss."

"Old friend kiss."

"Old boyfriend kiss? Or old friend-friend kiss."

"Just an old-old kiss." Kay stirred her coffee. "He's still the same. He said he'd call when he gets back from his tour, but I'm not counting on it."

"I hope he does call. It might shake Fenton up. You could use another man in your life."

"I have too many men in my life," Kay said, and she told Zabeth about Neal and Victor moving in.

"What were you thinking of?" Zabeth asked, astonished.

"Good question. I also have rabbits. Six baby rabbits and their feral mother in the drum tower, a huge snake in Nicky's room, a rat terrier in Victor's room ... "

Zabeth, unsmiling, held her hand up. "Stop. This is bad. What are you going to do?"

"Do? What can I do?"

"You can get them to leave!"

"How?"

"I don't know. Call the sheriff. Buy a shotgun." Zabeth turned to say something in swift stern Mandarin to the twins, causing them both to take dutiful sips of their cocoas, then spun back to Kay. "It's your house."

"Not really."

"Really." Before Kay could defend herself—and how, after all, could she defend herself?—and why should she have to?—Zabeth shot her a canny look.

"You like it, don't you?" Zabeth said. "Queen mother boss." She paused. "Martyr."

"What?"

"I bet you're feeding them gourmet meals."

"No."

" … and doing their laundry … "

"No!"

" … and slipping twenty-dollar bills into Neal's hoodie when he looks sad. Ha ha ha. Wendy and the Lost Boys. Well, I've said it before and I'll say it again, you're a nicer person than I am, Kay. But you are seriously insane. Hey, I know! Since you've already got a full house, let's have your party there."

"What party?"

"Your birthday party. Don't lie and say you forgot your own birthday? It's next week!"

"I didn't forget," Kay said truthfully. "But I don't want a party. Any other suggestions?"

"Yes. Why don't you have a birthday lunch with your father? Francis is smart. He'll tell you how to get rid of those squatters. I always see my father on my birthday. It's a tradition we've had since I was six. You could drive down to Carmel, have a fabulous lunch, get some good advice, then you could come home and have a fabulous dinner out with Dana and me and get even better advice. Sound like a deal?" She watched Kay's face then jabbed her wrist with a sharp fingernail. "Do it! Call the old guy. The worst he can say is no."

"Actually," Kay corrected her, "Dad can say lots worse than that."

"I like Francis," Zabeth reminded her. "I liked Ida too." She considered Kay over the rim of her coffee cup. "You never saw them the way I did."

"Well of course not. They weren't your parents!" Kay wanted to deflect the litany she knew was coming, but Zabeth had already launched into her version of Francis and Ida, who she called the Owl and the Pussycat, though the Pussycat, she granted, was a tigress and the Owl was a raptor. They were such a glamorous couple, Zabeth said, so witty, so intelligent, so much fun. Zabeth would have loved to have had parents like that, elegant parents who blew kisses back and forth to each other over their martinis. "They weren't just husband and wife," Zabeth said. "They were lovers!"

"'The children of lovers,'" Kay said, bitterly quoting something she had read long ago, "'are orphans.'" She glanced at her watch, rose, kissed the twins, hugged Zabeth, and threaded her way through the shoppers back to the piano. Zabeth was dense sometimes but she was right to sense that Kay did not want to call Francis. He was even worse on the phone than he was in person. And why would he want to see her on her birthday? He didn't care. He was the least sentimental person she had ever met. It was true he had blown kisses to Ida when she was alive, but he had married Glo the minute she was dead—so much for thinking of him as a "lover." She sat down at the piano and broke into a medley from *The King and I*, the last two words from "I Whistle a Happy Song" echoing in her head: *"I'm afraid."*

That evening she closeted herself in Ida's study. It was important to concentrate on the work she needed to do for the library.

She drafted a petition for the Friends of the Library, and started working on a talk to pitch to the Board of Supervisors. Surrounded by her mother's unfinished projects—the empty easel and tubes of unused paint, the potter's wheel, the six-page novels, the expensive cameras still in their boxes—she struggled to make the survival needs of her little library irresistible. Mrs. Holland, she thought with a pang, could have written this talk in her sleep—five years ago. Even now Mrs. Holland sometimes hit the nail on the head. That comment about a branch not being a tree ... there was something in that phrase that tugged at Kay's mind. There were other library branches, she knew, bigger, better ones, all over the country. She could move. Find a fully funded library somewhere else. But where? And how? The West Valley Branch needed her.

"*Time,*" she wrote, "*has not been kind to our West Valley Branch, but time is what it needs and deserves, time to develop its present resources, plan for its future productivity, and profit from its past successes ...*" Blah blah. Her words already sounded as if they'd been cribbed from one of the self-help books that she was addicted to. Maybe she needed a self-help book to break her addiction. Not that she had ever read any of those books all the way through. Who could? They were unreadable. She just liked having them, in the same way, she supposed, she used to like having a bottle of champagne in the refrigerator. Had she ever taken the *Miracle Mindfulness Makeover* back? Or was it still under her bed, opened to page 24?

She scowled, pushed back from the desk, and went out into the twilight to water the roses. Victor was lying flat in one of the lounge chairs by the pool, Ed on his chest, staring at the sky, and Neal was digging in the vegetable garden. What were they doing here? Neal should be married to a cheerful farm girl who spun wool from the hair of her own goats, and Victor should be sitting at home in his all-white living room with Stacy beside him, reading Scripture. She noticed the sandwich crusts on the pool table, the glasses of melted iced tea, the potato chip crumbs. Look away, she told herself. Don't clean it up.

"Babe?" Neal's reedy voice called from the garden.

"I am not your babe," she called back. "I never was. I never will be. My name is Kay. Call me Kay."

"Babe, I don't suppose you saved Goldie's afterbirth? No? I knew I should have reminded you. This patch could really use some added nutrients, especially if we're going to live off our own vegetables next year."

"We won't be here next year."

"We might," Neal said cheerfully. "The climate's changing. The economy's going."

"The Rapture," Victor agreed.

Kay, with a last dirty look at the dirty dishes on the pool table, fled to the music alcove to throw herself into the sonorous sanity of Beethoven. She waited until the chords cleared her head and calmed her heart. Then she got up and phoned her father to invite herself for lunch.

"Seems like a waste of a perfectly good birthday," Francis said, "but if you want to spend it in Carmel ... "

"I want to spend it with *you*," Kay corrected.

"No accounting for taste." But he sounded pleased. Glo, in the background, shrilled, "I suppose she'll want us to make reservations at Anton and Michael," and Francis replied, surprisingly, delightfully, "Aw shuddup." Turning back to the phone, he said, "Noon. Bring Nicky. We'll go to the club. And Kay, try, for once, to be on time."

WEEK FOUR

Her birthday morning dawned white with summer fog and Kay sat up in bed, hugged her knees, and looked out the window. Forty-five. Old! A year ago, she had spent her birthday with Charles and Nicky, the three of them taking turns quietly paddling the bay in a kayak. They'd picnicked on a deserted beach, napped on the sand, told knock-knock jokes to each other. She remembered the black-eyed seal that swam beside them on the way back to the launching ramp, and the crab fisherman who waved to them from his boat. She had just started seeing Fenton then; Charles had not yet started to talk about going away; Nicky had just begun guitar lessons. The library funding was not in danger, Victor's marriage seemed secure, Neal had a job and a place to live, and now? A year later?

She got out of bed, stumbled through a sunless salutation, tried to meditate, gave up, and went downstairs.

Nicky was still asleep but he had propped a card by the coffee pot with a drawing of her piano crowned with candles and *I LOVE YOU MOM* crayoned across the top. Kay smiled at the card and looked up, still smiling, as Victor stumbled into the kitchen, unshaven, rumpled, Ed yipping from the bedroom behind him.

"I'm driving down to see Dad today," she said. "Want to come?"

"To see Dad?"

"I know. But it's a nice drive. They're taking us to a club."

"Which one?" Victor pushed unwashed hair back from his swollen eyes and regarded her. "Pebble Beach? Carmel Valley?"

"I don't know, Dad didn't say."

"Pebble Beach would be primo. I bet Glo has a membership. Smartest thing Dad ever did was marry Glo."

"Why? Because she has money?"

"No! Land sakes! Because she's good for him." Victor picked up the cup of coffee she had just poured for herself, added three spoonfuls of sugar, and sipped. "Of course, Glo having money doesn't hurt," he added, opening the refrigerator door and rummaging around for the whipped cream.

"She's bought two cars from you already," Kay agreed. "And didn't you tell me she donated ten thousand dollars to Pastor Paulsen's Prayer-A-Thon-And-Barbecue?"

"I suppose you think she should be giving money to you instead?"

"No, don't worry, that won't ever happen. Glo doesn't like me."

"Well, she's a moral person. She was upset when you dumped Neal. We all were. You can't expect her to condone divorce."

"Ah. So that's why her first two husbands killed themselves?"

"Come on, Kay. Her first husband fell off a yacht and her second one … "

"Committed hari-kari with a steak knife in the bathroom? I'd say that was a pretty clear cut, if you'll excuse the pun, case of suicide."

"No wonder no one can talk to you," Victor said.

Kay didn't answer. She was remembering the last time she'd seen Glo. Glo and Francis had been dressed alike, in pale yellow cashmere sweaters and fawn flannel pants and they had stalked around the castle rooms, gathering up the few items they could use in Carmel. Glo's boney face had been set and stiff and Francis had hummed the first two lines of "Mairzy Doats" in the deadpan singsong that used to infuriate Ida. "Good thing you didn't get your musical talent from him," Ida used to tell Kay, fishing ice cubes out of her drink and throwing them at Francis, while Francis, deftly catching each one and dropping them into his own drink would say, "Good thing she didn't get *anything* from you," and then both he and Ida would throw their heads back and laugh, something Kay had never seen him do with Glo.

"And I don't agree that she's all that 'good' for Dad, either," she finished up. "He doesn't sound happy."

"He's not going to sound happy when he hears Nature Boy hasn't hung these cabinets yet," Victor said, turning to leave.

"Are you talking about Mr. Redpath?" Nicky, coming into the kitchen, raised his face for his morning kiss but Kay froze when she saw Orville draped around his wrists like handcuffs.

"I've told you and told you," she said. "The snake stays in his tank."

"Yes," Victor said, pausing in the doorway, "we *were* talking about Mr. Redpath."

"In. His. Tank." Kay watched as Nicky, nuzzling Orville's hideous head, reluctantly turned and left the kitchen. What was he getting from that snake? Was it his own personal *Keep Away* sign? His way of saying, *Mom, don't come closer*? He wouldn't lie with his head on her lap anymore, and she missed his warm smelly sweaty weight close beside her on the couch when they watched television or read at night. But he still lets me kiss him, she consoled herself. He isn't all grown up yet.

"You're having relations with the carpenter, aren't you?" Victor asked. He licked cream off his lips.

"Yes. I am. Fenton's my boyfriend. Come off it, Victor. Hey." She nudged her brother's bare foot with her own, tapping it until she evoked a wan smile back, a peace sign from the Old Vic, before his Conversion. "He doesn't stay overnight. We don't make out in front of Nicky. Though we are taking Nicky river rafting next weekend."

"Does your husband know?"

"Ex-husband," Kay said, "and no, I don't believe it has occurred to Neal that I have ever had relations with anyone, including him, and I would appreciate it if you do not mention it to him. Hey. Want to come today or not?" Her voice softened. "It's easier to visit Dad when it's both of us. And you need to get out of the house. And Glo's about ready for another new used car. And," she finished, "it's my birthday."

Victor looked up. "Are you going to make one of your birthday breakfasts?"

"What are those?"

"Pancakes. Every year on my birthday you made blueberry pancakes."

"But it's not your birthday. It's mine."

"You used to spell my name out in the batter. You used real maple syrup. You made cocoa with marshmallows. You used to fry ham steaks and give me the little white hambone to wear as a ring. Remember? Bacon's all right if we don't have ham. Why are you laughing? I always loved those birthday pancakes."

"Then you should make some."

"How? I can't cook."

"You could learn." She handed Victor the old *Fanny Farmer* cookbook just as Neal came up from downstairs. "Happy forty-eighth," Neal said and gave Kay a small box. Kay hesitated. Neal shouldn't be giving her gifts.

"Open it, Mom!" Nicky urged, coming in, snakeless, behind Neal.

"Well." Kay took it. "Thanks." She unwrapped the box, pulled out a strange looking sculpture, and looked up. "What is it?"

"I invented it," Neal said proudly. "It's a special mouth guard. So you won't grind your teeth in your sleep."

"I don't grind my teeth in my sleep."

"You used to."

"That was when we ... ." were married, Kay finished to herself. When I was starving to death of loneliness, when I chewed air in the dark while you lay silent beside me. She inserted the mouth guard and clowned for her family. "Thank you, Neal," she said, taking it out and returning it to the box. "Very thoughtful. Maybe I'll wear it when I see Dad this afternoon."

"Now if we could do something about your poor little mutilated hands," Neal said as he moved past her to put on a pot of water for one of his vile-smelling teas. "I've got some ideas but I don't have the formula right yet." Kay looked down; she could use a manicure but her cuticles were much better; wearing the nail polish helped; her nails had actually started to grow. Her hands didn't look great, but they were not "poor" or "little" and they were not "mutilated." Neal made everything so dark. "Be sure and give Francis my regards when you go down there today," Neal added. "I doubt I'll ever see him again."

"Why?"

"Oh babe. His cough."

"Dad's always had a cough."

"Just don't smoke with him. Okay? You always smoke with him."

"No I do n ... ."

"She doesn't remember to treat her body like a temple," Victor remarked, closing the cookbook and handing it back to her.

"Most temples are ruins," Kay pointed out.

"Birthday blues," Neal said gently. "Every year. Regular as clockwork. Worse now. With the change and all. Forty-eight's a dangerous age."

"I am not forty-eight," Kay snapped. "I'm only forty fi ... ." but Neal had already drifted back downstairs and Nicky and Victor had disappeared too. Kay went upstairs to check on Goldie and her litter, safely locked in the drum tower, did a few more sloppy salutations, and again tried to meditate. She probably wouldn't hear from Fenton on her birthday, but she had the river trip next week to look forward to, and it was ridiculous to think that she might hear from Biff, despite his promise, but she listened for the phone anyway. "No one called while I was in the shower, did they?" she asked when she came back downstairs.

"Some guy called on the landline collect," Victor said, not looking up from the cartoons he was watching with Nicky. "But we didn't accept."

"No name?"

"B-something. Sounded like a stoner."

Turning aside, Kay grinned and did a little dance. Not that it meant anything. She wasn't going to see Biff again. And, honestly: called *collect*? What a jerk. But it was nice he'd remembered, just the same.

Victor sold cars but he didn't like to drive them, so Kay accepted the keys and slid behind the wheel of the year-old silver Acura he had brought home from the lot. It was a two-hour drive to Carmel and she spent the first thirty miles trying to get used to the digital mysteries on the dash. She scarcely listened to Victor's complaints as he hunkered down in the passenger seat, surfacing only occasionally to hear that his back hurt, he couldn't sleep, his mouth was dry and he had a mysterious lump in his groin, possibly from lack of relations; there'd been a guy at his church who had died from that last year.

"Died of abstinence?" Kay glanced in the rearview mirror at Nicky stretched out in the back. Headphones plugged in, mouthing the words to some song she'd never heard of as he stared up at the roof. He seemed oblivious, but with Nicky you could never tell. There was a lot she did not want him to know about, and Victor's sex life, or lack of it, was high on the list.

"He and his wife quit having relations," Victor explained. "They already had six kids. So they took separate bedrooms. Started square dancing. And wham. Next thing you know? Prostate. Could you slow down? I'm getting carsick."

"Let me know when and I'll pull over." Kay glanced at his face, which was indeed pale. Victor had always thrown up as a child, depositing vomit neatly as a dog dropping a Frisbee right onto her lap. She remembered hopping by the side of the road with her dress held out while Ida covered her own mouth with a lipsticky handkerchief and Francis leaned against the car door smoking. It wasn't exactly child abuse and she supposed at some point someone must have pitied her and Victor enough to clean them both up. Or not.

She signaled for the Monterey exit and turned toward the artichoke fields near the coast. The soft sky and flat gray-green landscape soothed her, and she could already smell the sea. She had not yet let herself think about the actual afternoon lying ahead; she could not imagine that it would be, as Zabeth had insisted, "fun," but she hoped it would be bearable. She tugged the collar of her new linen shirt and smoothed her new linen slacks. They were supposed to look wrinkled, the salesgirl had said. That was the style.

"Do I look all right?" she asked.

Victor was trying to burp and didn't answer. He as always looked gorgeous. A shower, a shave, and the bloated zombie he'd been at breakfast had been transformed into a perfectly presentable if pale young man, golden hair cunningly curled, blue eyes clear. Ida's genes. So unfair. Kay still had no idea what he'd done to alienate the equally beautiful Stacy; she just continued to hope they'd work it out soon.

"Did you tell Dad about your separation?" she asked.

"It's not a separation."

"What is it?"

"Better pull over," Victor said.

Kay pulled over to the side of the road, got out, and lifted her face to the sky, trying to feel some sun through the overcast while Victor retched into a ditch. She knew the reason he was feeling sick was because he, too, was nervous about seeing Francis, and her own stomach, as always, roiled briefly in sympathy, but she swallowed hard and quelled it.

"Dad doesn't need to know about Stacy," Victor said, wiping his mouth with the tissue she gave him as he straightened.

"Okay," Kay agreed.

"He'll just tell me it's my fault. He always liked her better than me anyway. He'll take her side."

"Does she have a side?"

"Satan's side."

"Whose?" Nicky asked, leaning out the window.

Kay turned to him. "Looking forward to seeing your grandfather?" she asked.

"Sure," Nicky said. "Grandpa's funny."

"Funny? You don't remember the Indian wrist burns he gives you every time he shakes your hand? Or the Dutch rub when he pats your head? Or how about the time he threw you into the swimming pool and missed?"

"I remember you telling me about it," Nicky said. "But I don't remember it actually happening."

Kay nodded. Why should Nicky remember the pool incident? He had only been four. Francis had been drunk. They'd all been drunk. It had been one of those summer Sundays at her parents' that started with Bloody Marys, progressed to beer, went on to wine, segued into scotch. Francis had been uncharacteristically playful and when he picked Nicky up and tossed him toward the water, Nicky's head had clunked against the edge of the tile: the worst sound Kay had ever heard in her life. She remembered flinging herself into the car beside Francis, holding Nicky as, still drunk, Francis zigzagged toward Emergency. "We're lucky," Francis had breathed, when the doctor came to say there was no sign of concussion. Yes, Kay had thought, accepting the pronoun "we," for she felt as guilty as if she'd thrown Nicky onto the tile herself. She had meant to quit drinking that day. And she had—for a while. And then for another while and then for another while. Until now. Almost two and a half years sober, she thought, and, closing her eyes, offered a quick thank you. It was bad enough being who she was now. She never wanted to go back to who she had been before.

Victor slid back into the car, still clutching his stomach. "I think you must have put a bad egg or two into those pancakes you made me."

"You're right. Making those pancakes *was* bad. I've been sick about it myself all morning. And I've vowed never, ever, to make pancakes for you again."

"Please? My stomach? Could we just have silence?"

As she started the car up again, Kay glanced in the rearview mirror at Nicky, settling back with his headphones clamped on, his lips moving in some silent synchronization, and took in the sweet smile he gave back to her with grateful amazement.

Traffic clogged the narrow streets of Carmel-by-the-Sea and the sidewalks were already crowded with tourists. Kay had no idea why Francis had agreed to retire to this claustrophobic clutch of faux thatched cottages and trillion-dollar bungalows; it seemed absolutely the wrong place for him, but then the castle had been wrong too; perhaps Francis had never found a place where he belonged either. She tried to remember the directions to his new house—Carmel's homes had no street numbers—turned left, turned right, then right again, parking at last in front of a peaked stucco horror like the iced candy cottage in a fairy tale.

The mailbox, set under a shaggy cypress tree, was a miniature of the main house, the words *Wave Cave* painted on it in curvy letters. Kay glanced down at her wristwatch as she led the way up the flagstone pathway, past the stone dolphins, the brass deer, the marble sundial in the garden. Exactly noon. For once, Francis could not fault her for being late.

Glo met them at the door, unsmiling in a navy-blue pantsuit with brass nautical buttons. Her hair was set in stiff waves on either side of her pale face and her lips were painted in two straight streaks of red. Although she was ten years older than Kay, she had fewer wrinkles and Kay decided to spend some quality time before lunch going through the cosmetics in Glo's bathroom to see what she used.

"Francis is indisposed," Glo said now. "I tried to phone to tell you not to come." She paused and gave Kay an accusing look. "Your cell didn't pick up so I had to phone the house. Neal answered."

"Dad's living with us," Nicky agreed, looking around the dark living room with its Persian rugs and lacquered furniture. The last time he'd been here he had taken apart and carefully reassembled an old Chinese junk that Glo's great-great uncle had brought back from Shanghai in the '20s.

"And you didn't invite him to come with you?"

Kay opened her mouth to confess that she hadn't even thought of it, but Victor interrupted.

"Oh, you know Neal," he laughed, his nausea seemingly a thing of the past. "He had things to do. But he sends his love."

"He told me," Glo continued, eyes still on Kay, "that you've put him in the dungeon."

"He likes it there," Nicky said. "Hey, where's Grandpa? Is he sick?"

"Oh, who knows. The man's a drama king. He saw Dr. Deeds yesterday and he's been acting out ever since. You could all run up and say hello before you head back but don't stay too long. If you're hungry, there are drinks in the kitchen, ask Juanita or help yourself. I have some shopping to do. Goodbye."

"We're not going to the club?" Victor's disappointment made him sound ten years old.

"You still want lunch at the club?" Glo picked up her purse and strode toward the door. "Fine. Get in the car. Nicky?"

"Sure," Nicky said. "Mom?"

"I'll stay with Dad. Where *is* Dad?"

"Where he always is," Glo said. "Upstairs with the bird. Come along boys. I'm afraid Raoul is catering a wedding but we can at least get a salad."

"The famous Pebble Beach salad?" Victor asked, awed.

Upstairs with a bird? Nicky gave Kay a comical backward look as Victor pulled him out toward Glo's Jaguar. The front door slammed. Kay shivered. Talk about a socialite with no social skills. Then, alone, she looked around the dark house with its heavy beams and gabled windows. She could hear rapid fire Spanish coming from a radio in the kitchen but when she looked for Juanita—was that her name?—the kitchen was empty. The two downstairs bedrooms, both with twin beds, she noted, were empty too. She opened a door and peered into a pretty little library, shelved with leather-bound books that looked expensive and untouched. She headed toward the polished curved staircase. She had never been upstairs before and felt like a trespasser as she climbed past the wall hung with portraits of Glo's ancestors—toad-faced millionaires, smooth smiling philanthropists, brittle brunettes like Glo herself. Francis had told her once how Glo's family had made their money, but Kay couldn't remember now, something to do with the flower industry, two words that did not seem to belong to each other. There were no flowers in Glo's house, only huge pieces of furniture and cabinets filled with crystal and porcelain. Kay paused by a display case of obsidian owls on the landing and looked down the deserted hallway. The house was shabbier upstairs; the Persian runner was worn and boxes of Francis's architecture books, still unpacked, lined the walls. "Dad?" Silence. She raised her voice. "Dad?"

"Hushabush," Francis said. "You'll scare my familiar."

Following the sound of his voice, Kay saw there was yet another short flight of stairs at the end of the hall. She went up and peered into a small room set under the roof—it must be a maid's room—looking out toward the ocean. Her father sat in a rocking chair by the window. His knees were covered with an afghan, an oxygen tank stood unhooked at his side, and a large green parrot sat on his head.

Kay whistled. "Well, you've gone round the bend now, haven't you," she said.

"Not really," Francis answered mildly.

"Does he bite?"

"Of course he bites."

"Thanks for the warning. I'm not going near him." She stepped inside with caution. "I didn't think you liked birds. You didn't like Diablo."

"Who's Diablo?"

"My neighbor's pet rooster? Next door?"

"Oh yes. When you were living in the barrio. One of the best things about Raj is that he doesn't care whether I like him or not."

Week Four

The parrot was colorful without being handsome, his head ruffled as a dust mop, his button eyes set in a nest of wattles. Kay watched warily as he lifted one wrinkled charcoal colored claw after another and hopped stiffly off Francis's head to his shoulder. "Gently, gently," Francis crooned, patting its feathers.

"Nicky has a python," she offered.

"Now that's no good," Francis agreed.

"Neal brought home bunnies and Victor stole Stacy's terrier. He's a non-stop barker."

"You should take him up to that vet in Oxalis your mother liked so much."

"Right. Drive all the way to Oxalis in my free time."

"You can get up there and back in an hour if you don't stop at the outlets."

"I never stop at the outlets and I don't have an hour."

"Dr. Wallace is the vet's name, Kay. Nice guy. Scotsman. He'll know how to calm a nervous dog down." He chuckled throatily. "Your mother had a terrific crush on him. She was always trying to get him to give her free drugs."

Francis, Kay noticed, had begun to affect a low part and comb-over. He looked dapper as ever, despite the parrot, despite the afghan; his pink polo shirt was fresh, and he had stylish new frames for his glasses. She opened her mouth to ask how he was but he held up a hand.

"Shh," he said. "Can you hear the sea?"

Kay listened. She heard traffic, a blue jay, someone murdering a Scarlatti *Sarabande* on a distant piano. "No."

"Me either. Amazing. We're only eight blocks away from the ocean. Of course, I'm losing my hearing. The thing about Raj here," he continued, patting the bird again, "is this: he can hear just fine but he can't talk. He probably talked at one point, and he probably talked at length, because Jim Deeds took a look at him yesterday and said someone had cut his vocal cords."

"Birds don't have vocal cords."

"Exactly. Which makes me worry about Jim Deeds."

"Dr. Deeds is not a vet."

"Lucky for us," Francis said to the parrot, who preened.

"He's an oncologist. Dad? Why did Dr. Deeds come all the way down from San Francisco to see you here? Are you sick? Do you have cancer?"

"Honestly, Kay. Do you think I'd still smoke if I had cancer?"

Kay looked at the oxygen tank. "I don't know. What do you have?"

"Emphysema."

"Which is … ?"

"Worse than cancer."

"No, I mean … "

"Not my choice, to tell the truth. I always meant to freeze to death. I've designed a portfolio of icehouses, you know, always meant to build one, up in Aspen say, and lie down easy. But no. Emphysema, Kay, to answer your question, is a form of reverse drowning, as I understand it. Meaning you can take air in but you can't let air out. It's progressive. And there's no cure."

Kay turned back to the bird. "How did you get it?"

"Emphysema's not something you get, Kay; it's something you earn."

"No. I meant that thing. The parrot."

"Oh. Raj? He's an escapee. Just flew in the window the other day. Came to keep me company."

"Why do you need company? Do you live up here?" She looked around the room. The narrow bed under the eaves looked slept in; the covers were rumpled.

"Sometimes," Francis said. "Sometimes I am relegated to the attic, like old Ma Mamie … "

Kay waited. She had never heard of Ma Mamie.

"Your great grandmother," Francis said. "Crazy as a loon." He chuckled. "Used to get down on all fours and crawl around her bed barking like a dog. Hand me my cigarettes?"

"I don't see any."

"That's because they are hidden downstairs in milady's closet of winter clothes. First door to your right, walk in to your left, top shelf, look in the shoebox labeled *Prada*. Can do?"

"No," Kay said.

"What?"

"If you have emphysema, you should not be smoking."

"That is correct. Now hustle."

"Dad, I am not going to go get your cigarettes."

"What if I told you they were clove?"

"Are they clove?"

"Why don't you go down and find out."

Kay, reluctant, left him and descended the stairs until she came to a large cold room on the first landing. It was filled with packing boxes. She saw her own wedding gift to her father and Glo still in its wrapping paper, unopened. She had bought that gift years ago! Frowning, she touched the silver bow on top and read the card: *To Dad and Glo. Every blessing, love Kay.* She remembered how she had agonized before choosing the blue porcelain bowl, hoping to find a gift capable of capturing both her apology for bolting out of the courtroom at their wedding, and her sincere hopes for their happy union.

And she had been sincere, for a while, and Glo and Francis had been happy, for a while. The first year anyway. Maybe the second. They honeymooned in Paris, spent Christmas in London, Easter in Spain, took cruises down the Mexican coast, golf vacations in Hawaii. But they did not seem happy now. How could they? Francis was sick and Glo had the nursing skills of a spider. Still, there must be something there.

She turned to the closet and opened the door. She was braced for the crowded rack of Armani suits and furs in zippered bags but the shoes surprised her. Stack after stack of size 11 AA in four colors, black, navy, red, and brown. There were six boxes of Pradas on the top shelf and she did not find the cigarettes until she had looked through four of them. Why would Glo have stashed Francis's cigarettes up here instead of just throwing them away? Did she even know they were there? Probably not. Francis must have hidden them himself. Kay found an opened pack of something called Honeyrose and examined the print on the wrapping. No additives. No tar. No nicotine. Totally organic. She pushed the shoeboxes back in place and went back up the stairs.

"Ah," Francis said with satisfaction when she returned. He pried into the pack and deftly pulled out a Camel. "Care to join me? Or aren't you smoking these days?"

"I'm not smoking these days."

"So that's a no?"

"Yes."

"What?"

"Yes, that's a no."

"Well, have one anyway."

For a long while Kay and her father smoked in silence. Then Francis, exhaling, said, "So let's have it. What's wrong with you?"

"Nothing! Do I look like something's wrong with me?"

"You always look like something's wrong with you."

Kay opened her mouth to protest and Francis added, "You forgot to iron your clothes for one thing."

"I'm wearing linen. It's supposed to look like this."

"Like laundry? Your mother hated to iron too. Glo of course sends everything out. Even," his eyes widened with the wonder of it, "the sheets."

"Amazing," Kay muttered.

"Testy. Your mother was testy at your age too. I remember we went to an 'art party' of some sort at the HoHums and some famous poet no one has ever heard of, for very good reasons, got drunk and tried to kiss her. Ida threw her drink at his head." He laughed. "She was a devil, wasn't she?"

"You like devils," Kay said sadly.

"That's the truth."

She stubbed her cigarette out. The Camel had been all too predictable in its effect, and now she felt, in order, dizzy, dumb, and numbly desirous. She knew she'd crave another smoke in an hour, maybe less. What madness was this? Did she want to end up like Francis—with emphysema? She would have to phone Dr. Deeds when she got back to the castle. Francis was only seventy-six. He should be having some sort of life still. She picked up and promptly dropped the cord to the oxygen tank. "Is there anything I can do?" she asked.

"There's nothing anyone can do," Francis answered. "I did it all to myself. Well. Enough. How's the job? You do still have a job?"

"For now."

"And Nicholas?"

"Nicky's doing fine. He said to give you his love."

"I doubt he said those exact words, but no matter. And the homestead? Holding up?"

"Yes, but Dad, I ... "

"Are the kitchen cabinets hung yet?"

"They will be. Fenton does very careful work."

"So do glaciers. Tell him to look slippy. He's taken too long."

"Yes." She paused, then tried again. "Dad? I haven't heard from your realtor yet. He doesn't answer my calls. And I haven't heard from any buyers."

"What?"

105

"I said I'm wondering if the house is really for sale," Kay began, raising her voice, but Francis interrupted.

"You asked if there was anything you could do for me. There is one thing." He looked up at her as he stroked the greasy green feathers of the bird. "Milady has been on the warpath as you may have noticed and not without reason. I need to make what you AAers call amends. How would you feel about doing a little shopping?"

And that was how Kay found herself, half an hour later, her father's checkbook in hand, walking through the front door of the priciest jewelry store in town. She caught an image of herself in one of the four walls of mirrors as she entered, tangled hair, wrinkled shirt, scuffed shoes, sly happy grin. She hummed, eyes down, as she passed from one glass case to another, pausing at last before the display of red stones Francis had told her to find. "I'm looking for ruby earrings," she explained to the elegant young salesgirl.

"By all means," the girl said. "This way. Those," she added, as Kay hesitated at the display case, "are garnets." She led Kay through the heavily carpeted room to another counter. "For you?"

"No. For my stepmother. Mrs. MacLeod."

"Gloria?" The girl smiled. "Gloria was in the other day and she really liked these." She pulled out a pair of heavy gold encrusted stones that reminded Kay of something found in a tomb. "She tried them on three times but decided she couldn't afford them. Too bad too. They looked gorgeous on her."

"How much?" Kay asked. She filled out the blank check Francis had signed ("Keep it under three thousand," had been his only request), watched the girl wrap the gift in a gold bag with gold tissue, and left the store feeling as exhilarated as if she'd just robbed it. Stopping at an ice cream store, she debated about buying a six-dollar cone of something called Carmel Caramel Sea Salt Truffle Torte, opted for a four-dollar cone of plain vanilla frozen yogurt instead, and made her way back to the Wave Cave licking it, pretending she was a wealthy resident who belonged here and at the same time exulting in the fact that she did not. There had not been a single item in that jewelry store that she'd wanted. The clerk, noticing Ida's sapphire ring, had shown her a tennis bracelet to match but it looked scratchy and would flop down her wrist annoyingly, Kay knew, every time she played the piano.

It was great not to want things. She lingered outside shop windows. No to the hand-thrown pottery and hand-blown glass, no to the paintings of cypress trees at sunset, no to the cowboy boots and woolen capes and Panama hats, no to every single scented candle and fancy soap, and no to the gourmet dog biscuits, though she had, she patted her pocket, made a note of that nice vet up in Oxalis and would take Ed next week.

"I hope Glo likes these," she said, as she handed Francis the package. "They're sort of Roman looking. Big and square, set in gold."

"Oh, she won't like them," Francis said. "She'll take them back. My bride takes everything back. But that's not the point. She'll be temporarily mollified. *That* is the point."

"Sounds like a lot of trouble for nothing," Kay said.

"Not at all," Francis said. "Now. About your birthday. Surely you didn't come out all this way just to see your dear old Dad?"

"Of course I did."

Francis stretched his hand out. "Let's see that checkbook again."

"I don't want a check!"

"Who said you're getting one?"

Kay fished her father's checkbook out of her purse and handed it back, refusing to watch as he pulled out his gold pen and began to write. She walked to the window and stared at a wedge of ocean through the garden cypresses in the distance. "I didn't come for a present."

"It's your birthday, isn't it? Here. Take it. Enjoy."

Kay glanced down at the check. Four Thousand Five Hundred Dollars? A fortune! She had wanted to go to the symphony next week, and now she could, she had needed to buy new tires for the Honda, and now she could, she had put off paying Nicky's orthodontist, and now she could. "Dad ... " she stammered, overcome.

"A hundred dollars a year is about right, don't you think?" Francis said, before she could finish. "You *are* forty-five now? When I was forty-five, I had my own firm. And your mother," he added, "had her first amputation."

"I know. I'm lucky. I never forget how lucky I am to ... " *not be like her*, Kay finished in her head. "Thank you, Dad, thank you." Keeping her distance from Raj, she blew her father a kiss, tucked the check into her purse and looked at her watch. It was already after one. "You must be starving. Can I make you some lunch?"

"You can try. You won't find any food though."

And she didn't. Scavenging through the kitchen, Kay finally assembled a plate of various leftovers from Carmel's most expensive restaurants, mainly salads, most of them soggy. She found some imported cheese and toasted some stale bread and brought the plate back up. "Anything to drink?"

"Sure," Francis said, tapping another cigarette out on top of the oxygen tank. "Let's have champagne. It's your birthday and champagne is all Madame ever drinks; the refrigerator must be lousy with it."

Kay hesitated. She had seen a chilled bottle of *Veuve Cliquot* unopened on a refrigerator shelf.

"Unless you'd rather have a real drink?" Francis gave a thick slice of apple to Raj, who clasped it in his talon and pecked at it impatiently, spitting pieces out onto the wooden floor. "There's scotch downstairs, brandy, gin, whatever you want. Help yourself. But I think I'll stick with a little harmless champagne."

Harmless? Kay thought. *No thanks. Not for me.*

"Suit yourself," her father said.

"You okay?" Nicky's voice rose calm and quiet from the back seat as they headed home. Kay took her foot off the accelerator and slowed to the speed limit, meeting his steady eyes in the rearview mirror before searching the highway behind them for a police car. No one was coming. It was all right. This car was solid. It had only veered across the dividing line by a few inches. Victor, beside her, had not even noticed.

"Sorry," she chirped, a sour bubble rising high in her chest. She swallowed it down, aware of the complementary stink of tobacco in her throat as she did so, and threw her son a bright false grin. He did not grin back. There was no fooling Nicky. He had been watching her from the moment he and Glo and Victor returned from their lunch. Glo of course had not even looked at her, brushing past to set a white box of leftovers in the refrigerator, and Victor was, as always, preoccupied with his own concerns. He had been working figures out on a scrap of paper ever since they got in the car, humming to himself for the first time in weeks, and even though the tune was a dirge-like version of "Amazing Grace," it was good, Kay supposed, that he could sing at all. She had always admired her brother's voice, so sweet and true, and she missed the times he had leaned against the piano and sung along with her whenever she gave up on a difficult piece and broke into the Beatles. "What did you think of that crazy parrot?" she asked Victor now, careful not to slur.

"Doomed," Victor said, not looking up.

"Grandma Glo's going to call animal control while Grandpa's at the doctor's tomorrow," Nicky added, his voice drifting away as he settled back down in the back seat with his earphones.

"Good," Kay said. It was the first thing she'd heard about Glo that she approved of.

"Only Grandpa's going to hide Raj in the library. He says Glo has never read a book in her life and wouldn't think of looking in the library."

"He told you that?"

Nicky giggled, then silence.

Kay glanced at her brother. "How did it go with you and Dad today?"

"The usual. He only called me 'Vicky' twice. He referred to the dealership as 'the junk yard' and when I slipped and mentioned Stacy's name, he asked why I could never keep a woman."

"Ouch."

"I don't pay attention to him," Victor said. "'A soft answer turneth away wrath.'" He paused. "Dad give you a check?"

"He was over-generous," Kay admitted.

"He can afford to be," Victor said. "Anyway, you deserve it. Happy birthday, sis. Sorry I forgot earlier. Stacy always did those things, you know, birthdays, anniversaries." He was silent. "I don't think Dad knows how good he's got it. Glo is fantastic. Everyone at the club knows her. All through lunch it's *Yes, Mrs. MacLeod, Good to see you, Mrs. MacLeod.* And you know who was at another table? Clint Eastwood! Don't shake your head. You know who Clint Eastwood is. I met someone else too." He pulled a business card out and flicked it back and forth with his thumb. "One of the biggest divorce attorneys in the state. He's out of my price range by a couple mil. But as a friend of Glo's he said he'd help me with Stacy." He flicked the card a final time and put it back in his shirt pocket. "I'm going to wipe her out."

His voice was so low Kay wasn't sure she'd heard him correctly. She swallowed back another hiccup and kept her eyes on the road. *Wipe her out?* "I thought you didn't believe in divorce. You gave me nothing but grief when I left Neal. You said I was breaking a holy sacrament."

"You were. And I still can't believe you did it with a kit from Costco."

"You might want to consider a kit. My entire divorce only cost $150."

"You get what you pay for."

"Yes," she agreed, hoping Nicky wasn't listening. "It was worth every penny." This time her hiccup did bubble out, but neither Victor nor Nicky noticed.

Her mood plummeted predictably as she sobered and a nasty little headache began to pluck behind her eyelids. Guilt began its litany—why had she done it—why, after all those long healthy months of sobriety, had she taken a drink? No, not a drink. Four drinks. They had finished the bottle. Still wanting to please—and failing to please—her father? When would she learn? Could she learn? The afternoon had grayed over; Sunday traffic had increased. She headed toward Manzanita Heights in silence. She was scarcely aware of Victor crying quietly beside her but when she glanced over and saw his wet, mottled face she touched his wrist.

"Stacy loves you," she said. "It will work out."

"You don't know," he said bleakly.

And she didn't. She thought about the time last week when she'd run into Stacy in the department store. Her sister-in-law had been poring over infant layettes, a little smile on her face, and when she saw Kay, she had hugged her as if nothing was wrong. She had asked about Nicky and she had asked about Francis, and she had asked about Ed. She had not asked about Victor. If the separation was draining her, it didn't show; she looked rosy and round in a scoop-necked dress, the diamond crucifix Victor had given her for their tenth anniversary gleaming in her cleavage. Her pink polished nails had tapped the table of tiny outfits as Kay rattled on with news of the household. Kay had finally said, "Well, goodbye," and gone back to her piano, impressed by Stacy's reserve. How was it that some people were able to shut up? It must be a gift you were born with, Kay thought now, or perhaps, like the parrot, someone cut your vocal cords.

She edged the car into the castle driveway, parked, picked up her purse, the birthday check safely tucked inside, and slid out of the car. She needed an Alka Seltzer and a nap. Then she'd find an AA meeting. The thought of starting all over again, beginning with Step One, Day One, depressed her, and she groaned as she trudged up the walkway. Re-entry was tiresome, and it was humiliating. The last thing she needed was yet another one of those damn chips. I can do it on my own, she thought, as she stepped into the castle. I have the tools. All I have to do is use them. Starting—she glanced at her watch, suddenly remembering she was supposed to meet Dana and Zabeth at seven tonight for dinner—tomorrow.

The Cantina was crowded, dim, and noisy. "Remind me why we come here?" Kay shouted. "For the intimacy? The ambiance?"

"You come for the jukebox," Zabeth explained, licking the rim of her margarita with her short effective tongue as "La Bomba" blasted for the third time in twenty minutes. "Dana comes for the free drink that hot bartender is about to buy her. I come for the adults. This room is chock full of grownups. Not a four-year-old in sight."

Kay plunged a straw into her Diet Coke and thought with longing of the quiet bars where she and Charles used to meet and play pool and talk. She pulled his most recent postcard out of her shoulder bag and handed it to Dana, who dimpled helplessly as the bartender slid a free margarita in front of her. "Forgot your glasses?" Kay guessed.

"Read it to us," Dana suggested.

Kay leaned closer across the table. "It's Odysseus, waking up after a shipwreck, saying: '*Man of misery, whose land have I lit on now?*'"

"Man of misery," Zabeth repeated. She reached for the chips and salsa. "Sounds like your kind of guy, Kay."

"That would make me mad if it weren't true." Kay took a last look at the painting before slipping it back in her bag. "I wish Charles would come home."

"Right," Zabeth said. "He could move in with you."

"He'd be welcome," Kay said truthfully. "Except that my brother wouldn't let him. Victor thinks homosexuality is worse than evolution."

"Is Victor still there? For heaven's sake why?" Zabeth asked.

"Speaking of Victor," Dana said before Kay could answer, "I saw his wife at a restaurant last week. Having lunch with another man."

"What kind of other man?"

"I don't know. Red hair. Red face. Wedding ring."

"Pastor Paulsen," Kay nodded. "He's married."

"Everyone's married," Zabeth said, "but if his wife finds out he's seeing Stacy and kicks him out, he can move in with you too, right? Ha ha ha!" Zabeth rose, cell phone in hand, to step outside on the street where it was quieter and call home. For all her talk about being glad to be child free, she had already checked on the twins twice. She and Garret had hired a new nanny, "a free spirit," who only needed, Zabeth said, "a little management training," a skill, she added as she left, that Kay too could work on.

Kay turned to Dana. "Is Zabeth mad at me? She's being extra sharp tonight."

"She's worried," Dana said. "We both are."

"Because … ?"

"Because we don't like seeing you give your energy to people who don't deserve it. Or," Dana added, "need it." She pressed Kay's hand. "We've decided you're a female throw-back, and that's not a good thing. It's unhealthy. We want you to start saying no. The only person you have to take care of," and here Dana's voice wavered with the false regret of the childless, "is Nicky."

"It's because of Nicky!" Kay protested. "Nicky's the one who wants his father staying with us until he finds a place."

"And how is that working out?"

"Not great," Kay admitted. "He keeps forgetting to pick Nicky up after soccer practice, and he drifts off when Nicky's talking to him, just like he does with everyone. Last night," she remembered, "he turned the radio up to hear the ball game just as Nicky started to play a new piece for him on his guitar."

"Get rid of him," Dana said. Turning aside, she blew a languid kiss of thanks across the room to the bartender.

How? Kay thought. Neal insisted he was looking for a place, just hadn't found one, insisted he was looking for a job, just hadn't been hired yet. "Don't worry babe," he kept saying, in his weak womanish voice, "I'll be out of your hair soon." And Victor, either dead eyed in front of the television or cradling his Bible or locked in his room—how was she going to evict her own brother? Didn't he belong there as much as she did? Only of course she did not belong there at all.

"Well," she sighed, "it's only temporary. After the castle sells …"

"Are you sure it's even for sale?" Dana asked. "Maybe your dad wants to hold on to it."

Kay thought about this as Zabeth returned and set down a fresh frosted goblet. There was no sign Francis had ever wanted to "hold on" to anything he'd created. But he hadn't answered when she had asked about the sale that afternoon. Did he really not want to get rid of the castle? If he just wanted it to sit there she ought to forget getting any money and move out now. Oh what a mess. She could smell Zabeth's drink across the table, the celebratory summer scent of limes and tequila. She loved tequila. And it was her birthday. And she'd already gone off the wagon once that day in Carmel.

"I'll have one too," she said suddenly.

Charles's face flashed before her. If Charles was here he would punch her shoulder, hard, and she'd laugh and take her order back, but Charles wasn't here. He had forgotten her birthday. No phone call. No gift. Just these pretty painted postcards that said nothing, meant nothing. He had forgotten her.

"On the rocks," she added.

Neither Zabeth nor Dana said a word. They'd been with her before when she'd slipped. They knew she'd pull out of it. And what was one margarita? When her glass arrived she raised it in a toast, took the first electric sip, and looked around the noisy room packed with handsome young people. The Cantina was the biggest pick-up joint in the county and she didn't know why her friends had chosen it. Zabeth was happily married, Dana was happily single, and she had Fenton. Sort of. Taking another sip, Kay told her friends what Fenton's birthday gift had been: an Army surplus life jacket.

"Sexy," Dana drawled.

"I know. But I'll need it next week when we go river rafting. And on the romantic scale, you have to admit it scores higher than Neal's mouth guard."

"Not much," Zabeth said.

Week Four

Kay dropped her eyes and smoothed the tissue paper from her two friends' gifts in her lap; Zabeth had given her a leopard-print bikini, which she would never in a hundred years wear, and Dana had given her a huge gardenia-scented candle, which she would never in a hundred years light. Female throwback? Hardly.

No one knew her.

She licked the last few grains of salt off her margarita glass and studied her two friends, who did not look back. I should leave, she thought. I should just leave now, while there is time. I'll feel better tomorrow. She started to rise just as the waitress set her wine down. "From the bartender," the waitress said. "Happy birthday." Kay looked at the glass. Pale cheap sour Chardonnay. Her favorite. She could leave later.

She awoke early Monday to some all-too-familiar symptoms, not just the nausea and inflamed eyes and headache, but the riptides of shame at her failure to stay sober. She remembered ordering more wine, kissing the waiter, driving home with the parking brake on, and phoning Fenton at midnight to ask if he missed her. She had written a long loopy self-pitying letter to Charles that she had then torn up and she had almost gone into Nicky's room, hoping to sleep on his floor, stopped only by the thought of Orville.

Sitting up in bed, she ducked her head, clasped her hands, and launched into the Serenity Prayer, repeating it until her cell phone rang. She lurched to answer it. "Glo?" she said, instantly alarmed. "Is Dad all ri … ."

"You sneaky little bitch. I knew it was a bad idea to leave you alone with your father yesterday but it never occurred to me you would actually endanger his life nor did it occur to me you would actually steal from us."

Kay shook her head to try and clear it. Glo's voice was clipped and tense and Kay could hear her heels click as if she was pacing down the street; she must have taken the phone

outside, where Francis couldn't hear her; she was probably already dressed for another lunch at the club, her hair stiffly sprayed, her thin lips bright red, her fingernails, splayed against the golden chain of diamonds at her throat, red too.

"What are you talking about?"

"Don't even try to defend yourself. I found the cigarettes and I found the checkbook."

"I'm sorry about the cigarettes. Dad tricked me. But the checks, one was for my birthday and other was for a gift for you, I didn't steal … "

"No missy you didn't steal because I have cancelled both checks and I am about to phone the police. You should be getting a knock on your door any minute. This is grand theft we're talking about. I always knew you were out to get me, but I never thought you would stoop this low."

Kay, who was in fact stooped fairly low by then, crouched on the floor picking stray strands of alfalfa off the carpet, was speechless as Glo went on. "I don't think you understand how hard it is for Francis to make a healthy life for himself after fifty years with your crazy mother and the last thing he needs is a daughter who keeps trying to drag him back into the past. He's been coughing all night you'll be glad to know and his temperature is one hundred and two. He can't even talk. And Juanita says you ate everything in the refrigerator and went through my closet!"

Slowed by her hangover, Kay could only say, "This is all a horrible misunderstanding, I'm sure once Dad explains what happened you'll see … "

"I am not seeing anything, Kay. You cause nothing but trouble and if you set one foot in Carmel ever again, I will issue a restraining order so fast it will make your head spin. You are never, do you hear me, *never* to darken our door again!"

Click.

Kay stared at the phone in her hand. Why hadn't Francis explained things to Glo? Was he really coughing too hard to speak? He needed to see a doctor! She threw on a bathrobe and ran downstairs to rap on her brother's door. "Victor? Are you in there? Something really weird has happened and I don't know what to do."

"Have you looked at yourself this morning?" Victor's expression of distaste at her mussed hair and puffed eyes deepened as she told him about Glo's phone call. He leaned forward, Ed cradled in his arms, listening until she finished, then said, "Glo is the last person in the world we want to antagonize right now."

"I didn't antagonize her. I didn't do anything to her except buy her a hideous pair of ruby earrings."

"You never smile at her. You never call her to go shopping or have lunch. She was saying at the club yesterday that you have never once hugged her."

"Hug Glo?"

"See? She is not unintelligent, Kay. She is not insensitive."

"Victor, the woman just phoned to accuse me of grand theft and to tell me she's getting a restraining order if I try and see Dad again."

"A restraining order? Well," Victor said, "now you've done it. There goes my future at the Pebble Beach club. There goes my in with the divorce lawyer. Thanks a lot."

"*You're* okay. She still likes *you*. Phone her, won't you, she'll listen to you, and explain what happened!"

"No no," Victor whistled. "This is between you and her. I'm not getting involved in a cat fight."

"It's not a cat fight!"

"Count me out," Victor said. "You got yourself in this, you get yourself out." The doorbell rang just then and Ed scrambled to escape from Victor's arms. "Must be the cops," Victor said, setting him down. "You might want to comb your hair and wash your face before they haul you off to jail. What did you do last night anyway? Don't tell me you drank? Kay?" his voice followed her as she shunted Ed out of the way with her bare foot and went to answer the door. "Did you?"

The doorbell chimed again but by the time Kay got to the hall, Nicky was already there, greeting the driver of the carpool who was taking him to the first day of his summer school soccer camp. Nicky's jeans were clean, but his favorite tee-shirt was inside out, and the lunch bag he had packed himself was clearly filled with nothing but chips and cookies. His voice was cheerful as he said, "Bye Mom, I'll be back at four," but he didn't look at her before he stepped out the door. Still feeling drunk, unsteady and shaky, she showered, swallowed four aspirin, and dressed for work, waiting all the time for the phone to ring with Glo's apology, or, better yet, Francis's.

But the phone didn't ring. There was no email, no telegram, no flowers, nor any message when she got home from the library that night. It had been a difficult day. The copier had broken, someone had smeared shit on the wall of the men's bathroom, a sparrow had flown in through the open door and Kay had had to chase it out with a mop from the janitor's closet while the toddlers huddled under the Story Lady's black cloak and then, after the children left, Kay had to face the long overdue and highly distasteful task of firing Jolene. "You can't tell four-year-olds that a bird in the house means someone is going to die," Kay had explained. "I can't have you scaring children like that."

"I don't make these things up, you know," Jolene had retorted, flipping her cloak over her shoulders. "There is truth in these sayings. Someone *is* going to die." Her hooded eyes behind their tinted glasses settled on Kay, "Or maybe," she smiled, showing the sharp yellow teeth that she liked to bare during fairy-tale-time, "it's the library itself that is going to die. You will never replace me," she finished, as she gathered up her wicker baskets and bunches of dried herbs and set out the door. "By next week, you'll be begging me to come back. If the library is still here next week, that is. If the County doesn't close it down. Or if someone doesn't set it on fire."

Kay had locked the door behind her, then gone again to check her messages. Nothing. Not a single word from Fenton or Dana or Zabeth. They were all clearly sick of her. And yes, she was told, when she tried to cash it, that Glo had indeed cancelled the birthday check. It was useless. Kay tore it up and watched the pieces flutter into the recycling basket.

The capper was the postcard she received from Charles. He had painted a garden scene this time. On the back, again only a few lines from *The Odyssey*: " ... *leafy trees dangled their fruit from high aloft, pomegranates and pears, and apples glowing red ...*" What on earth did that have to do with her? What did it have to do with anything?

It was raining that evening as, still hungover, she put Ed on a leash and headed out to run the mountain trail behind the castle. Elbows pressed to her sides, she thought about Charles. He had been strangely sad in the months before he left, not as animated as usual, slower, sometimes coming over to her apartment and sitting quietly in the kitchen for hours, watching her cook and leafing through the magazines she brought home from the library. He had started to put on weight and refused to let her cut his dark curls which, to her dismay, he had started to tie back like Neal's, in a ponytail.

"What's going on?" she'd asked.

"Do you ever feel you're not living the life you were meant to live?" he'd answered.

"Are you kidding? All the time."

"What if you could do something about it?"

"Go back to being eighteen, you mean? Study hard, practice, stay in school, never take a drink, never run off with someone like Biff, never marry Neal, devote myself to music?"

He was silent.

"I'd probably end up playing in a second-rate orchestra somewhere," she finished.

"But you'd have mastered that Mozart piece."

"Yes." She turned to look at him. "What is it, Charles?"

"Oh," he'd said, "I might go away."

"For long?"

"As long as it takes."

"As long as *what* takes?"

"To change."

"But I don't want you to change."

"Tough," Charles had said and then both of them had laughed.

She paused to catch her breath on the trail and glanced up at the castle above. Something moved on the roof, disappearing behind a parapet. A raccoon? A rat? Shivering, she tugged at Ed's leash, trying to remember the myth of the pomegranate. Something about a goddess's daughter made to stay in the underworld half the year just because she ate a few seeds? That was as bad as having to return to AA just because you had a few drinks!

She came home, annoyed to see Neal, in lotus position on the Oriental rug, turning the pages of a tattered *Prevention* magazine, and Victor, pacing out by the swimming pool, muttering to himself. She propped Charles's postcard up on the kitchen counter and looked at it as she began to make Nicky's macaroni. The pomegranates on the painted tree, she saw, were exactly the color of Burgundy. Francis used to keep bottles of Burgundy down in the dungeon, she remembered, in a hidden alcove. Maybe the bottles were still there. It might help her hangover to have a small glass. Weren't women supposed to have one glass of red wine a night anyway? To give them heart? To give them strength?

WEEK FIVE

Fenton had a quiet step but a loud laugh and often his laugh was the only way Kay knew he was there. On the morning they were to leave for their river trip she heard him outside on the driveway with Victor, so she pulled the pan of brownies out of the oven, stirred the chili, added more wine to the marinade for the shish kabobs Fenton had said he liked, checked her lip gloss, and hurried out to the driveway to meet him. Leaning against his truck in the sun, his arms crossed high on his chest and his sunglasses pushed up on his forehead, Fenton looked dipped in gold, his curls cropped close around his tanned face, his strong neck, muscled arms and bare legs glinting already with a light sweat. "Hi," she said, coming up and nestling into his shoulder. "I've missed you!"

Fenton put his arm around her and looked down with a smile, but his eyes, she saw, kept the same false twinkle he'd been using with Victor; they didn't deepen for her, which was disturbing, because she knew, though he'd never said so, that he didn't like Victor. Stung but unable to show it, she pulled back, straightened and said, "We're all packed and ready to go. I've made about three pounds of brownies. We do need a lot of chocolate, right?"

"Gotta have chocolate," Fenton agreed in his easy way, dropping his arm.

Victor, about to leave for work, paused before getting into his car. "You *are* taking two tents, Kay? You're not both sleeping in the same tent?"

"I don't sleep in a tent," Fenton laughed.

"He sleeps under the stars," Kay explained. "Don't worry, Vic."

"It's not me I'm worried about," Victor said darkly. "It's your husband. And the example you're setting for your son." He frowned at them both and drove away.

Fenton laughed again and slapped her hip. It was a strong slap and she gasped as she rubbed it. "C'mon," Fenton said, "Let's pry that tater tot of yours away from his video games and hit the road." He hesitated. "Your husband's not inside, is he?"

"Neal's not my husband, Fenton, for the hundredth time, he's my ex. And you don't have to worry about him. I've already told him that you and I are," she hesitated, then went for it, "together."

Fenton didn't bolt at the loaded word. Encouraged, Kay continued, "And he's fine with it. At least," she amended, for it hadn't been clear that Neal had actually heard her, "he didn't say anything. Anyway, it's not as if he has any feelings for me anymore. Well, except for anger, hatred, resentment, fear, contempt, distrust and a deep-seated wish that I'd die and leave him full custody of Nicky. Other than that, I'd say we have a pretty darn good relationship."

"It's not that. I don't like the way he watches me when I work."

And when do you work? Kay thought. *You haven't been here once this week.* "Don't worry about Neal," she repeated. "He's actually been job hunting. I'm sure he'll be in his own place soon." Or would he? When she'd gone down to the dungeon to get more wine, her heart had seized at the sight of how clearly Neal had made himself at home; his television, computer, stereo, air humidifier, and water purifier were all hooked up and in place, he'd cleared a counter and filled it with surgical tools and decanters for his mysterious experiments and "inventions," the bookshelves were filled with health manuals, botany books, and vitamin bottles, and one of the posters from his old frame shop hung over his bed, the same one, she'd been saddened to see, that he'd always said reminded him of her, an Edward Hopper print of a slump-shouldered young woman in a red bathing suit reading a goodbye letter.

"You could make him leave, you know," Fenton said, as if reading her thoughts. "It's your house."

"Everyone seems to think that. But it's not true. It's my dad's house."

"Guess Nicky wants Neal here though, doesn't he. And if Nicky wants it, Nicky gets it."

Kay, surprised, glanced at him and met the same pleasant gold-flecked gaze.

"Shouldn't be hard for Neal to find a job," Fenton continued. "He had that frame shop for years. And he's got a college degree, right?"

Kay, uncomfortably aware that Fenton had never owned a shop and had never gone to college, murmured, "Right," and went back to the house to round up Nicky. She would deal with Neal when she got back. "Come on," she called, raising her voice over the sound of Ed yipping in staccato time inside Victor's locked room. "Let's go."

Nicky, sitting on his duffel bag playing a video game, looked up. "I don't want to," he said.

"Why? Because of Fenton?"

"He'll just tell me how fat I am."

"No he won't!"

"And you'll be all weird."

"No I won't. I'll be fine. Come on, bring your guitar. Bring your magic cards, your notebook, your Harry Potter, bring everything that will make this trip do-able for you, except for Orville." She crouched by his side. "Honey? I really want you to come. We haven't had a vacation since Charles left. And rafting down a river? Don't you think that will be fun?"

Nicky clumped to his feet, shouldered his pack, dragged after her, and watched as she gathered the food—so much food!— she had been cooking since dawn. She waited until his back was turned and then dropped two bottles of Burgundy into the hamper. She'd only been having one glass a night this last week, but Fenton might want something besides the twelve-pack she had bought him.

"All set, big boy?" Fenton's hand clamped on Nicky's neck and Nicky sagged at the knees, rolled his eyes and mouthed: *big boy?*

"He just means you're tall," Kay whispered, as they straggled with their camping equipment out to the car. "And strong, and ..."

"Weird," Nicky said.

"Here, take the window." Kay slid into the cab of the truck beside Fenton. The back was filled with fishing rods, the hamper and cooler she'd packed, and Fenton's inflatable raft. Peeking out of Nicky's backpack was a familiar toy: his old stuffed dinosaur. Boy, he really wasn't looking forward to this trip! She put one arm around her son and one around her lover but it wasn't a comfortable position for them or for her and after a few minutes her hands were back in her lap and she was once again making a conscious effort not to tear at her cuticles.

Trouble didn't start until they stopped for lunch a few hours later. Fenton didn't think Nicky should have two sandwiches and three brownies. Nicky didn't think Fenton should pull over on a residential street and "grab a little shut eye" on the front seat, which meant Nicky and Kay had to walk around the block until he woke up. Fenton didn't like the way Nicky groaned seeing the campground—a dusty strip along the river crowded with RVs and trucks—and he didn't understand why Nicky had to speak up and tell the camp host that he was eleven when he still looked like he was ten and ten would get him in for free. Nicky didn't see why Fenton liked lying so much, it wasn't as if Fenton was paying the camp fee in the first place, Kay was. Fenton drove around the camp twice before choosing a site next to three young blondes in bikinis, and when Kay protested that it was perhaps too close to other people, he said he liked "the view." Nicky disappeared into a latrine when it was time to set up the tent and while Fenton asked the blondes about good fishing sites, Kay popped M&Ms like uppers and drank one of Fenton's beers, which was all right, just one; she'd wait for her glass of wine until—she glanced at her wristwatch—six. She could last until six.

By mid-afternoon they had all fallen into a stoic lethargy. Kay had brought her knitting, but after two mistakes, she set it aside. She played five games of Hearts with Nicky, losing each time, had another beer, and inflated Fenton's rubber raft for him. She seconded Nicky when he said he'd rather practice his guitar than go out on the water, and waved goodbye from the bank as Fenton set out alone for some sunset fishing. As he drifted around the bend, she plopped down in the warm yellow sand by a clump of river willows, looked up at the sky, reached in her pocket, and snuck out a cigarette.

She probably didn't have to sneak. No one had said anything about her drinking or smoking this last week. Neal, usually the first to comment, had done nothing but sigh, Victor had been too self-absorbed to notice, Nicky seemed resigned, and Fenton had never taken her abstinence seriously.

She felt relaxed now, out here, by the riverbank. She watched the swallows dart across the water, smelled the sweet smoke from the other campers' barbecues, listened to the shouts of children from the shallows and Nicky's tentative chord changes from the tent behind her. It's easy to be happy, she reminded herself. Oddly, as the evening deepened, and she realized the swallows were actually bats, the smoke was marijuana, the children were screaming obscenities, and Nicky was playing "We Gotta Get Out of This Place," she did begin to feel happy. The situation was ridiculous—here she was, squatting alone on a riverbank fretting over her father, resenting her brother, feeling guilty about her ex-husband, worrying about her son, and annoyed with her boyfriend, while all around her the world stretched in its own bright beguiling mystery. She stubbed her cigarette out in the sand and laughed.

Fenton's big laugh boomed up the river and swallowed hers. She scrambled to her feet, took the rope he threw her and pulled the raft in to the beach. "Look what I caught!" Bare-chested and radiant, Fenton held up a shiny long trout, twisting on its hook. "Practically jumped into the boat at me."

"That is one awesome rainbow," one of the blondes from the next campsite said, stepping past Kay to look closer. "Wow! Lila! Lexie! You won't believe this."

Two other heavy-footed nymphs tramped up, all sunburned breasts and thighs, and Fenton, surrounded, beamed over their heads. "Take some photos, Kay, will you, I need a record of this. What do you think," he said to one of the blondes, "six pounds? Maybe seven? Ever see one so big?"

Kay dutifully clicked away with the camera as other campers came up to marvel at Fenton's catch. "You're going to eat good tonight," one of the men said, and Kay nodded, grateful for the cornmeal and bacon and lemons she had packed, hoping she would be able to pull off the recipe for hush puppies she had brought along as well.

"Oh, I wouldn't eat that fellow, if I was you," another man said. "That trout's a keeper."

"Grandpa Ghost," a woman agreed. "My husband's been trying to catch him for six years."

"You should take it straight to a taxidermist," one of the blondes breathed.

Fenton gave a somber nod and frowned at the fish still trying to swim through the air. Drops of red blood shot from its mouth and Kay felt sickened with pity for it. One minute it was free and proud in the cold fresh river, the next it was yanked up into the air, surrounded by these ugly gapers.

"What do you think," Fenton mused, as he brought the fish back to camp. "Cook it or keep it?"

"Honestly? I think if it's really Grandpa Ghost you should throw it back and let it live," Kay replied. Even Nicky groaned at that, and all three blondes gave her stony looks. But Fenton only laughed. "Empty the cooler, will you? It will be fine in there for a while until I decide what to do."

Empty the cooler? But then what would happen to the milk and cream and eggs and butter and bacon and lettuce and fruit and marinated lamb and spiced chili and all the other costly, carefully prepared, gourmet foods she had brought? "Hurry," Fenton said, beaming down at his fish. Reluctantly, Kay and Nicky took all the food out and helped Fenton lug the cooler down to the bank where he filled it with river water, worried the barb out of the trout's mouth and laid the fish in like a raging baby. Then he walked around with Kay's phone, taking photos.

"You girls got any illegal substances you're willing to share?" he asked one of the blondes and a few minutes later he was over at their campsite, talking animatedly about just where he had been on the river and just what bait he had used when the fool fish "practically jumped right into the boat." Kay poured her long-awaited glass of wine, started the fire to grill the kabobs and corn and while Nicky sat in the shadows eating his way through the tub of brownies, she drank her way through the rest of the wine bottle, trying not listen to the laughter from the blondes or the thrashing in the cooler. Fenton returned at last, reeking of pot, smiling and chatty. Kay drained her thermos cup and leaned forward, looking into the campfire. Her head was spinning, her stomach was cramping, her thoughts were hormonal, and her throat thronged with dark words. She always knew when she shouldn't open her mouth and she knew it now.

"Cooked or kept," she said, savoring Fenton's phrase before succumbing to the darkness. "Sort of like our relationship. I mean, you don't seem able to make up your mind whether you're with me or not."

"What are you talking about?" Fenton laughed.

"Us. You and me! What do you think? Do you think we have a relationship?"

"I'm not going there," Fenton warned.

"Why not? You haven't been *here*."

"Just because I talked to some girls ... "

"I don't care about those girls, Fenton."

Fenton let the lie go, then, quiet, asked, "What do you care about?"

Nicky rose, clapped on his headphones, and slipped into the tent.

"I just want to know why you are keeping me in the cooler until you decide what to do with me."

Fenton laughed. "Do you think you're a fish?"

"Yes. Why not? I feel hooked. I feel trapped. You haven't put any energy into keeping me but you haven't let me go either. Or maybe you do want to let me go but you want me to figure it out by myself. You want me to break up with you which I would do except I can't because we're not together in the first place."

"I don't know what you're talking about," Fenton said.

"I'm talking about ... " Kay stopped, then blurted, "We haven't made love in three weeks."

"Whose fault is that? I'm not the one whose brother acts like the Ayatollah. I'm not the one who has an ex-husband prowling around the house every night I stay over."

"So it is hard for you being there."

"You bet it's hard."

"Then why don't you ever ask me to your house? I have never been to your house, Fenton. I have no idea where you live. For all I know you have a wife and six children."

Fenton laughed.

"What's so funny about having a wife and children?"

"It's the last thing I'd ever want," Fenton said. "Believe me."

"So what do you want? Do you want to be with me?"

"I don't have any complaints."

"What does that mean?"

"Kay?"

"What?"

"Go to bed. Sleep it off." He rose to kiss her but she moved away and stood over the cooler instead.

"You know what I'm really mad about?" she said. "That time we went out to that oyster restaurant and you found a pearl in your oyster and you didn't give it to me."

"That was months ago!"

"My point exactly. Months ago, and nothing's changed. The waitress came over and the cook came out and all the other people in the restaurant were going *Look he found a pearl* and what did you do? Wrapped it in a paper napkin and put it in your pocket. I should have left you then."

"What are you talking about?"

"I want to know who you gave that pearl to."

"I didn't give it to anyone. To tell the truth, I forgot all about it. It's probably still in that shirt. No. It's not. I remember I got paint on that shirt and had to throw it away."

"You threw it away? Fenton. Listen. You do not take care of your things." Kay paused, lowered her head, tried to focus through the blur of wine and firelight that made the night shadows dance too darkly. She had something important to say. "I," she managed with forced dignity, "am one of the things you do not take care of." Dizzy, she sank beside him by the fire, dropped her head and hugged her knees. "Sorry. I hate talking like this. No wonder you don't love me." She waited. Either now he'd say he loved her or he'd say nothing. A minute passed. He said nothing. But the next minute he reached out and brushed her hair with his hand and tipped her face up and gave her a sweet short kiss.

"You're not yourself when you drink this much," he pointed out.

"No, I am myself. That's the problem. The only time I say the things I really think is when I'm drunk. The rest of the time I lie." She sighed, disgusted by the entire exchange, not just by what she'd said already but what she was about say next. "You really didn't give that pearl to anyone else?"

"There is no one else. Now you better get to bed in your tent with your son. I've got to build a weir in the river to contain the fish. I'll see you in the morning."

But the fish was gone in the morning. Nicky was the first to see the raccoon tracks in the sand leading to the little dam in the riverbank Fenton had thrown together in the dark. He and Kay knew enough not to say anything when Fenton got up, but Fenton just scratched his head and said, "Huh."

Just like the pearl, Kay thought, *something precious lost but what the huh*. She swallowed a palmful of aspirin with her black coffee and tried to be cheerful as she flipped pancakes over the fire. Still, what a terrible way for that old warrior trout to go—first bashing itself stupid against the white walls of the cooler and then being eaten alive. She shook her head when Fenton offered her a beer—no more drinking! No more smoking! She would get back into AA (only did they have to call it The Program? it sounded so Soviet) as soon as she got home. She'd knock Victor off his pulpit, she'd kick Neal out of the house. Once those two were gone, maybe she and Fenton would be a couple like other couples, normal people who spent their weekends together in healthy activities like they were doing today: loading the raft with fruit and crackers and cheese and setting out on the river so they could shoot the rapids.

Shoot the rapids?

"I don't want to," Nicky said for the fourth time.

"All you have to do," Fenton repeated, ignoring him, "is row like I showed you, so when I shout 'left' you row left—and you too, Kay, are you listening?—and when I shout 'right' you move to the other side of the boat. Got it?"

Nicky shrugged and ducked as Fenton roughed his hair. "All set? Everyone got their life jacket on? Let's go!"

He shoved them off and they floated around the bend, leaving the campground behind. In ten minutes they could have been in an earlier century: steep walls of forest rose on either side. The morning air smelled crisp and tangy, brown rocks gleamed below the clear green water, herons fished on the banks and turtles sunned on half-submerged logs. Fenton's square shoulders and tanned arms made a brave figurehead at the prow of the boat and Kay was filled with pride in him and in Nicky too, for Nicky, also sitting in front of her, had caught the rhythm of the rowing faster than she and had started to hum, enjoying himself.

"We're coming to a little run now," Fenton warned, looking back with a grin.

Nicky laughed as they rippled over a shallow rushing current and Kay laughed too.

"Now we come to some real fun," Fenton called, and suddenly they were in a churning rocky wash that wasn't Kay's idea of fun at all, but she followed Fenton's orders and helped pole a safe route past brush and boulders, landing in a quiet pool at the end of the rapids. Rounding another bend, they saw the three blondes struggling in the water, trying to get their overturned raft upright. "Here," Fenton said, gesturing Nicky to come sit in front and take his place, "you two steer us over to the bank and I'll catch up with you." He stripped off his life jacket and Kay twisted in her seat to watch him dive in, swim over to the blondes, right their raft with one easy lift and then—*a little too easily*, she thought—hoist the laughing girls in, one by one. He gave their raft a shove to set it off, waved, and swam back to where Kay and Nicky paddled in the shallows. He emerged, grinning, golden, gorgeous, pleased with himself, and reminding Kay, for some sour reason, of a yellow lab that had successfully retrieved a thrown stick. "Our hero," she said and he took her words, as he should have, literally—to her relief, for the last thing she needed to show this morning was more of last night's nastiness.

"It was nothing," he said, and settled back in the raft, with a pat on Nicky's shoulder and a "Good navigating, dude," which made Nicky puff with pride.

It's working, Kay thought. *We're getting along. We're having a happy day. It can be done.*

They stopped for lunch on a little island. Still hungover, Kay waited until Nicky went down to the water's edge to practice skipping rocks the way Fenton had taught him, then she napped in the sun, her head on Fenton's warm shoulder. Her drowsiness continued even after they got back into the raft. "We'll hit the big rapids pretty soon, kids, so get ready," Fenton said, his voice tight with excitement, but Kay couldn't sense any approaching rapids in the broad expanse of sunlit water on either side of their rubber craft. Enjoying the feeling of being ferried without effort past obstacle after obstacle, she laid her oar in her lap and played at princess, trailing one hand in the water.

Next thing, without warning, she was in the water, bounced out of her seat like a tiddlywink, moving fast in a torrent of cold wet noise toward a barricade of logs and grey rocks. She could see the raft just ahead but when she tried to grab it her hand slipped off the wet side, and something hard in the charging water banged against her bad shoulder, then her knee, then tumbled her forward. "Mom fell in!" Nicky shouted and Fenton turned around with a distracted look, hooked her by her life jacket, lifted her up and plopped her back in the raft before turning back to the front and poling them safely past the boulders and down a crashing drop into another pocket of quiet green water.

She didn't speak on the van that ferried them back to the campground, choked with gratitude and with an animal adoration of Fenton. He really was her hero. He pushed her head off his shoulder. "Thing to do when you fall in like that is keep your feet pointed downriver," he told her. He pressed both palms against the small of his back, twisted back and forth, and looked at her without smiling. "How much do you weigh anyway?"

"I don't know."

"Because I think you threw my back out."

"Really? I did?"

"It hurts like hell."

"I'm sorry! You don't think it was lifting those three girls … ?"

"No, my back felt fine then. But it sure as hell hurts now. God. You're going to have to drive us home, Kay."

"We're not staying another night?"

"With me feeling like this? I don't think so."

"Maybe if you lie flat for a while and rest?"

Fenton, lips pressed tight, shook his head and Kay could do nothing but say "I'm sorry" again, two words she should put on a tee-shirt and wear every day. She helped him out of the shuttle and back to the campsite, where he lay in regal splendor under a cottonwood tree, smoking a joint one of the blondes brought over, while she and Nicky deflated the raft, threw away the ruined food and tried to figure out how to collapse and fold up the tent. After hoisting the hibachi into the truck bed, Kay trudged off to the latrine. She saw herself reflected in the aluminum mirror there—nose a triangle of bright red, eyes hooded and bloodshot, hair a tangle, lips scaly, legs and arms bruised and bleeding from her river run, wrinkled shorts, wobbly thighs, baggy boobs, tee-shirt smudged with dirt—the Devil's dream date. She made a face, wiggled her fingers by her ears, and did a quick little hate dance before a footstep at the latrine entrance made her pull herself together.

"Mom? What do you want me to do with all these books and board games you brought?"

"Burn them."

"What?"

"Nothing, Nick. Hang on. I'll be right there."

She came out to see Nicky leaning against the truck, looking forlorn with his guitar at his feet. She went up and stood beside him. "Thank you for being such a good sport this weekend, honey. I'm sorry it hasn't been much fun."

"I'm just glad you didn't drown," Nicky said.

"You are?" Tears stung her eyes and she blinked them back, relieved that he was looking over at the campsite, and not at her.

"Do you think Fenton's going to get arrested for drugs?" he asked.

"Not unless someone turns him in. Tempted?"

Nicky shook his head. She followed his eyes and saw Fenton slowly rising to his feet, one hand on the small of his back, the other on the shoulder of the youngest blonde. He looked old all of a sudden, standing next to the girl, his eyes dilated, lips parted in a sloppy smile. "I think I like him better when he's high," Nicky said. "He's not so nervous."

"Fenton? Nervous? He's one of the most relaxed people I know."

Nicky broke into an exact imitation of Fenton's loud laugh and Kay, surprised, said, "You're right."

"Dad says he's probably got ADD and that's why he can't finish anything he starts."

Your Dad is not one to talk, Kay thought, but all she said was, "Speaking of finishing, let's pack up what's left and head back." Her eye fell on something tangled on the grass near the cooler. Perfect. Charles's scarf, wine stained, grass stained, brownie stained, filthy. She yanked the knitting up and shoved it into her backpack. She'd throw it all out, begin again; she had more of the same yarn at home. But how many times did she have to start over until she got it right?

It was almost ten at night before Kay, shoulder aching, knees throbbing, pulled the truck into the castle driveway. Fenton woke up, as he always did, sweetly and easily, and said, "I can take it from here, Kay, so you guys get your stuff and I'll bring the cooler and the rest of the things back to you as soon as I feel better. Be good." He slid into the driver's seat as Kay slid out and gave a jaunty half honk as he pulled out of the driveway. Relieved for once to see him go, Kay watched his lights disappear down the hill then turned and limped after her son toward the house.

"Hi Dad," she heard him say. "Hi Uncle Victor. Hi Grandpa."

Grandpa?

At first she couldn't see him. The Great Room was sacked. Dirty cups and glasses ringed the tops of the antique chests and crusts of pizza and watermelon rind littered the heavy mahogany table. The glass doors leading out to the pool were wide open and a wet towel lay on the parquet floor. The room smelled of male sweat, garlic, tobacco, and what Kay supposed was parrot shit. When she heard the familiar rattle of ice cubes, she swiveled to see her father half-hidden in a corner by the window, stocking feet propped up in his leather recliner, smoking a cigarette, drinking a bourbon, and working a *New York Times* crossword puzzle with the gold pen he always said the Shah of Iran had given him. It was as if time had stopped, as if he'd never buried Ida, never married Glo, never left the castle at all. Kay stepped forward, easing her backpack off her sore shoulders.

"Hey," she said, her voice cautious.

"Hey yourself." Francis looked up. His blue eyes were clear; his skin was rosy. He looked nothing like the frail old man in the attic she had left in Carmel last week. Kay sent a wary smile toward the top of his head then scanned the room. Victor was flopped on the floor, holding Ed; Neal, on his knees, was installing a huge new television set, greasy tools spread in a radius around him on the Oriental carpet. The parrot swung on the chandelier, biting at loose crystals. She did not see any luggage and there was no sign of her stepmother. The oxygen tank gleamed by Francis's chair but it was, she saw, again unplugged. Nicky, standing sturdily beside her, asked what she could not bring herself to say: "What are you doing here, Grandpa?"

"I live here." Francis reached out and flicked Nicky's nose. "What are *you* doing here? Thought you weren't coming back until tomorrow."

"We had to leave early because Mom fell out of the boat and broke Fenton's back."

Francis, interested, said, "How did she do that?"

"She weighed too much when he pulled her out of the river."

Neal with a sleepy blink looked up from his tools. "You'd think a carpenter would know how to lift a dead weight properly. It's in the knees."

Francis said only what he'd said all of Kay's life: "Typical," as he filled another space in his crossword. Kay crossed her arms. No one had asked if she was hurt from her fall, no one cared if Fenton's back was truly broken, no one was happy to see her, and Nicky, for the first time ever, had sold her out. It didn't matter that he now shot her an apologetic look. The last thing she needed was a child who said "sorry." She turned back to her father. *Typical*, she reasoned, was at least a primitive form of conversation.

"So you *are* talking to me?" she asked.

Francis looked up. "Why wouldn't I be talking to you?"

"Glo said … "

"I've told you, Kay, no one pays attention to Glo."

"I do," Victor said.

"Yes, but you don't count." Francis took a sip of bourbon and went back to his crossword puzzle.

"Is she here?" Kay, arms still crossed, glanced at the closed door leading to the master bedroom.

"Nope. She had better things to do."

"Glo's at her three-hundred-acre ranch in New Mexico," Victor said, his voice hushed with reverence. "Olympic size swimming pool. Riding stable full of thoroughbreds. Peacocks. Llamas. Alpacas. She invited me and Neal to go dove hunting next fall. I don't know why Dad didn't want to go down there with her tonight."

"Llamas," Francis said, winking at Nicky, "give me the woolies."

Kay took a quick breath. "Is this because of me?"

Francis looked up. "Why on earth would anything be because of you?"

"Because Glo thinks I stole from your checking account?"

138

"You did?" Nicky echoed. "You stole from Grandpa's checking account?"

"No I did not steal from Grandpa, Nicky. Do you think we'd still be here if I had?"

"No. You'd be in jail."

"No. I'd be in Paris."

"But you wouldn't be in Carmel," Victor sang.

Kay turned back to her father. "You did talk to her, Dad, didn't you? You did explain things?"

Francis shrugged. "My bride hears what she wants to hear."

"But … "

Francis flapped a hand in dismissal. "Don't worry, Kay. You worry too much."

"She said she was going to get a restraining order against me. She said I was never to darken her door again!"

Francis threw his head back and laughed out loud. "Never darken her door?" He wiped his eyes. "The junk that woman watches on TV. Speaking of which, what do you think of your new boob tube?"

Kay looked at the monster Neal was assembling. "The castle already has a TV."

"Not a sixty-five-inch state-of-the-art 3-D LCD plasma flatscreen," Victor breathed, as he rolled over, Ed in arms, to watch Neal work.

Kay frowned. The old TV was inconspicuous, tucked into a corner where Nicky could watch it in peace and where the noise would not filter into the house. This new one would dominate the entire room. It would be the first thing the realtors would see when they walked in the door. It already blocked the view of the mountain. She shuddered as Victor, with a flourish, hit the remote control and the screen filled with robots shooting ray guns at each other. "Thank you, Grandpa," said Nicky.

"Not at all, Nicholas," Francis answered. "Enjoy."

Kay turned. It was late, she was tired. "I've had a horrible two days," she said. "I'm going upstairs to my room to cry."

"Cry? Well, that's better than hitting the piano keys like you used to," Francis said. "Or," turning to Nicky, "does she still do that?"

Nicky, the little traitor, nodded. "She uses her fist."

"Some things never change. Speaking of changing," Francis continued, "the boys and I couldn't find any sheets or pillowcases for my room. I'll need towels as well. You haven't used the good yellow towels, have you, Kay?"

"No Dad, I have not touched the good yellow towels."

"I'll need them," Francis said. "And sheets? For my bed?"

Kay, exasperated, gestured at Victor, who was still fixated on the television, then at Neal, who was gathering his tools, then at Nicky as he slipped out of the doorway. "Can't someone else make your bed up? My shoulder is killing me."

"Mild exercise is the best thing for an injury," Neal advised.

"Lifting weights helps," Victor agreed. "That's what I do."

"Now," her father ordered, but it took the long cough that followed to propel her into action. She limped down the hall, opened the heavy doors to her parents' old room, and stalled. She had not come in here once since she'd moved back. This was the room where her mother had suffered, this was the room where her mother had died. Kay had entered this room every day during Ida's last illness, bringing tea and magazines and flowers, offering chirpy news about Nicky's accomplishments, gossip from the library. She had fed her mother carefully, smoothing the napkin under her chin and coaxing her mouth open for each bite. She had read to her, sung to her, changed her diapers for her, and, most important, she had listened to her. She had heard the whole story of Ida's disappointed life, all the adventures Ida could have had if she had not married Francis, had two children, slipped on a stair, broken her back, lost her health, her youth,

140

and all her hopes. "I have never done anything with my life," Ida sobbed once and Kay had wanted to say *You had us.* But she knew her mother would only blink at that, confused. As Francis had just pointed out, she and Victor didn't count. They didn't matter. Hesitant, Kay remained standing in the doorway, waiting for her mother's ghost to manifest with all its needs and sorrows, but the room stayed empty. She limped quickly across the huge expanse of Persian carpet to open the windows. The scent of night jasmine from the garden flew in. Of course mosquitoes could fly in now too, or one of the bats Nicky swore swooped over the swimming pool at night. Be fine if they did. Give the parrot something to squawk about, she thought, as, shoulder aching, she stretched fresh sheets over the king-sized mattress, dusted the dressers and tables, and hung the good yellow towels up in the cracked marble bath.

"Thought we'd lost you in there," Francis said when she came out. He held a prescription up in his hand. "I know it's late, but I need this filled tonight. And here's a grocery list, but it can wait until tomorrow."

Kay looked down at the list in his clear block print: Carrots, apples, sunflower seeds, cashews. *"Groceries" for the parrot? Damn right it could wait until tomorrow.*

"Hurry on now. The pharmacy in Rancho Valdez stays open all night but I don't, and I'll need those pills before I go to bed." He coughed again and Kay felt herself shorten. It was almost physical, the way she sank into her shoes. Her parents' authority, coupled with their fragility, had always cut her down to size, and her size now seemed to be her height at age four, the year her mother first handed Victor to her and said, "Here. You take him."

In a four-year-old's high voice, she looked at her hulking healthy sibling staring open mouthed at the television screen and said, "Why can't Victor go?"

"I don't know if you recall, but the last time I sent Victor to the pharmacy he ended up in drug court."

"That was twenty years ago."

"Like I say. Some things never change."

Kay glanced again at her brother. He had turned from the TV, and was examining Francis with the hurt look she had seen on his face as a teenager.

"I have changed, Dad," Victor said. "I'm not the same person."

"That's right. You're not. I forgot. You've been reborn." Francis waved a hand at Kay. "Run along now."

"No." Kay felt her body begin to shake and she hugged herself to stop it. "It can wait. I'll phone the pharmacy and have them deliver."

Francis smiled pleasantly, parted his lips and said, "What?"

Kay opened her mouth to repeat her refusal, but suddenly it was not just her body shaking, it was the world, for without warning the chandelier started to tremble, Ida's portrait swung sideways over the mantle, the television lurched to one side and Ed howled as plates crashed in the kitchen. Kay grabbed a Nicky too surprised to move and hunched with him under the doorframe. The earthquake was short and the three men sat on calmly until it stopped. Then: "Felt like a one point two," Neal said, adjusting the television.

"The Lord's preview," Victor predicted.

"This place is built on a rock," Francis said. "Oh Kay," he added, "put cigarettes on that list. And Victor? The remote if you don't mind."

It was after midnight before she got back from the pharmacy and made it up the tower stairs to her room. Every part of her body ached. She wanted to sleep for a week. She stripped out of her camping clothes, took a hot shower, and flopped onto the bed. Turning over on her side, she heard the quiet throb of a car pulling out of the driveway—Victor, off on his nightly vigil to drive up and down the street outside his old house, hoping Stacy would run out, fall to her knees, and beg forgiveness. She thought of Neal, down in the dungeon, bent over one of his weird homeopathic experiments, and of Nicky, sneaking through the pantry in search of any chips or cookies hidden on the shelves. She thought of Fenton too—wherever he was, perhaps lying in bed with all three of those blondes. Restless, her mind came back to Francis, his wondering face as he said, "Why would anything be because of you?"

She turned over, too tense to sleep. If only Charles was here! *I did what you always told me to do,* she'd say, *I stood up for myself—and what happened? The earth shook. But nothing else did!* Charles would look at her, seriously, not laughing for once. Perhaps he'd tell her to grab Nicky and get the hell out while the going was good. *Lambkin,* he'd say, *enough is enough.* And it was. What was she waiting for? Permission? From whom?

When the phone in the kitchen rang, she pulled the pillow off her face, rolled over, sat up, and hurried down the stairs. Charles always knew when she needed him; he was psychic that way. But the operator's voice asking if she would accept a collect call reminded her that Charles would never phone collect. "Listen to this, Karoony," Biff said.

The opening bars of "On Green Dolphin Street" came through the receiver, Biff humming along, his voice close to her ear. Kay listened, alert, unsmiling. She knew every nuance of Eric Dolphy's bass clarinet. "Made me think of you," he said as the song ended. "Remember?" Silent, she nodded, but before she could answer his next question, "How are you doing?" Biff began to tell her what *he* had been doing: winding up his tour, heading back down from Denver, thinking about hooking up with some other musicians and making a new C.D. "I was wondering if we could get together when I get back." His voice dropped, seemed to come closer. "I've missed you."

"Since when?"

"Since the first night I met you."

"I'm hanging up now."

"That's all right. I'll call again."

Was he that desperate? Was she? Rubbing her stiff shoulder, Kay plodded back up the stairs. The last thing she needed was to fall back into lust with Mr. Wrong. Not that Biff was really a threat. Too immature, too uncommitted. In many ways he made Fenton look like a prince. Still, unable to sleep, she could not get "On Green Dolphin Street" out of her head. The melody had brought back those late spring evenings in Berkeley, when Biff was young and beautiful, sitting beside her on the fire escape, playing his clarinet, while she sat with her arms around her knees and listened, feeling as she'd never felt before or since—free, joyful, fearless. She turned over, humming a few bars of the melody into her pillow.

WEEK SIX

Francis was an early riser, and the following Saturday Kay was not surprised to find him smoking in the Great Room at six, a crossword puzzle open on his lap, Raj on his shoulder. She brought him a cup of coffee and sat down beside him. He took in her baseball cap, dark glasses, and baggy jeans. "Off to see your addict friends?"

"I don't have any 'addict friends,' Dad."

"Really? You may be missing something. Your Aunt Arlene might have lived to see thirty if she'd had a cult to go to."

"I have an Aunt Arlene?"

"Had. I doubt that she's still with us."

"But you don't know?"

He shrugged. "She looked like you," he said.

Kay waited for more, filling in the silence with possible adjectives: *dumpy, frumpy, stumpy, lumpy,* but all Francis said, after a moment, was, "She had beautiful skin."

"Do you have other sisters?"

"Well, there's Jackie."

"And Jackie is where?"

"Last I heard, Jackie was living in a trailer in Bakersfield with another woman. She weighed three hundred pounds but that may have gone up." He shook his head and wrote a word down on the puzzle. "She was a pretty child. Slim. Not stocky like Nicholas. Who knows how these things happen."

Kay started to snap, *Nicky isn't stocky*, but stopped. Where had all these new family members come from? All she knew about her father's history was what Ida had told her—that Francis had grown up an orphan in Colorado, that he'd won a scholarship to MIT when he was sixteen, that he had earned his degree in architecture when he was barely twenty. He had deflected her childhood questions so summarily that Kay had long ago assumed his family was dead. "You mentioned your grandmother when I saw you in Carmel," she said. "The one who lived in the attic?"

"Ma Mamie," Francis nodded. "Woof woof."

"Woof woof?"

"She used to get down on all fours and bark at us."

"Bark at you and your sisters?"

"And my brothers. She'd bark and then she'd pee on the floor."

"You had brothers?"

"Well, yes ... let's see ... Kip, Mick, Harry. Harry's still in Aspen. You could look him up if you wanted to meet someone willing to whine you out of your last dime."

"So you didn't grow up in an orphanage?"

"Where did you get that idea? No, I grew up in a regular family, just like you did."

"Ha."

Francis regarded her, his blue eyes steady. "You may not appreciate this, Kay, because you have always had a roof over your head and food on the table. You also as I recall had ballet lessons, horseback lessons, archery camp, a swimming pool, and twelve years of piano instruction."

"And you didn't have any of that?"

146

"I had other things."

"Such as?"

Francis thought. "Construction materials," he said at last.

Kay waited. That was all. She tried to imagine Francis growing up in a noisy jumble of brothers and sisters. He must have hated it. *I would have loved it*, she thought. I *could have used "a regular family."*

"Do I really look like Arlene?" she asked as she rose to go.

"Ida had the looks, didn't she," Francis said without answering. "Beautiful face. Wasted on Victor." He reached for his coffee, took a small swallow, and set it down. For the first time Kay noticed the silver flask by the cup. "Oh, by the way," he added, "did you know you had a snake in the house?"

Several, she thought, but, "Yes," she said. "Orville. He lives in Nicky's room."

"Not anymore he doesn't. I saw him slithering down the hall an hour ago."

"He got out? Where was he going? My God. Can snakes climb stairs?"

"Snakes can do anything. Better watch where you walk. It's a jungle in here."

"Yes," Kay agreed. "It is."

She knew she was supposed to look for "similarities not differences" at her AA meetings but that morning nothing made sense. The first speaker had problems with his shower head: "Every morning I get a blast of water straight in the face because I never remember to turn the shower head to the side before I turn the tap on." He paused. "It makes me want to kill myself."

Everyone nodded as if it were the most normal thing in the world to want to kill yourself after a dunking and for a moment

Kay almost felt sane. She listened as a bearded man confessed he once stood on a table beneath a whirling ceiling fan trying to cut his head off with the blades and a tattooed woman followed by saying she had tried to set herself on fire in her wedding dress but her Higher Power must have been looking out for her because her Bic was out of fluid. When another woman said she'd recently bought twelve bottles of vanilla extract at the IGA and told the checker she needed them because she ran a wedding cake business, Kay put her face in her hands. What could she possibly add to any of this? She had done a lot of stupid things in her life but she had never felt suicidal. Or had she? She remembered the car accident after Francis and Glo's wedding, that sudden reckless twist she took speeding off a country road in the moonlight; she thought of her tumble out of Fenton's boat into the rocky rush of the river. She kept silent throughout the remainder of the shares, but at the end of the meeting she forced herself to rise and announce she had completed seven days of sobriety. Accepting a hug from a radiant man in a soiled Grateful Dead t-shirt who held her too close, she managed to mutter "Thank you," before extricating herself.

"Don't thank me," the man admonished. "Thank your Higher Power."

And she would. If she could. If she knew who her Higher Power was. She returned to the house to find Nicky, blinking back tears, scouring the castle for his snake—Orville better not be Nicky's Higher Power. Victor had left for the dealership, leaving a yapping terrier and the entire kitchen trashed behind him. She did not want anything to do with Victor's Higher Power. Neal looked up with a melancholy nod as he sat breakfasting on greenish grains: she wasn't sure Neal even had a Higher Power. As for Francis's Higher Power? That capricious cynic in the sky? No thanks. She bent to rub Ed's hard head and offer him a biscuit. Ed stopped yipping long enough to gulp it down. *Oh no, Kay* thought, *What if I'm Ed's Higher Power? And if I am, shouldn't I do something to help him? Stop his endless barking?*

The drive to Oxalis took, as Francis had said, less than an hour and Dr. Wallace was, as he'd also said, a nice guy. Kay watched the veterinarian's large hands move over Ed's quaking body, pressing against the tiny ribs and peering into each ear. Ed, who had whimpered and choked during the entire drive, now stood like a photographer's fashion model, gazing up at his handler with shining eyes.

"He likes you," Kay said, amazed.

Dr. Wallace nodded without looking up. "He's a good little guy. Nervous. But still not as antsy as your parents' old poodle."

"You remember Coco?"

"I remember your mother." Dr. Wallace looked at her over Ed's head and Kay blushed. It wasn't just that Donald Wallace was good looking—not tall, but broad shouldered with deep-set hazel eyes—but that, probably from working with the wounded and wordless for so long, he invited instant intimacy. "Formidable lady."

"Formidable," Kay repeated, grateful.

"Now as for Mr. Ed here. You say he barks constantly unless he's held?"

"Yes. Sharp regular staccato yips. He doesn't quit until he's picked up."

"And you let him get away with it?"

"Let him?"

"Aren't you tired of carryin' a cairn?"

"Who's a terror of a terrier? Yes. I am."

Dr. Wallace's laugh rang out so heartily that his nurse poked her head into the examination room, curious. "You're a clever one," he said to Kay, and his tone was so warm, pleasant, and admiring that she almost looked over her shoulder to see who he was talking about. "Tell me," he said, "has anyone tried to train him? Your husband maybe?"

"I'm not married."

"So no shock collar, behavior therapy ... "

"I said I'm *not* married," Kay joked, happy when again his laugh rang out.

"Oh wait," he said chuckling. "What's this?" He picked up one of Ed's paws and bent over it, suddenly serious. "Scar tissue. An old foxtail injury. Looks like he hurt himself a while ago, liked the attention, and has been requesting it ever since. Odd," he said, frowning. "Dogs don't usually hang on to old hurts like that. People do. But dogs?" He scratched his head. A well-shaped head, Kay noted, with a thatch of thick auburn hair. Was *he* married? No ring. But a man this attractive would have to have an adoring wife. "Does he have a job?"

"Ed?"

"Dogs like having something to do. Who gets the paper every morning?"

"We don't take a paper."

"Don't you want to know what's going on in the world?"

"No. It's all bad, isn't it?"

"Living in a bubble is bad. Look. You have a dog toy or two, don't you? Ask someone to throw it to Ed three or four times a day. Not you. No throwing for you until your shoulder gets better. Be sure and reward Ed with a treat when he comes back with the toy, but don't pick him up. If the barking doesn't cease in a week or two bring him back. Now do you mind just slipping your sweater down a bit so I can take a look at that shoulder? That's right. The right one. Good. Ah. How long has it been troubling you?"

"Years," Kay admitted. "But it's been worse since I fell in the river."

That laugh again. Happy. Non-judgmental, as if it were a perfectly normal thing to fall in a river. "And you've been living with the pain?"

"Yes, I ... "

"You might want to call my orthopedic surgeon and get it operated on, you know. Here," he scribbled a name on a scrap of paper, "no need for a rare blossom like you to live like Ed now, is there?"

"No."

"Good lass. And a great tattoo. Never examined a blue horse before."

Kay, blushing again, took the leash he handed her, conscious of the brief brush of his fingers over hers as they both set Ed down on all fours on the floor. At the doorway she paused, "Do you ever treat parrots?"

"You have a parrot?"

"No, I mean, well, my dad has a parrot. He named him Raj."

"What does Raj say?"

"He doesn't say anything! He can't talk."

"That's just because no one's taught him."

"Really?"

"Sure. All parrots talk. All they need is some loving encouragement."

"Loving encouragement," Kay repeated.

"Sit down with him when you get home," Dr. Wallace advised, "and teach him to say oh, how about, 'Pretty Girl.' It's a start. You can teach him to squawk out your other attributes later."

"My other ... " Kay stopped herself, laughed. "I'm the parrot now."

"I've always wanted one," Dr. Wallace smiled. "But my ex-wife had severe ornithophobia."

Ex? Well, not everyone can be a rare blossom. Kay led Ed out on the leash and was so impressed by his new obedience that she took a wrong turn leaving the animal hospital and found her-self driving through the shady streets of Oxalis, a small college town she'd never visited before. It seemed to be going through a growth spurt—there were new shops and coffee houses on the main street and—she slowed—construction was underway for a new library. It was going to be a huge library, six times the size of the West Valley Branch. She whistled. It was good to see that some counties supported their public libraries, she thought, and she slowed again to admire a green-shuttered cottage on a side street that reminded her of the one she and Nicky had once sketched. Curious, she parked, pushed through the gate and walked up the broken path to the door. The cottage looked as if it had been abandoned for years; the roof was mossy but the walls didn't slant; the foundation seemed to be sound. Peering through an empty window she saw a large sunlit room with a warm wooden floor, a stone fireplace, built-in bookcases. She walked around to the back; an old-fashioned patio and barbecue pit, a trellis heavy with ancient wisteria. By the time she sped away, Ed barking again, she was happy, happy just knowing that such a house, in such a town, with such a man as Dr. Donald Wallace, existed.

"Welcome to Palace Pigsty," she warned Fenton when he came to the back door the next day, ready to finish up the kitchen cabi-nets. "It's been wild around here."

"I like wild," Fenton reminded her. His hair was tousled, his work shirt was unbuttoned, his leather tool belt hung low on his hips. She had tried to break up with him twice over the phone this last week but had not been able to say the words. Now, with him gloriously before her, breaking up seemed even more diffi-cult. She began to tell him that they had to talk soon, but just as she opened her mouth, Francis came into the kitchen. She introduced the two men, proud of Fenton for standing up straight and holding out his hand.

"So you're the Apache," Francis said, ignoring the hand. "Heard a lot about you. Haven't liked what I've heard."

Fenton, tall, easy, laughed.

"You're fired."

"Sir?"

"You were retained to install six kitchen cabinets and hang a kitchen door. That was two months ago. I see three cabinets and no door. My grandson tells me you use the verb 'waltz.' You apparently waltz to work and waltz home again fifteen minutes later. Is that correct?"

"My back," Fenton began.

"Back schmack," Francis said. "Get out."

"Dad!"

Francis raised an eyebrow but before Kay could plead his case, Fenton had begun to gather his tools with an economy of movement she had never seen in him before. "I'll need my ladder," he muttered as he brushed by her.

"By the pool," she whispered. "I took it down from the tower window."

"I'll finish the cabinets myself," Francis said. "Maybe you could clean the garage out for me, Kay. I'll want a workspace." He disappeared out the back door Fenton had in fact still not replaced and Kay turned to hurry out to the pool to help with the ladder. It was heavy and she had struggled trying to lay it flat behind the rose bushes before her father saw it propped against her window. She stepped out into the garden just in time to watch Fenton hoist it on his broad shoulders and then, with no expression, crumple to his knees with two sharp cracks on the concrete, then tip face forward into the swimming pool, the ladder crashing on top of him.

Kay rode in the ambulance, holding Fenton's hand, which twitched with pain and something else: fury. Fenton was angrier than she had ever seen him—at her father for calling him an Apache when his heritage was Pawnee, at Neal for diving in and dragging him the entire length of the pool with the chokehold he claimed would do the least damage to his spine, at Nicky who had seen him fall in the water and laughed, at Victor for saying the Lord moved in mysterious ways, and, of course, at her. "Why couldn't you have let the ladder stay where it was?" he growled. "It was picking it up that made me lose my balance."

Kay pulled her hand back. "Actually," she said, remembering Neal, "it was not using your knees to lift properly that made you lose your balance."

"Well, I won't be using my knees for much now, will I," he said, and turned his head away. Kay looked as the cords in his tanned throat pulsed with swallowed tears and reached for his hand again. She hated herself for what she was about to say, but she said it anyway.

"I'm sorry," she said.

They waited three hours in the hospital before he was X-rayed and diagnosed with two cracked patellae and put in braces. "He can go home," the doctor said, "but he needs to stay in bed for two weeks with both legs elevated and he won't be able to bend them or climb stairs for another month."

"Then I can't go home," Fenton said flatly.

"Why is that?" a pretty nurse asked.

"Because I live in a tree house."

"Like Tarzan," the nurse giggled.

"A what?" Kay leaned close. "Did you say a tree house?"

Fenton gave her a cold look.

"I'd ask you to stay with me," the nurse said, "only my husband wouldn't like it."

No one will like it if he stays with me, Kay thought. *I won't like it myself. But where else can he go?* She looked down at Fenton lying as still—and still as beautiful—as a vandalized statue. The little room Ida had called The Knight's Nook was empty; one of Ida's hospice nurses had slept there years ago and it still held a cot. It was warm, dry; it had its own entrance, it was close to a downstairs bathroom. "There's an empty room at the castle," she said at last. "It's on the ground floor. You can stay there."

"Your father won't let me."

"He never goes downstairs," Kay said. "You won't even see him."

Fenton was silent a long time and then: "I guess that could work."

No gratitude? No thank you? No *why are you being so good to me when I have been so bad to you?* Could she finally just accept that this handsome, lonesome, sad and nervous man was not for her and never had been? Fenton, catching her expression, turned his head aside in a quick, proud gesture that reminded her at once of Ida. Maybe it was a yoga move taught only in hospitals. The Wounded Warrior.

Excusing herself, Kay rose to phone her father, who said only, "Why not, the more the scarier."

As usual, she couldn't tell how serious Francis was so she paused and said, "You're sure?"

"Nicholas here won't like it, but then Nicholas doesn't have a vote, do you kid," and when she did talk to Nicky, a second later, he did indeed groan.

"How long?" he asked.

"A month, the doctor said. Maybe more."

"So no more brilliant camping trips?"

"Nope. You're safe."

"Me?" Nicky barked his new rude laugh. "You're the one who's not safe, Mom."

When she came back from the phone, she wheeled Fenton out to the car, easing him in, her own back pinging and pinching under his weight, drove him up the mountain and settled him into his new room, with Victor and Neal looking on and giving useless advice as she helped him hobble on his crutches to the cot. "I'll need some things from the tree house," he told her as he settled, groaning, under the down comforter she tucked around him. "Can you bring them?"

Later, after he'd slipped into sleep, she took the directions he'd given her and drove his truck out to the western edge of the county. She turned off the freeway and followed a rural road through forests and vineyards, then veered onto a gravel strip that led past an abandoned trailer, a burnt-out shack, an outhouse, a locked tool shed, and ended before a grove of giant oak trees with a flight of rough wooden stairs up one trunk leading to a swinging rope ladder leading in turn to a structure on another trunk that looked like a miniature Swiss chalet. She parked, got out, and gazed up with wonder. Dad would never have fired Fenton if he'd seen this, she thought. He would have recognized a fellow architect and been impressed. Or—taking in the unfinished exterior, the duct-taped rain gutter—maybe not. Hiking up her skirt, Kay climbed the ladder. The key was where Fenton told her it would be, inside an empty paint can on the narrow front deck, and she eased the door open and stepped in.

The one room under the peaked roof was light and airy, furnished only with a cast iron wood stove, a pallet piled with sleeping bags, a folding table, a bamboo rocking chair, a plastic tub filled with dirty dishes, a camp stove, an assortment of Coleman lanterns and a scatter of building manuals, maps, and power tools. Fishing rods, skis, a bow and arrow, work clothes and winter jackets hung off the rafters. She saw a pile of tee-shirts and jeans tossed in a corner, among them the leather bomber jacket she'd scrimped to buy him for his birthday. She hung it up, then stuffed other clothes she thought he'd need into a pillowcase, trying to remember what he'd asked her to bring. That book on the hikers lost on Mt. Everest, some underwear, his sweatshirt, his toothbrush, the brown shaving kit—he'd repeated "the brown one not the black one" twice—so it must be important and of course it was the one thing she couldn't find, until, on all fours, she saw it under his bed, drew it out, and peered inside, unsurprised to see it contained two full baggies of pot, a clip, a bong, and some papers. Resigned, she dropped it into the pillowcase too. What difference did it make, as long as he only smoked in the Nook?

She lingered a while, reading his mail, going through his receipts, poking through pockets of his jackets, and then, because she would never be here again, washing his dishes from the barrel of rainwater and putting them away on the shelves, all the time looking for a sign of herself, her place in his life. There was nothing. There was no picture of her, no mark on his Sierra Club calendar with her name. Her carefully chosen cards and notes had not been kept, and though there were a few names of other women jumbled in with his bills and invoices there was no sign he had ever phoned them back or taken them out. A box by his phone held invitations it seemed he'd never answered, a single toothbrush sat by his sink. She picked up a book on Thoreau and saw a quote underlined in thick carpenter's pencil: "I love to be alone. I have never found a companion that was so companionable as solitude." Okay, she thought. Solitude. Not bikinied blondes or pretty nurses. Not me. Solitude. But the battered silver baby cup with the name *Pamela* engraved on it? The book titled *How To Get the Love You Deserve* in his bathroom—a book she'd been meaning to read herself? The metal lunch box filled with turquoise pawn jewelry she had never seen him wear? The Celine Dion disc in his CD player?

Who was he? She knew his apple-cedar smell, the old burn scar from a welding accident on his inner arm, the deep dents in his buttocks, the warm touch of his broad, plaster-stained fingers, every inch of his astonishing face. She knew he had grown up poor, living on state cheese and food coupons. His father had disappeared long ago; his mother died young. He had a sister in the military, a much older cousin who had once played pro ball in Seattle, a high school shop teacher who had encouraged him to go into the trades and with whom he still kept in touch. She remembered the first time she'd seen him, the day he came to soundproof the music room at the library. She'd been stunned by his broad shoulders, his gold-flecked eyes. She'd fallen in lust, not love. And he? She tried to think of any compliments he'd given her, any reason to think he cared more than he showed. "I like you because you're not spoiled," he'd said to her once. And, another time, "Being with you is almost as good as being alone." She flushed, remembering her drunken diatribe by the river. Madness. She and Fenton were never meant to be a couple.

She sat for a while on his rocking chair, looking out at the pattern of leaves through the windows, listening to the wind and the crows. Fenton had done what she had not yet managed to do—he had made a home for himself. Too bad there was no room in it for anyone else. She rose at last and locked the door behind her.

WEEK SEVEN

Ten Easy Steps to Fearless Public Speaking was full of good advice and Kay studied the book faithfully every night before her presentation to the County Board, practicing eye contact in front of the mirror and forcing her frozen lips into a warm, confident, encouraging grimace behind the wheel of her car as she drove to work. She learned that the word for this particular terror was "Glossophobia"—"glossa" from the Greek for "tongue," "phobos" from the Greek for "dread"—and that it was the second most common fear in the world. She taped herself on Nicky's recorder and although she listened to her own too-sweet, too-soft voice, cringing, with both hands over her ears, she thought her points for saving the library were intelligent, practical, and well made. She visualized applause—grateful Board members coming up to her afterward to say she had really opened their eyes and changed their minds. Standing behind her desk at the library the afternoon before her talk, she reviewed the ten steps for a final time, then reached for her pen and added a few more:

11. *Don't pee down your leg.*

12. *Wear a sanitary pad in case you pee down your leg anyway.*

13. *Don't faint.*
14. *Wear clean underwear in case you faint anyway.*
And, finally:
15. *Remember that this talk is not about you. No one cares about you. It's about the library. Give it your best shot.*

That helped.

"You're cheerful today," Lois Hayes said, checking the return shelf to see if, by some fluke, *The Miraculous Mindfulness Makeover* had finally arrived. "We're all looking forward to your presentation tonight. We're counting on you!"

"I'm counting on *you*," Kay said. "I want you all to hoot and holler at every point I make. We need to show the Board real solidarity on this thing."

"We will," Lois promised.

And, really, what could go wrong? Her speech was fine. Dana and Zabeth had both read it and approved it, and, to cement their approval, had even taken her shopping for a new outfit: a black jacket, a short black skirt, a white lace camisole, and cherry red pumps, dressing her, as she pointed out, exactly like a library book, black and white and not read all over. Dana lent her an ebony comb for her hair; unsmiling, Zabeth lent her a silver bracelet for her wrist. By the time she dressed and came downstairs Thursday evening, speech in hand, she looked far more put together than she felt. Neither Francis nor Nicky glanced up from the video game they were playing together and neither Neal nor Victor wished her luck as she asked each of them to move their cars so she could get out of the driveway and make it to the Courthouse on time, though both said, as they came in, that her right rear tire was low. Ed sniffed the high heels she was wearing, and went back to lie down in front of the fireplace. "He's not barking," Kay noticed.

"He hasn't barked since you brought him back from the vet's," Francis said, moving a joystick over an exploding tank.

Kay felt a pulse of pleasure remembering the hazel-eyed veterinarian. "Dr. Wallace is a genius," she agreed.

"No," Nicky said, not looking up. "Dad's the genius. He gave Ed some special medicine."

Neal beamed, eyes bright behind his smudged sunglasses. "You won't believe it," he began, and Kay didn't, as Neal, excited, explained that he had been harvesting impatiens petals and mint from the neighborhood gardens in Manzanita Heights at dawn and then distilling them "down to their essence" in his little lab in the dungeon. "I've added some roots and herbs and a few secret ingredients," he said proudly, "and I've been giving Ed a vial a day."

Ed, hearing his name, tumbled over on his back, paws in the air, eyes closed. He looked almost cute. Neal's formula had transformed him from a yippy little nerve ending to a cuddly, relaxed, semi-normal puppy dog.

"You should try it," Neal finished.

"Right," Kay said, picking up her purse.

"No, really. No offense babe, but I can smell b.o. on you. You've always had performance anxiety; you've always gone to pieces whenever you've had to do anything in public."

"That's not true."

"You couldn't sleep for days before you gave a concert. You duck out of parties. And our wedding?" Neal looked at her tenderly. "It had to be at City Hall because you didn't want anyone to see you walk down the aisle? Wait here," he instructed. "I'll give you a vial."

"Give her two," Francis called from the game table. "She's bigger than Ed."

Flower water? Dog Dew? Totally organic, Neal had said. Weed juice and ginseng. Best stuff for nerves, Neal had said. But what did Neal know about nerves? Kay parked behind the Courthouse, gathered her notes, and, trembling, sweating, stomach reeling, pulled the stopper out of one brown bottle and sniffed it. She had not had a drink since she had returned from the river trip. It had been easy. She had not wanted one. She didn't want one now. She just wanted to stop shaking. She thought of Ed, his transformation from devil to darling—perhaps this stuff really worked? Trembling so badly she almost spilled it, she lifted the vial to her lips, shut her eyes, and downed the liquid in a single draught. Sour. Nasty. Nothing flower-like about it. But her throat relaxed and a soft fire warmed her almost at once. She mainlined the Serenity Prayer for a few seconds, then, remembering that she was, indeed, bigger than Ed, uncorked the other vial and downed it too, waiting for the second wave of warmth to weight her veins and steady her heartbeat. Then she slid out of the car and walked toward the Courthouse. In her nervousness driving here she had failed to notice what a beautiful night it was, the sky still holding gold from the sunset, the silver moon low on the horizon and right beside it, in the last wash of the afternoon's light blue, Venus, the wishing star. Kay stopped, pressed a hand to her heart, and felt her eyes water as she wished, hard, for the care and safety of The West Valley Branch Library. She wiped away a tear, turned and smiled, surprised to see Lois Hayes right behind her. "Losh!" That didn't sound right. She tried again. "Losh? Wyer you here?"

Lois stepped back. "Why am I here? I came to support you."

"You did?" Tears again. How kind of Lois! Why had she never liked her? The beady eyes weren't unkind and the quick tic of the narrow lips was perfectly natural: Lois wasn't judging her. Lois was supporting her!

"Are you okay?" Lois asked.

"I'm wonderful!" Kay said—or thought she said. She couldn't tell. Lois didn't look convinced. But it was true—she *was* wonderful. Bold and brave and bright and able to march right through the Courthouse doors and give the most impassioned, convincing, articulate argument for saving the library that the goddamn fucking Cunty Board of Stupidvisors had ever … uh-oh.

"You don't look good. Do you want me to give the speech for you?"

Mustering every muscle in her stricken mouth—no wonder Ed couldn't yip—Kay tried to say, "No thank you. I'll be fine. I can give my own talk," but ended up simply shaking her head.

She waited until Lois, with a final backward frown, headed off toward the meeting room, then she turned and staggered in the direction of her car, got lost, found it after circling the parking lot, got in, turned the key, found an exit, drove around the corner, opened the door, threw up on the pavement, drove down another block, parked, and passed out.

She came to an hour later with the moon in her eyes, vomit in her hair, and the familiar realization that she had ruined her life. Once again. She looked at the two empty brown bottles lying on top of *Ten Easy Steps to Fearless Public Speaking* and began to shiver. Goodbye library. Goodbye job. Shame made her curl around herself and rock back and forth on the car seat, too sickened to sit up. This was worse than her birthday. Far worse because she knew better now. She knew better than to touch any substance that promised escape. What had Charles's latest postcard shown? A scene from the Lotus Eaters section of *The Odyssey*—a lush golden peach and on the back: *Those who ate the honey-sweet fruit no longer wished to sail for home* … She'd thought at the time it just meant Charles was going to stay in Greece forever, but she saw now he had been trying to warn her. Charles had always been prescient. But if he knew she was having a hard time, why hadn't he come home to help her get through it?

Shakily, she sat up, turned the key, the dead-end street ahead of her darkly lustrous through her tears. She couldn't blame Charles. She couldn't blame Neal. She would have to take full responsibility for this disaster. It was no one's fault but her own. She would have to *sail for home* and face the music. She would be calm, she would be sensible, she would be mature.

Screaming at Neal took the last of her strength and the sly way Neal listened, eyes downcast, half-smiling, clearly proud of his "invention," took the last of her patience. He was fascinated by her symptoms and questioned her closely: nausea, followed by an actual blackout? "I need to do some adjusting," he murmured. "The proportions are off."

"Everything's off!" Kay raged, pacing around the dungeon. "Stop gloating, damn it, Neal! You've squatted here for months, you haven't found a job or another place to live, you're setting a terrible example for our son, and you used me for what is probably a highly illegal experiment, just to see what would happen. You are the single most selfish short-sighted unfeeling immature individual I've ever known."

Neal shrugged, and his shrug meant what it had always meant: *so what?* So what if I'm not perfect? So what if I make mistakes? The two words of mental health, *So What*, available to everyone in the world, it seemed, Kay thought, but her.

"I'm sorry, babe. I thought you'd be proud of me. You always wanted me to do something I liked. That's all you talked about when we were married. And I like working with plants. I'm good at it. Look at you: the proof's in the pudding."

Kay, exhausted, sank down onto the seat of her mother's old wheelchair. "What does that mean?"

"It's means you're amazing right now. Articulate. Focused. Passionate. No more stage fright. You really responded to the medication I gave you."

"You didn't give me 'medication,' Neal. You gave me poison. And I've always been articulate, focused, and passionate. When I'm drunk. Which I probably still am."

Neal, smiling his downward smile, shook his head. "The dog wasn't *poisoned*. Ed was *improved*. I'm on the right track, babe, except," his smile faded, "I may have to use less locoweed."

"You're kidding—you put *locoweed* in that stuff? What else did you put in?"

"Let's see." As he ticked the ingredients off on his fingers, Kay stared at him. She did not hear "morning dew." She did not hear "impatiens petals." This round-shouldered, gray-haired, slow-speaking madman reciting a list of toxins had once been her husband. She had loved him, she had supported him, she had trusted him. She glanced over at the lab he had set up on the counter by the sink: amber dropper bottles, glass funnels, coffee filters, glass bowls, bottles of spring water, copper pans, a jumble of powders and pills from the health food store where he'd last worked and, yes, liquor bottles, two of them.

Kay heaved herself off the wheelchair without a word.

"Kay, listen, once I get it patented, this formula is going to take us places."

"Not us. You. Straight. To. Jail."

"Why do you always have to be so negative?"

"I don't know. It's one of life's mysteries." She clumped back up the dungeon stairs to find Francis. She found him sitting in his chair, feeding peeled grapes to the parrot.

"You actually drank that stuff?" he asked when she told him what had happened.

"Of course. You're the one who told him to double the portion."

"I never thought you'd actually drink it, Kay. It's for dogs."

"I couldn't give my presentation. I got sick on the street. I couldn't see to drive. You know what's in Neal's formula? Valerian, absinthe, brandy, opium, strychnine, and, get this, locoweed."

"My brandy?"

"Probably. There's a whole stash of stuff down in the dungeon and Neal can't afford to buy anything."

"I hope he didn't use the Courvoisier your mother and I brought back from Paris. The absinthe, well, that was just a joke. Ida liked to shock people, you know. Raj would have liked your mother. Wouldn't you, Raj?" He held out his hand, letting the parrot pick through the grapes. "Look," he said, delighted. "He only takes the red ones!"

"So you're not going to make Neal dismantle his distillery? You're not even going to talk to him?"

"Neal's not a child, Kay. And he's certainly not my child. If I'm going to talk to anyone, I'm going to talk to you."

"So do it," Kay said.

Francis looked up, mild. "I just did. Oh. By the way. A know-it-all named Lois Hayes phoned. She said the Board meeting was cancelled. Apparently, all the members had dinner earlier at some oyster restaurant tonight and they all got food poisoning. She said she had no idea that you'd eaten with them; she said she was surprised that you were that close to the enemy."

Kay stared. "Cancelled?" Dizzy, she steadied herself on the back of a chair. "You know what that means? That means I'm saved."

"Not you too," Francis said.

"It's a miracle," Kay marveled.

"Well keep it to yourself," Francis said, and fed the parrot another grape.

Loud splashing from the swimming pool brought her, blinking, to the tower window the next day. It was past noon. Pushing her hair back from her swollen eyes, she opened the window and peered out.

Zabeth and Dana sat side by side at the pool's edge, watching Zeng and Zai splash in the shallow end with a strange man, no, not a man, that was Nicky with them, swinging the twins around in the water. Kay had totally forgotten that she had invited her friends over for a swim today. How pretty they looked, sleek and tanned, in their fancy sunglasses and skimpy swimsuits. She looked down at her own rumpled robe and shrugged. She would join them as soon as she'd had some coffee. They could celebrate her successful reprieve. Thinking of her reprieve she bent her head and pressed her hands together. Whatever angel of goodness had prompted the entire Board of Supervisors to eat bad oysters was an angel she was willing to honor forever.

Her almost holy sense of gratitude was challenged by the mess in the kitchen. The counters were littered with broken eggshells and the floor was sticky with watermelon seeds. Pushing aside the clutter, she filled her coffee cup and carried it past the newspapers, clothes, shoes, glasses, plates, loose change, and sports equipment scattered over the floor of the Great Room, careful not to step where Ed had pooped on the parquet. The parrot watched with wary black eyes as she passed by its perch on the landing and Goldie hissed as she pushed open the closed door to the drum tower and bent to pour kibble into her bowl. The kits were fluffier by now, open-eyed and clumsily active, but they were not pretty and Kay did not love them. As soon as they were weaned, they were headed to the animal shelter. If Orville didn't get them first. For Orville—she glanced around nervously—was still loose inside the castle.

Back in her own wonderfully empty room, she heard a familiar deep laugh from outside and looked out the window again.

Bare-chested, crutches propped to one side, Fenton sat in the sun, with Ed, still stoned, lying under his chair. Neal was out there too, in a scarecrow's straw hat, digging another hole in the garden. And who was that old fellow in the white linen pants handing Zabeth a tall drink with a slice of lemon in it: Francis? All dressed up like a gay plantation owner? And the muscular blonde crouching down to talk to Dana? That was Victor? Closing her eyes, Kay tried to recapture the sense of reprieve and thanksgiving she had felt a few minutes before, but her head still throbbed from last night's potion. Music would help. She'd go to the music room and work on that sonata she was having so much trouble with and she would not wonder what Fenton was laughing about—again?!!—or why Zabeth was going ha ha ha in that donkey bray of hers or why Dana thought she could get away with a bikini at her age, or why anyone thought it was a smart idea to entrust an eleven-year-old boy with life-guarding two manic tots and—opening her eyes again—who was that? She leaned forward, scowling as a submerged swimmer she had not seen before burst out of the water right next to Nicky, dreads dripping, breasts plumply popping out of a see-through brassiere: Chiana? Chiana was Zabeth's "free-spirited" new nanny?

Kay pulled on her ancient red Speedo, popped four aspirin, grabbed a towel, and went downstairs.

"This is one of those golden afternoons," Zabeth said later, "that I'll want to play back like a movie next winter, when the weather is lousy and Garret's home with the flu and the twins are driving me crazy." She said this leaning back in a lounge chair in her tiny black one-piece, a twin nestled under each silver bangled arm, smiling at Francis, who looked up from his crossword puzzle, leaned over, and tapped each twin on the nose with his pen in an affectionate way, Kay was sure, he never had done to either her or Victor.

"It is," Dana agreed, from her seat under the sun umbrella. "Golden, totally golden." She turned to Fenton. "Kay's father tells me you're an Anasazi," she purred. "Did you go on a vision quest?"

Instead of slugging her, Fenton inexplicably smiled and shifted his gleaming shoulders. "I sailed alone for six months through the Pacific," he began. For shame, Kay thought. Shouldn't he at least have the decency to observe a short period of mourning before he moved on? After all, she had not yet officially broken up with him. Then again, she reminded herself, she had never officially been with him.

"Every day will be this golden one day," Victor said.

"What's he talking about?" Zabeth asked Kay.

"The Rupture."

"My witty sister," Victor said. "She means The Rapture," he explained to Zabeth.

Zabeth laughed. "You don't really believe any of that, do you Victor?"

"Yes," Victor said simply. "I do."

"I just hope when the world ends," Dana smiled, "that it will find me hiking the Pacific Coast Trail."

"I rode most of it once on my mountain bike," Fenton chimed in in a sturdy baritone.

"I love mountain biking," Dana purred.

"You do? I can't get Kay to even get on a bike."

"That's a shame because they are such a healthy and environmentally sustainable way to get around. And they keep you," Dana stretched out one leg that had been toned, to Kay's knowledge, by liposuction, "so fit. I just got a Ferrari," she added.

Fenton whistled.

"I actually have two. I need to get rid of one. I'll probably end up giving it away to someone. I don't suppose you … ?"

"He'd love to," Kay said loudly, sitting up to rub sunblock on her own white un-liposuctioned legs. "But as you can see, he's in severe pain from two serious knee injuries. You'll have to pedal for him."

Both turned to look at her. She put her head back down on the towel.

"Those of you left behind," Victor continued, "are going to need to start arming yourselves. You will need rifles and handguns as well as butcher knives. Fenton, you have a crossbow, which is good. Neal, you need to start practicing with that machete. But guns are the main thing. Luckily some of us have been going out to the shooting range every day. Nicky's getting pretty good."

Kay sat up again. "You've been taking Nicky to a shooting range? Neal? Did you know about this?"

"Here she goes," Victor began.

"Thar she blows," Francis echoed.

"Over-reacting," Neal summed up. "We didn't tell you because we know how you'd get, Kay. Don't worry," he added. "Your brother and father and I have talked about this. We'll take full responsibility."

"I forbid it," Kay said.

There was silence. Then as if on cue, Francis, Victor, and Neal said her name together in the same breath, with the same grave tone: "Kay." When had the three of them agreed on anything? And why hadn't Nicky told her about this? They had always been so open with each other. Hadn't they? *Honey*, she wanted to call, *get out of the pool, you've been in long enough.* But he wasn't six years old anymore; he was almost twelve and his laugh, as he batted a ball back to Chiana, was almost as alarmingly deep as Fenton's. It was clear he had no intention of getting out of the pool.

"I forbid it," she repeated.

She tore at a cuticle as Victor, returning to his favorite subject, went on for a few more minutes about Armageddon. "Every major infrastructure is going to collapse," he predicted, his voice reverential as he described the downfall of phone lines, media, transportation and internet systems. Summing up, he turned to Zabeth. "You were saying you'll be home next winter with a sick husband and kids? Trust me. There will be an armed mob outside your door. Your husband's a pharmacist, right? They'll be wanting drugs, and you," he turned to Dana, "sitting up there in your condo with all those bikes, will be a sitting duck for bandits."

"Sounds exciting," Chiana called from the pool. "Where will I be?"

"If you're smart," Victor said, "you'll be in church. The churches will be protected. Bring plenty of cash, keep a weapon on you at all times, and stay close to the altar. As for provisions, those of you left behind are going to find that food will be scarce ... "

"We'll be fine here. We'll have the garden." Neal removed the piece of hay he was chewing on to turn to Kay and add, "The chickens are coming tomorrow, babe. Rhode Island Reds, good layers, six of them."

"Very funny," Kay said. "When is the cow coming?"

"We're not zoned for cows."

Kay put her hands over her eyes. She literally felt her head had just separated from her neck, bounced as high as Nicky's beach-ball, and exploded. *I can't do this anymore*, she thought. *I can't, I can't, I can't.* Feeling drops of water on her chest, she looked up to see Chiana standing above her, toweling herself as if slowly stroking down a pony.

"I know you," Chiana said.

"No, actually, you don't."

"Yes, I do." Chiana squatted beside her, pubic hair tufting out of the crotch of her underpants. "You're a Friend of Bill's. I've seen you at meetings." She put a finger to her lips. "Don't worry.

I'll protect your anonymity. You've got an awesome son," she added as she straightened, "and an awesome house too. Nicky says it's a sort of hotel. Can people stay here?"

"No."

"Too bad. I'd love to crash here."

I'm sure you would, Kay thought. *And I'm sure you are*, she thought later, as Dana said she was sorry for flirting with Fenton and *I hope you did*, she thought, as Zabeth, laughing, said she was afraid she'd gotten a sunburn. "It's just that I thought you two were over," Dana said as she kissed Kay goodbye in the hall. "It's just that I always have fun talking to Francis," Zabeth said, as she belted the twins into their car seats.

It's just that you can both go to hell, Kay thought. So much for a day of grace, gratitude, and thanksgiving. It was clear that she wasn't needed here. And if she wasn't needed, what was the point? Was there a point? She looked around to see if Nicky wanted to take a drive with her, but she couldn't find him. Just as well. It was a long drive to Oxalis.

Her phone kept beeping once she was in the car, however, and she never made it out of the county. Francis phoned to remind her that Raj needed sunflower seeds and he needed scotch, and Victor emailed to tell her that Fenton had drunk the last of his, Victor's, special chocolate milk, so could she pick up a carton, and Nicky texted to ask if he could go to the new Star Wars movie with Chiana (NO), who knew the theater owner and could get them in for free (I SAID NO). Kay went to the market and returned, dismayed to see there were still cars in the driveway. Victor had been bringing home loaners from the dealership for Francis to consider and she saw a black Jaguar, a silver BMW, Neal's van and a dented blue sedan of some sort blocking her place, so that once again she had to park on the street. Pushing open the heavy front door with her uninjured shoulder and balancing the grocery bags in both arms she was puzzled to hear Mozart—the same sonata she had been struggling with—pouring from the piano.

Coming in, she dropped the groceries on the kitchen counter and hurried upstairs toward the music alcove. She pushed aside the velvet drapes, caught her breath, and leaned against the wall to watch. Biff looked even thinner than he had at the Rode House, and, unfairly, even younger, his straight hair falling across his lean face, his black tee-shirt frayed at the neck, and his feet, she glanced down, yes, bare. She did not expect him to acknowledge her, he never did when he was playing, but the glazed look he raised from the keyboard seemed to include her. He finished the piece with a quiet, perfect flourish, and smiled.

"I let myself in," he said. "I hope you don't mind. I called to a kid on the roof and he said you'd be back soon, so ... " he shrugged, grinned, "I took advantage."

"Nicky was on the roof?"

"Guess so. Who's Nicky?"

"My son. Who is about to be grounded. He knows he's not supposed to climb up there. I guess he's mad at me for ruining his first date." Kay paused. "I didn't think I'd see you again."

Biff laughed. "I said I'd come back; didn't you believe me? God, this place. It's as if time stopped." He looked around, showing Kay one perfect ear and exposing the small star arrangement of moles she used to kiss on his throat. "I keep expecting the Dragon to slink in with her drink and ask me to play 'I Feel Pretty.' She's not here, is she?"

"No," Kay said, "she's not."

"And your father?" Biff asked, rising to follow her down the stairs to the kitchen.

"You'll meet him if you're staying for dinner."

"Dinner? No no, I don't want to put you out, I just dropped by to say howdy, see how you are. Though now that I see what you've got in this grocery bag … Johnny Walker?" He whistled. "And what's this, macaroni? Don't tell me you still make that great macaroni and cheese? With pancetta, was it? And breadcrumbs?" He grinned at her astonished face. "I told you. I remember everything about you."

Yes, Kay thought, everything except who my son is and that my mother died. The rest he remembers the same way he remembers the scores to Mozart sonatas: automatically. "The silver is in the top drawer," she said. "Why don't you set the table? There will be seven of us."

"Seven?"

"It's a long story. And they may not all show. No one in this house eats at the same time."

But that night they did. Nicky came in first, flushed from his afternoon in the pool, sullen that Kay hadn't let him go to the movies with Chiana, and defensive about being caught on the roof. "It's perfectly safe, Mom," he said, shooting a dark look at Biff.

"Safe as the shooting range?" Kay snapped.

"Safer. I was on the flat part."

"There is no flat part."

"Whatever." Nicky slumped into a chair and examined his dinner to make sure it came from the Kraft box she'd made separately for him. "Who's the new guy?"

"Biff Kelly," Biff said. He picked up one of Nicky's hands before the startled boy could yank it away and turned it over, palm up. "Awesome callouses, man. Guitar? Cool. Want me to show you some chords I picked up from Santana?"

"No," Nicky said. "Who's Santana?"

"Just another devil worshipper," Victor said, coming in, sitting down, and, helping himself to Kay's casserole. "This is the third night she's made pasta," he said to Biff, adding, "Got my money?"

"Sure do." Biff slapped a hundred-dollar bill down on the table and Kay watched Victor calculate whether it was worth asking for twenty-three years of interest as well, relieved when he simply nodded and pocketed it. "That your blue Suburu? You used to drive a VW van when you were fornicating with my sister."

"You know," Biff said, leaning forward, "I sold that van for twenty thousand dollars five years ago, can you believe it?"

"Car collectors are crazy," Victor agreed.

"You fornicated with my mother?" Nicky asked.

"No, no ... " Kay started.

"We lived together," Biff clarified.

"When?" Neal asked, coming into the dining room. He was still in his straw hat, Kay saw, and his nails were dirty. "You never told me you lived with anyone before, Kay."

"Yes I did."

"You never told me," Nicky said.

"It doesn't affect you. You weren't born. I was eighteen."

"You should have seen your mama," Biff said to Nicky. "Hair down to here, slim as an eel. A real beauty. And," he added firmly, helping himself to seconds, "she still is."

"Slim as an eel?" Neal repeated. "Huh. Guess I missed that phase. Of course, her digestive enzymes ... " He patted his own slack stomach, said, "She bloats," and reached for the salad.

"Chiana's eighteen," Nicky said.

"No, she is not, honey," Kay said. "She's closer to thirty."

"Which one's Chiana?" Neal looked up, a leaf of lettuce between his lips.

"The one in Kay's AA group," Victor said.

"AA," Biff nodded, glancing at Kay. "Cool."

"Kay doesn't need AA," Neal said, starting to chew. "She needs B3."

"Chiana sure doesn't look thirty," this from Fenton hobbling toward them on his crutches. "How old would you say that woman Dana is, Kay?"

"No one knows," Kay said. "Fenton, this is Biff, he's visiting from ... where are you visiting from, Biff?"

"I live on the road," Biff said, grinning and once again rising to shake Fenton's hand.

"Fenton lives in a tree," Nicky said, innocent eyes on his plate. "Like a monkey."

"You're the monkey," Fenton laughed and Nicky, surprisingly, laughed back.

"Organ grinders used to have monkeys," Francis said, his light drawl cutting through the laughter as he came in to take his place at the head of the table. "Sometimes you couldn't tell which was the musician, the little man or the little ape."

This time Biff rose more slowly and when he looked at Francis his smile was uncertain. "It's good to see you again, sir," he said, holding out his hand.

"I'm afraid I can't return the sentiment." Francis pulled out his chair, stubbed his cigarette out and set his drink down. "I do remember the way you treated my daughter, Mr. Kelly. I didn't like it at the time and I don't like it now. If it were up to me," Francis continued, "I'd throw you out right now."

Kay put down her fork and glanced at Victor, who met her look with equal surprise. Francis had never defended either one of them before. For a second, she had a flash of the father she had always wanted Francis to be: the gentle powerful guardian who took care of his kids. But ... had Francis really not liked the way Biff had abandoned her? At the time, she recalled, he'd been pleased. At the time, she recalled, he'd been at least partly responsible for Biff's departure.

"But it's not up to me to throw you out," Francis continued, "it's up to Kay. And my daughter likes to take in strays. So join the crowd. Sit down. Eat your noodles."

"Thank you, sir."

Francis turned to Kay. "You might want to open some wine. This seems to be a reunion of sorts."

Kay escaped to the alcove in the dungeon. She grabbed the first bottle she found and started back up the stairs, pausing outside the dining room door for a moment to remind herself that the wine pressed against her side would be no kinder to her than the men at the table. I don't have to drink it, she realized. I never have to drink alcohol again. She felt her shoulders drop with relief. Why had this simple thought never occurred to her before? Because it was too simple? And was it too simple because she was still nauseated from last night's fiasco? Probably, she decided. But for whatever reason, for tonight at least, it was working.

After dinner Francis rose, gave the table his usual words of goodnight, "I've had a wonderful evening. Unfortunately, this wasn't it," and went to bed, but the "reunion" continued. Biff's stories about famous musicians he'd known and worked with seemed to keep the others entertained. He had learned from his mistake mentioning Santana to Nicky, Kay noticed, and tailored his references to his audience, telling Fenton about the time he'd opened for Guy Clark, and Victor about his stint as organist at the largest Lutheran church in St. Paul, and complaining to Neal about the eight-string banjo he'd invented that he wished he'd had the foresight to patent. Kay, washing dishes at the kitchen sink, was both comforted and troubled by the murmur of male voices and laughter coming from the Great Hall. It was admirable, the way Biff had not let Francis intimidate him, but a little too easy, the way Biff had made himself at home. He was a con artist and con artists, she reminded herself, usually give as good as they get. Her lips lifted as she remembered the quiet way he'd said: *a real beauty.* She heard a step behind her and turned to see Nicky checking the ice cream in the freezer.

"All I bought is bubblegum," she warned him. "It's the only flavor I can resist."

Nicky opened the carton, peered in at the blue and pink goo, and said, "You know, Fenton's right, I've probably had enough to eat tonight. Think I'll resist too."

"'Fenton's right?' I've never heard you say that before."

"You've probably never heard anyone say it before. Just don't let him know I did."

"I won't. And Nicky? I mean it about the roof. I used to go up there too, when I was your age, but that was a long time ago, when the roof was new. There's moss on those slates now; there are a hundred places where you could slip and fall. It worries me. It worries me almost as much as the shooting range. I don't want you to go to either of those places again. Okay?"

Silence.

"Okay?"

"Mom, I said okay."

No, actually you didn't, Kay thought, as she watched him leave. Had he been losing weight? He looked slimmer. She slipped a cigarette out of a pack her father had left open on the counter, examined it, slipped it right back in again, and went to sit outside by the pool, trying to ignore all the glasses, plates, beer bottles and strewn towels still left from the afternoon's party. Lying back in the lounge, she looked up at the dark shape of the mountain against the stars, trying to still her thoughts. Biff's reappearance was nothing to get agitated about. An old friend, much changed, older, even his talent—his Mozart had been a bit too fast, too bright—diminished. He couldn't possibly break her heart again. Still—she wondered if it was true, what Ida had told her just before she died: that Biff had accepted money from Francis to leave her. How much money would that have been? A hundred dollars? A thousand? Had her father bankrolled Biff's flight with the waitress? That tough curvy dimpled little waitress?

"Lena," Kay remembered, when Biff stepped outside and joined her in the dark. "Lena Polanski. Whatever happened to her? She played the saxophone I remember. Wasn't she trying to get on *Saturday Night Live*?"

"She auditioned. We both did. But we never made it." Biff perched on a deck chair beside her. "There's a lot we haven't talked about," he said.

Kay waited. But that was all he said. The sounds of the summer night hummed around them, insects, an owl call, the whir of the pool filter, a quiet splash, perhaps one of the bats dipping in for a drink. Victor's car started up as he left for his nightly cruise by Stacy's house, and deep inside the castle Nicky began to practice some new chords that did, yes, sound a bit like Santana's.

"Let's start by talking about Lena Polanski," Kay suggested.

"Oh Karoony. Move over so I can lay down beside you. Lena died ten years after we were married. She had heart trouble."

"You married her? And you lasted ten years?"

"Is there an echo out here?"

"I didn't think you'd stay married to anyone for ten years."

"We only lived together for three of those years. If that makes you feel better." Biff turned his head and she felt his eyes on her face. "What else do you need to know?"

"Did you and Lena have children?"

Now it was Biff's turn to be silent.

"Yes? No?"

"I have two little girls. Not with Lena. They're with their mothers."

"Mothers? Plural?"

"I send them money. I see them when I can."

How old are they where do they live what are their names when was the last time you saw them? Kay asked none of this. From the

179

way Biff shifted on the chaise and blinked up at the stars she knew he wouldn't answer. Biff had never hesitated to say, "I don't want to talk about that," and get up and leave. Lying still by his side she cleared her throat to ask one last question. "Did my father pay you to run out on me?"

"God no!" Biff's voice rose in such righteous indignation that Kay guessed he was lying, but then again, she had never known when Biff was or wasn't lying so why would she be right this time? "Who told you such a thing? Your mother? That woman was a witch, Kay. I'm not kidding. She would do anything to control you. And your father is just as bad. You got dealt a bum hand there, Karoony. Man." He whistled. Then, in a lower voice, "No one could pay me to—what did you call it? *Run out on* you? I never *ran out on* you."

"I don't know what else you'd call it. I came home from work one night and you were gone."

"It wasn't an easy decision. Damn! Don't you remember the note I left you?"

Yes, she remembered the note, a generic message in pencil: *It isn't you, it's me*, left on the pillow. It wasn't until three days later that she found out Biff had left town with Lena. Sassy brassy Lena with her hoarse voice and round hips, Lena whom she had tried to hate and tried to blame even though she had known, all the time, that Biff's note lied. Biff *had* left because of her. In asking for his attention, reassurance, affection, she had asked for too much. He had nothing to give but his love for music, his bravado, and his energetic involvement in life.

"I am sorry Lena died," she said, after a while.

A soft snore was the only response; Biff had always been able to fall asleep as fast as a cat. She got up and looked down at his face, no longer the face of the boy who had abandoned her, but the lips as always lifted in a sweet bow. Biff, who smiled in his sleep. She picked a dry towel off a chair and draped it over him. It was after midnight. She supposed he could stay here until morning.

Three hours later she felt the tower room bed sag as Biff slipped in beside her. "Freezing out there," he whispered, and to demonstrate he rubbed his chilled feet against the backs of her calves and put his cold arm around her waist.

"Biff," Kay said, groggily slapping his arm back, "get out of my room."

"C'mon, one night. I won't touch you. Look. No hands."

"What's that?"

"Oh, just ignore him."

"Out, Biff. I mean it."

"Please? I just want to sleep next to you. You have no idea; you are the best person to sleep next to. It's true. There's something about you. Restful. Restful and healthful and wholesome. I feel safe with you. C'mon, Kay, let me stay. At least until I get warm? It's cold out there on that long dark road."

"What long dark road?"

Biff was silent, then, in a hurt voice: "You have no idea how long I've traveled or how much dark I've traveled through. I hope you never find out." He put his hand on her waist again and leaned close to her ear. "I'll keep to my side of the bed. I promise."

Kay was silent. Hadn't she once wanted this? She had fantasized about Biff's return for years. In her fantasies, however, it was a contrite, broken man who begged forgiveness on his knees. Not this jaunty intruder whose dick, she could feel, was once again bobbing against her hips. She sat up and reached for the light but as she did she remembered a phrase she had copied out of *The Mindfulness* book: *Never say no to an offer of love.*

But was this an "offer?" And was it, had it ever been, "love?"

WEEK EIGHT

"Biff Kelly." Zabeth fixed her small, pretty, bloodshot eyes on Kay's averted face. "You've outdone yourself now, girl. I thought it would be good for you to sleep with him once or twice. But I never thought you'd actually let him move in with you."

"Just for a while, until he goes on tour. Don't look at me like that."

"Are you giving him money?"

"Zabeth! Come on."

"Are you?"

Kay looked around the restaurant for rescue. Sometimes being with Zabeth was like being locked in a squad car. When had she turned into such a moral authority? She was worse than Victor. There was no need to tell her about the impacted molar Biff couldn't afford to have pulled a few days ago, or the clutch going out in his car. Zabeth rattled an armful of silver bracelets in front of her face to regain her attention.

"What does Francis think?"

"About what?"

"About your bringing in … " Zabeth put down her martini to make a show of counting on her heavily beringed fingers, "a fourth derelict?"

"I thought you liked Biff!"

"I do. He's cute. He's charming. He may even be the genius he says he is. But he's as wrong for you as Fenton was. You *are* through with Fenton? Because I don't know if you've noticed, but Dana's after him."

"That doesn't mean she's going to get him."

"Oh no? Ha ha ha."

Kay stirred her Diet Coke in silence. Zabeth was acting like this because Kay had missed the twins' ballet recital last night—Francis had been coughing so hard she hadn't dared leave him—and she had cancelled their movie date the night before because Biff had borrowed her car—and she had had to cut a phone call short because Victor kept interrupting to ask where the butter was—and Fenton had accidentally dropped her phone when he tried to photograph a hummingbird outside his window. "I've been a bad friend," she apologized.

Zabeth leaned across the restaurant table, her voice hard and clear. "That's not the problem," she said. "You've been a good friend—to the wrong people. What's the matter with you these days?"

Kay shrugged and rubbed her forehead. She wanted to blame the castle. She wanted to explain that ever since she'd returned there, she had been under some sort of dark spell. She had regressed to her child self. She had felt shorter, squatter, stupider from the minute that carved front door first clanged behind her, and week by week it had only gotten worse. The light in the castle was dim, the echoing rooms were cold. The air was still laced with the pervasive undercurrent of her mother's perfume, mixed with new odors of dog, parrot, cigarette smoke, and male musk. It was hard to breathe there. Hard to laugh. Hard to think clearly. Everywhere she looked there was something that needed to be cleaned, something that needed to be fixed, someone who needed attending to. Francis was ill, Victor was having a breakdown, Neal was unemployed, Fenton was crippled, Biff was broke. She hadn't played the piano for weeks, she hadn't finished reading *The Odyssey*, she hadn't returned all her self-help books, she wasn't running, her knitting was a tangled mess, she'd stopped house hunting, and, although she wasn't drinking, she no longer went to AA meetings. "I don't know what's wrong with me," she admitted. "Maybe I should see a therapist again. Or hire an exorcist."

"How about just hiring an eviction service?"

"I can't kick everyone out, Zabeth."

"Sure you can. Look." Zabeth reached over and pressed her hand. "I've known you a long time. You're a good person. I've seen you 'be good' to everyone from the Jehovah's Witnesses who come to your door to that homeless guy you let sleep in the library. Don't shake your head; everyone knows you let him sleep there. But lately it's gotten out of hand. Last year you had your own place, you were independent, you were fun to be with, and now, frankly, you're a drag. If you really want to keep your job, find a decent man, and move out on your own, as you say you do, then: do it. Get cracking. Stop waiting on other people. If you can't get them to leave, why don't you leave? Stop being so fucking nice." She finished her martini, set her glass down, and pushed the check toward Kay. "You'll have to treat today; I left my wallet at the office."

Kay started to laugh, but one look at Zabeth gathering her jacket and briefcase together told her that her friend wasn't kidding. Zabeth, who charged four hundred dollars an hour for legal fees, probably felt that she had given Kay valuable free advice with her "get cracking" crack. Well, maybe she had.

"We have to talk," she told Biff when he came into her room later that night.

"Okay," he smiled, sitting down beside her, taking her hand, and looking around the room. "I like the paintings in here," he said. "Who did them?"

"My best friend."

"Talented gal."

"No. A guy. My best friend's gay."

"I was gay for a while."

Kay, curious, waited, but Biff had nothing to add, so she continued, "His name is Charles Lichtman and he left last spring to 'find himself.'"

"Want to help me find myself?" Biff asked, placing her hand on his crotch.

"No," she said, pulling her hand back. "In fact, that's what we need to talk about. You're going to have to find another place to live, Biff. You can't stay here anymore. And I can't sleep with you anymore."

"Okay," Biff agreed, yawning and standing to drop his clothes on the floor. "I'll leave tomorrow. But that doesn't mean I can't sleep with you tonight, does it?" He drew her down on the bed beside him and pulled the covers over them both. "Does it?"

"Yes," Kay began, but Biff had already fallen asleep. She stared down at his face, the pixie eyebrows, the perfect ears, the long lower lip she had once adored. She remembered confessing to Charles that when Biff had left her, years ago, she had been so heartbroken she had wanted to die. "You'd kill yourself for someone named Biff?" Charles had teased. She had laughed then but she sighed now, for the truth was she missed that old passion. Biff, always adaptable, woke and sighed with her, then he cupped her breast, kissed the tattoo on her shoulder, opened his eyes slyly, and looked up. "I don't remember this little blue horse."

Week Eight

"It's my lucky charm." She wanted to tell him more. She wanted to tell him about the moonlit horse that had appeared out of nowhere and led her to safety across the snowfield after her drunken car crash, but Biff had already stopped listening and begun to hum one of the hymns his new band was putting together. Spirituality, he'd told her, was the coming thing; religion was hot. His band would hit the charts playing old standards with new twists; using sitars and celestas and hand organs, they would play in churches all over the world.

"Everyone's heard 'Amazing Grace' on a Scottish bagpipe," he told her sleepily, his hand moving over her shoulder. "But no one has heard 'Are You Washed in the Blood' on a bagpipe."

"I met a Scotsman recently," Kay began, but Biff, still humming, had swung his leg over her thighs. "A veterinarian," she finished, to herself. Donald Wallace's voice and face had flitted in and out of her thoughts ever since the trip to Oxalis. He seemed—she was probably wrong—like the perfect man, capable, calm, and caring. She pushed him out of her thoughts and she was about push Biff off too when she realized it wouldn't be necessary. He was asleep again.

Easing into an upright position, she picked up *The Odyssey*, which she was determined to finish. She opened to Book Ten, and soon found herself swept up by the narrative, applauding the way Circe briskly turned Odysseus's sailors into pigs and mocked them as they rolled in the mud. Still, she noticed that even that stern goddess softened when Odysseus, always cagey, always clever, wept, and soon, too soon, Circe was changing the swine back into men again, bathing them, dressing them, feeding them … sleeping with them?

"Karoony?" Biff, awake, began singing softly in her ear. Despite herself, Kay let him draw her down—one last time, what could it hurt, he'd be gone tomorrow—and tried not to hear the other familiar sound coming up from downstairs.

Week Eight

Francis. Coughing. Always coughing.

"I'm worried about Dad." She dropped by Victor's dealership at lunch the next day, impressed, as always, by how pleasant his office was, clean and airy, unlike the clutter he lived in at the castle, and how nice he looked, in his sports jacket and open necked shirt, his polished shoes on his polished desk as he leaned back to listen to her. She, by contrast, felt rumpled and ruffled after her morning at work, shoulder aching from shelving and nerves thinned from training seniors how to use the new computer program. She pushed her hair back and started to say more but Victor held a finger up, needing to take a phone message. His voice on the speaker phone was deep and cheery, and Kay, on hold, waited. One of Ida's last paintings, a respectable attempt at overripe strawberries, hung on the wall, next to Victor's Salesman of the Year award, and, on his desk, a bright color photo of Victor alone on a golf course. The photos of Stacy were gone.

"Dad's getting worse," she continued when Victor set the phone down. "He doesn't eat, his color's bad, he must go through a fifth of whiskey a day, and all those cigarettes? He refuses to see Dr. Deeds. So what do you think? Should we phone Glo? I can't, you know. She won't talk to me. You'll have to."

"I already did," Victor said.

"That's great! What did she say? Is she coming back?"

"Actually, we only talked about trading in her BMW."

"So she doesn't know how ill he is? Will you phone her again?"

"I can't. She's not at the ranch anymore. She went to a spiritual retreat in Palm Beach."

"They have spiritual retreats in Palm Beach?"

"Laugh."

187

"Sorry. I just want to know if we should get Dad to a hospital. Victor? Are you all right?"

"Do I look all right?"

Kay studied her brother. Victor had stopped crying weeks ago. His eyes were clear, his skin was rosy, his hair was glossy, his hands were manicured, but his full lips had diminished to one hard angry line and his stare was cold.

"No," she decided.

"My wife has defied her Savior and defiled her body, and you? You have been having unholy congress under your father's roof with two different men. No is right, Kay."

"Okay. I'm leaving now. Just wanted to see if you'd help me out with Dad."

"Mother would be turning over in her grave."

"Neal is turning her grave over for her, remember? He's even composting it. Look, Victor, if you're so miserable, why don't you take Ed and leave?"

"Why don't you?"

"I'm going to," Kay said. "The minute the castle sells."

"It's not going to sell."

"Why not?"

"It's not for sale."

"Ah." Kay sat back down.

"Dad hasn't done a thing with it. He is just sitting on it." Victor's voice rose, aggrieved. "He could make a killing right now with the market the way it is. He could sell it and have enough left over after taxes to set us both up; we'd never have to worry … well, why bother. Dad's Dad. He never has given us anything, has he?"

"Life."

"You can get 'life'—if that's what you want to call it—from a test tube, Kay. From a dirty filthy test tube. Ask Stacy if you want to know more about 'life.' She's an expert."

Week Eight

Kay, troubled, rose as Victor reached across his desk to take another call. So all this time Francis *had* been lying to her? What was going on?

There was time to catch an AA meeting before returning to work, a new one Kay had never been to; it might be tolerable. She found the meeting room, came in late, and took a seat in back. The topic seemed to be "boarders." A surprise. A relief. A subject she could talk about. She raised her hand.

"I have five boarders," she began. "Sorry. I'm Kay and I'm an alcoholic." She paused for the chorus of *Hi Kays* and continued, "They are all men and they are all living with me. Every night when I come home from work I walk into a dumpster—there is mess everywhere, television blasting, a python loose somewhere under the floorboards, a parrot on the chandelier, a doped-up dog locked in a room down the hall, oh and another room full of wild rabbits, there are cars parked every which way in the driveway, beer cans, ashtrays, bar bells … no one cleans, no one cooks, they all eat separate meals at separate times and leave their messes behind and it is driving me crazy. I'm worn out. I haven't been getting enough rest, I've been sleeping with someone I shouldn't be sleeping with, my girlfriends are disgusted with me, my best friend has disappeared, my father has flat-out lied to me, I will probably lose my job soon—and I don't know why! I don't know why I'm doing any of this! I have asked them to leave, they have not left, I have set up rules, they have not followed them. I don't know how I got into this mess or how I am going to get out of it! But," triumphant finale, "I'm not drinking! So. I just wanted to say that. Thank you."

The silence continued until an older woman in a velvet tam sitting next to her said softly, "Glad you're here, Kay," and someone else began to speak. Kay sat back in a flurry of relief that changed into confusion and then into acute physical pain when she realized that the topic was Establishing Borders not Putting Up with Boarders. This, she decided as she left, was one meeting she was never going to return to.

She remained in pain all the way to work, thinking not just of her stupid mistake but of the fact that she had done exactly what she most hated hearing others do at AA meetings: she had complained—whined—and she had bragged. It was horrible; it was scary; it meant that, at long last, she belonged.

She parked behind the library, pulling weeds off the sides of the path as she walked up to the door. The shabby little building, in the afternoon's clear light, looked exactly like what it was: a shabby little building. It was in need of paint, repairs, and landscaping, and the interior, as she stepped inside, felt cramped, dingy and ill-furnished. Was the County Board right? Should it be torn down, the land sold, a shopping center built here instead? This library was, after all, just a "branch," not, as Mrs. Holland had pointed out, a "tree." Shouldn't she move on to a bigger, better-paying job? What difference would it make? She didn't really help anyone. The homeless could nap at the bus station as comfortably as they could here, the addicts could find gas station bathrooms to shoot up in, the teenagers could ask their parents for assistance with their term papers and the seniors could go to the community college for help with their tax forms. Essentially, she did the same crap here she did at the castle. She picked things up and she put them away. Over and over and over again.

"You're late," Lois Hayes observed, joining her at the front door. "Dr. Chester from the Board of Supervisors called. They're meeting tonight."

"Tonight?"

"At seven. They can't secure the room at the Courthouse so they are all coming here to hear you."

"My God." Kay looked around at the carts of unshelved books, the posters for last winter's concerts and lectures still tacked to the bulletin boards, the overflowing waste baskets, the drooping ferns on the front desk. "Okay, let's get busy. Would you call the Friends of the Library and tell them to come tonight and support us? And oh. Here." Kay reached into her purse and pulled out *The Miraculous Mindfulness Makeover* which she'd found in the piano bench that morning. The cover only had a few coffee stains, the pages secreted only a few buttered bagel crumbs, and the chapter she had dog-eared, the third one, on self-worth, wouldn't be one Lois Hayes needed. "Someone finally brought it back," Kay said.

"Someone," Lois repeated drily. But she took it.

"Your dad may be a great architect," Fenton complained that afternoon, as Kay pushed him around the mountain trail in Ida's old wheelchair. "But he does not know how to hammer a nail in straight and those cabinets are all going to have to be done over. And that guy Biff you seem to like so much? What's he doing here anyway? He's no better. And Victor! Has Victor ever done anything with his hands? I'm thinking if I could get Nicky to help me, watch out, there's a pothole, Kay, the two of us could get the work done in a week."

"I didn't think you and Nicky got along."

"Nicky gets along with everyone."

"Everyone except me. He's barely talked to me since I said no to the shooting range." Rubbing her sore shoulder, Kay braked Fenton by the overlook and crouched by his side to take in the vista of the valley below. "He *has* stopped going to the shooting range?"

Fenton didn't answer but after a minute he covered her hand with his and gave it a brotherly squeeze. His big hand, after weeks of disuse, was almost soft now; hers, after weeks of dishes, laundry, and housekeeping, was rougher.

"I've been giving him a few carpentry lessons," Fenton said. "We're starting simple. He's learning to make a box for his stash."

"Stash?" Kay repeated, just as Fenton cupped his ear and turned to her, eyes glowing.

"Hear that?" He brought a finger to his lips, then, radiant, "A Western Tanager. He should be headed down to Mexico by now. And look." He laughed softly and Kay followed his eyes to the trail's edge where a handsome buck with a huge rack stood poised, looking back at Fenton with dark unfrightened eyes for a moment before wheeling around and disappearing into the woods.

"I'm thinking twenty dollars an hour," Fenton said.

"For … ?"

"The carpentry lessons."

"You want to be paid for having Nicky help you do work you should have finished yourself a month ago?"

"Don't raise your voice, Kay. You'll scare the butterflies. Look, there's a Monarch. I'll talk to Neal. Maybe we can work out a trade."

Neal and Fenton working out a trade: there was a picture. Kay, dressed for the Board presentation, came downstairs and paused in the doorway to watch them as they stood in the garden. Was it her imagination or had they started to look alike? Neal had tanned, working outside, and Fenton had paled, lying in bed. How they managed to communicate without actually speaking was a wonder but they seemed to have reached some accord, for after a moment they shook hands. What a relief. Two grown men making decisions about the education of a boy: just the way things should be. Impressed, she saw Neal hand Fenton the long garden hose, but her smile faded as Fenton plunged the nozzle down a hole in the kale patch. Neal walked to the water tap, turned it on full blast, walked toward another hole, raised the shovel over his head, waited, and, a minute later, smashed down hard on something in the ground. Goodbye Mr. Gopher.

"I *hate* that!" Kay turned to see Nicky and automatically dug into her purse for his dollar, but Nicky seemed to have lost interest in the Hate Jar and walked past her silently carrying his guitar. Plopping cross-legged on the floor beside Francis, who sat in his leather armchair, surrounded by his arsenal of whisky, cigarettes, and crosswords, and topped by his parrot, Nicky slowly began to pick out notes to a song Kay didn't recognize. She listened a minute, confused by the harsh jangle of strange chords. Victor, coming in from work, brushed past her to pluck the remote from its place by Francis's ashtray and turn on the television.

"Bad news," Victor announced, as he announced every night. "Riots in Athens. Look at that." He pointed to a grainy video clip of angry crowds surging down a street, waving placards. "Isn't Greece where your friend Charles went, Kay? He's probably trampled to death by now. And look at this: huge flood in Biafra. Who would want to live in Biafra? We're next, you know, big earthquake here any minute, that last one was just an intro, this mountain we're sitting on is dormant, sure, but it could blow, it could blow any second ... " He rocked back on his heels, muttering, "Cop killing, look at that, school shooting, car bombs, forest fires—I tell you guys, 'Now is the judgement of this world.'"

He didn't notice when Nicky stood up, pale, looked straight at Kay and said: "I don't want to hear all this. I'm just a kid."

"I know, honey. And your Uncle Victor's just an idiot. Don't pay any attention to ... "

"Can't you stop him?"

"No, she can't. But I can," Francis said, and clicked the television off. "Go to your room, Victor. Nicholas, go find your snake. Kay, go save your library." He started to say more but was caught up in a spasm of coughing. Kay paused, hesitant to touch him.

"Please use your oxygen tank," she pleaded. "It will help."

"Stopping smoking will help. Stopping drinking will help." Neal, coming in from the garden, ignored Francis and spoke directly to Kay. "Your father should be walking three miles every morning. He should be having a warm water enema every day. He should be eating sour goat curd and drinking cold-pressed juice. I've told you all this and you ignore me. Let me throw some amaranth and anise seed in the blender and whip him up a smoothie."

"Dad's not having anything you 'whip up,' Neal!"

"Don't shout." Neal turned to Victor and raised his hand, the dead gopher dangling. "Hey, what do you think? Would Ed like this?"

Victor's eyes shone. "Let's find out."

Kay watched as the two men hurried out to the back yard, whistling to Ed, who was almost as stoned as Fenton, both of them sitting by the pool in the twilight. One of Biff's jazzed-up spirituals began to pour out from a kazoo upstairs. Wasn't Biff gone? He should be packing all his instruments up by now.

"I'm leaving," she said. "Wish me luck?"

No one answered.

Somehow driving to the library to speak wasn't as terrifying as driving to the Courthouse to speak and as Kay greeted the Board Members and led them to the comfortable chairs she'd pulled from the Music Room she found she was far less frightened than she had been the week before. The library looked almost pretty in the setting sun; the yellow roses she had arranged in a glass vase glimmered in the golden light and Lois Hayes's gingersnap cookies scented the air. Standing tall, Kay pressed her hands together, took a deep breath, and smiled around the assembled group, relieved and touched to see that both Zabeth and Dana had come to support her, and grateful for the large group of Friends and other patrons from the community that she recognized. The Nordrums, hand in hand, beamed at her from the front row, and one of the Rode brothers (she could never tell them apart) had showed up. A dark shadow weaving swiftly through the back of the room caught her eye, but it was just Jolene in her Story Lady hat and cloak; good of Jolene to come, she thought, after being fired.

"Thank you for being here tonight to listen to our plea for saving the West Valley Branch," Kay began. She picked up her notes, scanned them, and set them down. She would read from the speech, with its carefully researched, but deadly dry, statistics, later. What she wanted to say now she wanted to say from the heart. She spread out her hands. "We have a genuine treasure in this place. No other library in the county has such a devoted clientele, such a unique collection of art, science, and music books, such consistently high circulation figures. Almost everyone living here in West Valley is an active card holder, our rooms are always full. People come here to read, to learn, to use our computers, to listen to music, to watch movies; seniors and teens come to attend our free lecture programs—we not only have slide shows on travel, we offer free talks on diversity and race, nonviolent communications, and global warming—the community's children come for our books and videos and the Story Hour we hold every ... " Kay paused, startled, as Mrs. Holland materialized through the front door and shuffled toward her. Uh-oh, she thought, stepping forward to introduce her, hoping no one else noticed that the purple velour sweat suit the old woman was wearing was two sizes too big, that the dingy men's socks on her feet were serving as shoes, that her hair was uncombed and her eyes were unfocused. "Mrs. Holland," she said, reaching out to clasp her veined hand and draw her forward, "managed this branch capably and creatively for twenty-five years. She inaugurated both the film series and the lecture series and she finessed the book budgets so intelligently that we were able to expand our collections without ... "

"What is that doing here?" Mrs. Holland said, looking not at Kay, but behind her, to the vase of roses on the desk. "This is not a flower shop." She picked up the vase before Kay could reach it and turned it upside down, spilling roses and water onto the floor and spattering Kay's red pumps. "This is a ... " she paused, sneezed.

"Life saver," a dark thrilling voice finished from the back. "A single vase of water saved the life of the poor little crippled Everson girl. It was all that stood between that blind six-year-old child and a flaming inferno." Jolene spread her cloak out as the Board of Supervisors, stunned, turned to look up at her. "Little Janie Everson, imagine, six years old and only one leg, alone in a cabin way out in the woods when a hot ember from her drunken father's wood stove hit the braided rag rug her dead mother had made and started to smolder. Now most little blind crippled girls, they wouldn't know what to do, but Janie took one sniff of them noxious fumes, grabbed that vase full of her dead mama's funeral lilies and threw it on the rug and put that fire right out. If she hadn't had her wits about her, she and her drunk Daddy would have been burnt to a crisp. I tell you this now because this building," Jolene finished, her voice dropping, "needs more than a few vases. It is a fire trap and one day it and everyone in it will be going up in smoke." She snapped her long fingers, flipped her cape over her shoulder, turned on her heel, and strode out. "Whoosh."

"The library is inspected every year," Kay said, her voice steady in the ensuing silence. "We are totally up to code." She pressed Mrs. Holland's hand and led her carefully to the distraught attendant who was waiting in the doorway to take her back to the rest home. "Mrs. Holland personally supervised the alarm system, the sprinkler system, and the extinguishers. The building is safe and stable; it sustained no damage at all during our recent earthquake. Fires are not our worries. Revenue cuts are our worries." She reached for her typed notes then and read clearly and steadily for the next ten minutes without further interruption. She and Lois Hayes fielded the few questions that came after the talk and she handed copies of her speech out to the Board members as they rose to leave. "Very interesting," Dr. Chester said. "Very," he hesitated, "colorful."

"Thank you," Kay said. She tried not to collapse when Zabeth and Dana hugged her, and she tried not to notice when a grandmotherly Board member, standing at the rack of craft books, slipped a quilting manual under her coat. After everyone left, she knelt and gathered bits of the broken vase up and mopped the floor. The roses she retrieved to bring home with her. She would dry them and keep them forever as a memento to one of the worst nights of her life. She paused before the Greek display and spoke to the painted postcards. "You shoulda been here, Charles," she said. "You're missing all the fun."

WEEK NINE

If Charles was having fun in Greece, he wasn't telling her about it. The postcards continued to come, each one more beautiful, and more enigmatic, than the one before. The newest one, showing a white-washed guesthouse smothered in bougainvillea with *Eleni Studios* scrolled across the arch in bright blue script, was especially irritating, for inside Charles had cribbed another line from Homer: *Making for home, by the wrong way, on the wrong courses*—which meant he wouldn't be back anytime soon. There was no one she could call, no one she could talk to about him. A new book, one she had ordered months ago, had arrived at the library that morning. Called *What to Do When a Friendship Fails*, she had brought it home with her, hoping it might offer insight. A set of test questions called "Do You Know Your Friend?" compelled her now to reach for pen and paper.

What is your friend's full name, where does it come from, and what does it mean?

"Charles" meant "free man," Kay knew that, and "Lichtman" meant "candle maker" or "bringer of light." It was a Dutch name. Or French. Or German. Or Jewish. Was Charles Jewish? As for a middle name—did he have a middle name? He signed his paintings CAL so the A must stand for something. Arnold? Alfred? Well. Funny. He had never told her his middle name. She had never asked. What sort of a friend *was* she?

Frowning, Kay skimmed through the other questions. She knew Charles's shoe size (10), his favorite food (pesto pizza), his least favorite food (shrimp), his birth sign (Libra), his allergies (penicillin). She knew he'd grown up in Ohio, gone to UCLA on a painting scholarship, studied with a famous lyrical abstract artist in Germany, taught at the Art Institute. He'd had one gallery opening in New Mexico and other gallery openings up and down the West Coast. She could describe his height (5'10") and his weight (145) and his black curls, honey-colored skin and hazel—or were they brown?—anyway, his hazel-brown eyes. He was in good shape, bicycled and kayaked and went to the gym regularly. He was a terrific pool player. He didn't have a favorite color, he liked them all, and he was equally indiscriminate about movies and would sit through anything. His favorite book? *The Odyssey*, she wrote, and sighed.

Who is the love of your friend's life?

That was easy. Jimmie Halloran, a North Beach sculptor. Kay had heard a lot about Jimmie, but she'd never known him; he'd died before she met Charles. That was five years ago. Had Charles had lovers since? He was beautiful, smart, talented—surely he had not been celibate the whole time she had known him? He had many male friends but he never talked about having crushes on any of them or going out on dates or sleeping with anyone. She'd just assumed he wanted to be private about his sex life, that he went to clubs and met men on his own. She'd been too polite to pry. Too polite? Or too scared to find out, to know about his real life? Or—be honest—too hopeful that perhaps he wasn't gay at all, but would suddenly reveal deep sexual feelings for her, for Kay?

What was the happiest moment in your friend's life?
Had he told her?
What was the saddest moment in your friend's life?
Had she asked?
How have you helped make your friend's life happier?
Well, she had posed for him. She had sat before his easel for hours, self-consciously nude, holding her stomach in the whole time, and the portrait had won a prize and been sold at a gallery to some collector, so that was good, though she could not bear to look at the painting herself and was glad it was gone. She always washed his car and cleaned his house whenever his back went out. She let him beat her at Scrabble, not that she actually "let" him. Oh. And she played the piano for him. He loved that. He could listen to her for hours. He said it was the best cure for his depression.
What does your friend get depressed about?
?
What does your friend like about you?
?
What do you like about your friend?
Everything!
What is the one word you would use to describe your friend?
Motherly.
Motherly? Kay put the pen down. That was a weird word choice but it was the first word that had occurred to her. Not "motherly" in the way Ida was motherly—commanding and demanding and controlling—but motherly like the women she had always loved in books, like Marmee in *Little Women*, for instance. Charles was thoughtful, competent, brisk, and kind. He smelled good. He made the best chicken soup; he gave the best foot massages. In the months before he'd left for Thailand, he had come over to her apartment frequently. He hadn't wanted to go to concerts or movies or museums or take

one of their long rambling walks. He made sushi one night, she remembered; he gave Nicky a cute faux hawk haircut and one long rainy evening he taught her to knit. He hadn't talked much. And all the time she had nattered on and on about her problems with Fenton, with Neal, with her job. She must have bored him silly.

She closed her eyes, trying to remember the day he had left. It had been last Valentine's Day, which had stung, for she had counted on spending the evening with him on the sofa picking through a heart shaped box of See's chocolates and watching *The Philadelphia Story*. Instead, she had gone over to help him pack, surprised by how little he was taking. His suitcase held hardly any clothes and when she marveled at the shirts and jeans he'd put in a pile for the Goodwill, he told her to help herself. She had; she'd been wearing one of his soft flannel shirts ever since. He'd put his paintings and books and his bike in storage, he told her, and he had sublet his flat.

"For a simple holiday to Thailand?" she had asked, astonished.

"Not so simple, Kay. And not a holiday."

"That's right; you have that painting class. But you're not going to stay there after the class ends, are you?"

"Probably not there, no."

"Where?"

"Don't know yet."

"But you *are* coming back here?"

"Gonna try."

"Wow. I'm getting worried, Charles."

"Sorry, lambkin. I don't have any answers yet. When I do, I'll let you know."

"So I'll just have to sit and wait?"

"No. You'll be busy taking care of Nicky and learning that sonata and running the library and going to AA meetings and breaking up with Fenton and saving your money to buy a house of your own in a good school district with a studio in back where I can work."

She'd laughed. So he was coming back. But why—she had to ask this again—was he leaving in the first place?

"I told you. I need to change."

"Change what?"

"Myself."

"But … ? Forgive me, Charles, but you're the most perfect person I know."

"Look at the people you know."

"Ha."

"Just wish me luck, okay? There is something I need to do and I need to do it now. I've waited long enough. Come on now. Smile. Give me a hug."

She had. A wonderful hug. A strong-armed rock-from-side-to-side hug with a ripple of loving laughter that went straight from his heart to hers followed by a pat on the back that was … motherly.

And then he was gone.

And he had stayed gone.

She looked at the test questions, gave herself a big fat F, crumpled the paper, and tossed it in the waste basket. She would be a better friend in the future. She wouldn't talk about herself, wouldn't complain. She would bake Charles an applesauce cake when he came back, he loved applesauce cake, she would wind the beautiful scarf she would definitely have finished knitting by then around his beautiful neck, she would play that Mozart piece perfectly, rippling through those difficult arpeggios without a stumble, she would listen without interruption, speak without rancor; she would not ask if he still loved her or why he'd stayed away so long. She rose, inspired, and walked to the music alcove to start practicing those arpeggios, but stopped in the doorway, shocked to see that Biff was in there, setting up his band instruments.

"What are you doing?"

"Oh, hi Kay. I just came in to rehearse, hope that's all right."

"No, it's not all right. I agreed you could stay this one extra week but the rule about not using my music room still holds, Biff. It's my room. It's my place. Out."

Biff laughed, amused. "I didn't know it mattered so much to you."

"It does."

"Got it. Okay if I just play one ... "

"No!"

"Okay, darlin', okay. But it's not as if you've been seriously working in here."

"You've no idea how serious I've been."

She watched as Biff gathered up his kazoo and his trombone. Still smiling, he edged past her to take them up to the drum tower. "I'll have to come back for the bass," he said.

"And the three guitars."

He chuckled. "And the dulcimer."

It didn't take Biff long to set up in the drum tower and the house, to Victor's satisfaction at least, soon began to rock with church music. Kay tried to shut it out and focus on the Mozart but it was impossible. The castle was a volcano of discordant sounds. Fenton and Nicky, down in the Knight's Nook, couldn't hear anything over the whine of their power tools as they worked on Nicky's carpentry projects; Neal whistled tunelessly from the vegetable patch, the television blared sports, the radio blared Christian rock. Kay gave up and went downstairs. Francis was just deftly replacing his hearing aid with ear plugs as she walked into the living room.

"You might want to leave those in. Dr. Deeds is coming by later to see you," she told him.

"Old Jim? Whatever for?" he asked, raising his eyebrows.

"He misses you," Kay said. "Your warmth. Your charm."

"You called him?"

Kay nodded.

Her father chuckled. "Did he sound surprised to hear I'm still here? He only gave me six weeks, you know."

"Six weeks for what?"

Francis didn't answer. "Your boyfriend is murdering 'Holy, Holy, Holy' up there isn't he."

"He's not my boyfriend," Kay corrected, relieved to realize that was true. Exhausted, she sat down beside her father. "Remember the way Stacy used to sing that hymn? Plain and true, from the heart, in that sweet voice of hers."

"I talked to Stacy the other day." Francis lit a cigarette, blew out two steady streams from his nostrils, and took a sip of the whiskey she saw he had beside him. Who was pouring his drinks? She had been monitoring it all week to see he never got alcohol before five. Victor wouldn't. Fenton couldn't. Nicky? "We had a nice conversation."

Her eyes on the almost empty glass, Kay said, "Stacy doesn't have conversations."

"She does if you know what to ask her."

"What did you ask her?"

"Who the father was."

"I knew it I knew it I knew it. She's pregnant. Oh boy."

"Close. Girl. Due in November."

"It's that creep Pastor Paulsen, isn't it! He has five kids already."

"No, actually, it's Victor."

Kay waited.

"If you'll recall, your brother was once, among other things, a sperm donor." Francis tapped one cigarette out and lit another.

Kay frowned, remembering her brother in his twenties—his gangsta sunglasses, long golden hair, his Genghis Khan tee-shirt that boasted *FATHER TO MILLIONS*. "You knew about that?"

"Of course. Your mother didn't, though she might have been delighted. Ida was unpredictable that way. And of course, she was always hoping Victor would start to put *something* in the bank."

Kay's mind was jumping. "Are you're saying that Stacy went to Victor's doctor, or Victor's sperm banker, or whatever, and got herself impregnated?"

"Correct."

"Wow. Good for Stacy! But I don't understand. Why isn't Victor thrilled? They've wanted a baby for years."

"Because she went behind his back and without his permission and because Victor considers his old sperm 'unclean,'" Francis quoted drily.

"Because the sample was submitted before he was saved?"

"Right. He's convinced Stacy has been impregnated with the anti-Christ and will give birth to the 'Devil's spawn.'"

"But that's crazy."

"No doubt. But it's consistent."

"I wonder," Kay said, thinking aloud, "if this isn't more about Victor's pride being hurt than about any 'unclean' donations. I bet he's simply waiting for Stacy to say she's sorry."

"Oh, I think your brother's heard you say you're sorry too often to ever want to hear the words from anyone else."

"How," Kay asked, impressed, "did you manage to make Victor's problems my fault?"

"No one else wants them." Francis's voice was dry but his eyes were twinkling; he was having fun. In a terrible way, she was too. These insane exchanges with her father were like jousting matches, only he fought with a rapier, she with a popsicle stick. She sat still, refusing to be routed. Sometimes just a stubborn refusal to leave could make him start to talk like a human.

"Did you tell Stacy that Victor drives by her house every night hoping that she'll come out and ask him to return? Did you tell her that all he talks about is Armageddon, gloom and doom, that he sees everything in black and white, that he cries all the time, that he's miserable?"

"That he hasn't changed in forty years, you mean?"

"You know what I think? I think Victor will be fine once he sees the baby," Kay said. "No one can resist a baby. Everything will change once he realizes he's a parent."

"I don't recall that being the case for either your mother or ..."

"Present company excepted, okay? Enough!"

Francis chuckled. "What about Nicholas's father?"

"Neal?"

"Nicholas's father."

"Neal *is* Nicky's father." Kay stared at Francis. "I was faithful to Neal the entire time we were married."

"Making up for it these days, aren't you?" Francis said, picking up his pen again.

"I'm not doing anything I'm ashamed of."

The raised eyebrow, the pursed lips.

"Okay, a few things I'm ashamed of. Anyway," daringly, disrespectfully, "weren't you having an affair with Glo when you were still married to Mom?"

"That poor girl," Francis said.

"Mom?"

"Oh no, Ida was tough. I mean Glo." Francis tapped the puzzle with his pen. "I'm afraid Glo got more than she signed up for when she married me. She was a debutante, you know. Golden girl. Never had children, never had to work. Her life was one long party. She never counted on this, being stuck with a sick old man." He shook his head. "And now, if you'll excuse me, Kay, I am going to put my earplugs back in."

Kay, dismissed, rose to go, but paused in the doorway. "Even with your earplugs in you are going to have to hear your own cough, Dad. It's bad. Dr. Deeds is going to hear it too."

"Which one?" Francis pointed to the parrot and Raj, on cue, tipped his head and coughed.

"I always said that bird could learn," Francis said, proud. "All it takes is patience. Patience and," as he and Raj coughed together, "practice." He looked up. "Good news about Nicholas's parentage," he added.

"It's not news," Kay snapped.

"Not to you, perhaps. For the rest of us, it's a welcome revelation."

"Well how about the 'revelation' that the castle is not even on the market?"

"You just figured that out?"

"You mean it's true? All this time you've lied to me?"

"In a manner of speaking."

"Why? What's the point?" She threw her arms up in a dramatic gesture so like one of Ida's that she was not surprised to catch the merry eye of the painted portrait still hanging off-center above the fireplace. "I don't understand. What are we all doing here?"

"Where else would we be?"

"I could think of a thousand places!"

"Go forth my child and seek them out."

"I'm going to," Kay said. "I'm not staying here. If you're not really selling this place, I am taking Nicky and we are moving out."

"Hold your horses," Francis said. "I am selling the castle."

"When?"

"That's none of your business."

"Actually," Kay reminded him, "it is."

No answer. Just an empty glass, held up for a refill.

"No way," Kay told him and escaped back to the music alcove, enraged to see Biff back in there, talking on the phone. "Out!" she barked. He looked up at her with a sweet, rapt, faraway smile as she stormed up to her bedroom and tried to knit a few rows on Charles's scarf to calm herself. Her heart was racing and her head smoldered with a thousand little fires. No more, she thought. No more home-cooked meals. No more tables set with flowers and linen, no more attempts at polite conversation, no more doing everyone's dishes afterward, alone, in the kitchen. No more rants from Neal, sermons from Victor, "suggestions" from Fenton, surprise revelations from Francis or loveless love-making with Biff. She was through.

She reached for her laptop, downloaded some local rental listings, and, unable to find Nicky anywhere, grabbed her purse and left the house alone to go check a few of the addresses out. But when she got in her car, she found she could not turn the key. The fight, if that's what it was, with Francis had drained her. She just sat in the driveway, behind the wheel. She saw lights flick on and off throughout the castle, listened to male voices rise and fall, heard blasts of television sitcoms and Christian talk shows; she smelled burnt toast from the kitchen and chlorine from the pool and manure from the vegetable patch, she watched the sky darken behind the turrets, saw the stars come out, felt the wind rise. It took Nicky's worried voice, calling "Mom," to finally rouse her, and when his voice rose to another louder, more insistent "Mom," she sighed and reached for the door, but when he started screaming "Mom! Mom! Mom!" she leapt from the car and raced back to the castle. She tore up the stairs past the music alcove where Biff was still talking on the phone, and arrived breathless at the open door of the drum tower. "The bunnies," Nicky was crying. "Ed's got the bunnies."

A flurry of hissing, yelps, barks, whimpers. Kay pulled Nicky out of the way as Ed charged past with a bloody kit dangling from his jaws, Goldie right behind him as he disappeared through the open door of the music alcove. Biff dropped the phone and laughed in amazement as Ed wheeled around with Goldie clamped to the top of his head, kicking with her hind legs at his eyes. The parrot, coughing, flew back and forth above them, shitting on everything.

"We need the hose," Biff shouted over the noise. He opened the music alcove window and leaned out. "Hose," he called down to Neal.

"You can't bring a hose in here!" Kay cried. "Mom's harp! My piano!" but Neal had already thrown the extended garden hose through the open window. "Turn it on!" Victor yelled from the stairwell. "Don't!" Kay called, just as Biff aimed a strong stream into the room. Blood and water sprayed all over as Goldie, drenched and hissing, leapt off Ed's head and disappeared down the stairs and Ed, both eyes bleeding, sped after her, the dead kit still in his mouth. "He's blinded," Victor said, his voice accusatory. "Kay, get a towel." When Kay didn't move, Biff handed her the still-shooting hose, which she aimed out the window. She felt something rocket over her head and looking up saw Raj take off toward the mountain. She heard a laugh behind her, then another, then another. She turned. Francis, Fenton, and Neal stood in the doorway.

"Short, brutal, and nasty," Francis said. He lit a cigarette and shook his head.

"That's what happens when you take someone off meds too fast," Neal said. "I told Victor that Ed needed to be brought down slowly."

"Far out," Fenton agreed. "Hey Nick," he added. "Look who I found in my room." He unwrapped Orville from around his bare shoulders and held him out to Nicky as if offering a lei. "Came right up to me. I think he missed you."

Nicky took the snake, purred a muted endearment to it as it draped around his own neck, then stared at Kay with huge hot eyes. "Mom?" Nicky said. "Why didn't you stop it?"

"What could I do, honey?"

"What you always do," Nicky said. "Nothing." Stroking Orville's flat head he turned and went down the stairs.

Kay looked after him, stunned. The doorbell rang.

"Doorbell," Neal said.

"Doorbell," Francis repeated.

"Someone's at the door, Kay," Fenton explained.

She should have turned the hose on all of them then but she didn't. She threw it back out the window, shouldered her way down the stairs, pushed past the pizza delivery girl at the front door, got into her car, drove to the library, found the postcard showing *Eleni Studios* in Paros, called the airport and left to find Charles in Greece.

WEEK TEN

It was the most daring thing she had ever done, and the dumbest. She had no address for Charles, no phone number. She had never been out of the country before, and Greece, with its unfamiliar alphabet, economic instability, political riots, and sweltering summer weather, was hardly the best place to start. She had packed in a hurry, taking her knitting and her old swimsuit but forgetting her sandals and toothbrush. Charles had insisted she get her passport when he got his last year, so at least she had that, but she had less than one hundred dollars in her wallet and only one credit card. She phoned Lois Hayes from the Athens airport, asking her to fill in at the library, and she phoned Nicky to tell him where she was and not to worry, she'd be back in a few days, but the phone at the castle rang unanswered. She dialed again and again until Victor picked it up, said, "Kay's not here," and was about to hang up when she stopped him. "Greece?" he repeated. "That's insane. Who's going to take care of Dad if you're in Greece? Dr. Deeds said he needs to stay on oxygen and take some special meds. And no, I don't know where Nicky is. Here. Talk to Neal, I don't think he even knows you left." Neal, who repeated "Nicky?" as if he didn't know who Nicky was, let alone where he was, said he'd ask Fenton, and Fenton, taking the phone, said that Nick had gone to the Nordrums' for the day but not to worry, he'd be home soon, and they'd all take good care of him until Kay got back. "We'll see," Fenton said, in his easy drawl, "that he has a good time."

"I don't want him to have a good time," Kay explained, cupping the phone to protect it from the din of foreign sounds and voices that surrounded her. "I want him to eat three healthy meals a day and get to bed on time and attend soccer camp and I do not want him playing violent video games or going to movies with Chiana or firing guns."

"I'm not the one who takes him to the shooting range, Kay."

"That's right. You're the one who's teaching him how to kill with a bow and arrow."

"And a Bowie."

"A what?"

"A knife."

Kay hung up, fumbled through her purse for Charles's last postcard, turned it over, memorized the postmark, found an information booth, and got directions from an English speaker on catching the ferry to Paros. Using the airport bathroom to wash up after the long flight, she leaned over the sink to stare into the mirror like she used to when she was drunk. She felt drunk. What was she doing here, why had she come, where was she going, and how would she get there? No matter, she thought, looking away. Charles would tell her, once she found him; Charles would explain everything.

Counting on his counsel, she headed toward the port, somehow got on and off several wrong busses, flagged down taxis, tugged her suitcase over narrow sidewalks littered with orange peels and broken glass, sidestepped sleeping dogs and cars parked on the curbs and made it to the ferry landing, stumbling on to the right dock at the right time. She followed the other passengers up the ramp and onto the ferry and spent the trip at the railing in a trance, watching misty islands float by on the flat blue sea. She suspected she was in shock, but she was too shocked to question it.

She let herself be swept down the ramp with the other passengers when the ferry docked and followed a burly driver to his taxi. Silent, she showed him the painting of *Eleni Studios* on the postcard, which he seemed to recognize with an unsurprised shrug, and sank back in the seat, staring out the window as they left the port town behind and circled up a stony mountain terraced with olive and citrus trees. The road curved after ten minutes and then dipped into a village and she leaned forward to take in the boxy white houses with their flat roofs, blue shutters, walled gardens and planters overflowing with pink and red geraniums. The driver pulled into a flagstone turnaround, parked, accepted some of the money she held out, and pointed toward a set of stone steps descending between two whitewashed walls. Then he got back into his cab, reversed, and left her standing alone.

She looked around. A warm wind tugged at her jacket and she shivered, wondering, for the first time, if Charles would be glad to see her. He had never liked surprises, she remembered, had always issued invitations a few days in advance, and here she was, running to him unannounced like a child with a bleeding knee. But what could she do? He'd been gone three months; he'd sent her no phone number, no actual address. If he was horrified by her appearance, so be it. She hadn't horrified enough people in her life; it was time to start. Defiant, she picked up her suitcase and started down the stairs. A small white cat with pale green eyes immediately leapt from a wall and strode toward her possessively, rubbing against her ankles and mewing a harsh imperative. Kay stopped in her tracks. She was sick of animals and this cat was repulsive. Its ribs showed, its short tail stuck straight out, there was a pink patch of ringworm on its neck and a bleeding abscess

213

on its ear. Hoping it wasn't a bad omen, she stepped around it, crossed the flagstones to the two-story white house with *Eleni Studios* scripted in blue on the side, lifted a doorknocker in the shape of a hand, dropped it, and waited for Charles to come out and either hug her or yell at her.

The door was opened by a plump young woman in sequined jeans and an orange sweatshirt, whose abundant hennaed hair was pulled back in sparkly barrettes. "Hello," Kay said, trying to look over the woman's shoulder. "My friend Charles is renting a room here. May I see him please?" When the woman didn't answer, she added, "Do you speak English?"

"Yes, I speak English good, thank you. My name is Eleni but what name your friend?"

"Charles?" Kay repeated. Seeing the woman's blank face, she wished she had remembered to bring a photograph. "I know he's been staying here. Look." She pulled out the postcard and showed it to Eleni, and then, dipping into her purse, brought out a sheaf of the other cards. "He sent me paintings of your garden. Your pomegranate tree."

Eleni shot Kay a sudden shy smile. "The painter."

"The painter!" Kay agreed with relief.

"Okay, please to come in. And you," Eleni said, thrusting a broom at the white cat, "be out." She drew Kay inside with a warm strong hand, closed the door firmly behind her, and led her into a small sunny room filled with plants and mismatched furniture. Kay stepped forward happily only to see that the room was deserted. "I don't ... " she began, turning with her question.

"Over here!" Eleni said, impatient, and Kay saw that she was not pointing at any of the overstuffed couches but at the wall. Stepping closer, she saw two unframed oil paintings propped on a bookshelf. One was a portrait of Eleni, standing with her hands on her hips, laughing in the sun. The other showed a tall broad-shouldered woman seated in front of an easel. Both were clearly works of Charles's—there was his familiar *CAL* in the corner.

"Nice," Kay said, "but I don't understand. Where is he?"

"Gone."

"Gone? You mean down to the village? Out at the beach? Will he be back soon?"

"No no. Gone."

"Dead?!"

Eleni laughed. "No no, just," she looked helpless, "gone."

"I came all this way … " Kay began, her voice breaking, and then, recovering herself, "Do you know where he went?"

Eleni shook her head and spread her hands out, empty.

"No forwarding address? No message saying where to reach him? Did he leave with anyone else? No? He went alone?" Kay tried to think. "May I see his room please?"

"Sure. No problem." Eleni led her through a series of dim cluttered rooms that smelled of cigarettes and soup and, without a word, up a flight of outside marble stairs to a floor of small apartments. Only one of the rooms seemed to be occupied. Dazed, Kay thought she saw a dark silhouette moving back and forth before a window but the impatient voice saying something in Greek on the telephone did not belong to Charles. "Alkis," Eleni explained as they passed, which must have been the man's name. "Boat broke." Eleni unlocked number nine, strode inside, threw open the shutters, and Kay swayed again. The room smelled like Charles—that familiar mix of turpentine and clove gum. It was clear he had been here. And it was clear he had left. The room was completely empty. She looked around at the white walls, wooden floor, neatly made bed. Blue and white plaid curtains were pulled back across tall glass doors leading to a narrow balcony. A small bathroom contained a seatless toilet, a handheld shower, a chipped sink. There was not a scrap of soap, a forgotten sock, nothing of Charles's had been left behind. Kay sank down on the edge of the bed.

"Can I stay here?" she asked. "Just for a few days. I will pay, of course." She paused, struck by the truth of what she was about to say next. "I didn't think this through very well. I have no place else to go."

"Happy have you," Eleni said warmly, and left. Kay sat on, unable to move. The afternoon sun slanted in through the open window. After a while she stepped out to the balcony to watch white doves swooping back and forth over the village roofs. Some spicy cinnamon scent came from a neighboring kitchen, Alkis's deep voice down the hall rose and fell, and a quiet wind brought the fresh scent of the sea. These were the sights and sounds and smells Charles had known and she drew them in as if they could bring him closer. What bad timing she had! To arrive just as he left! Why oh why all her life had she been too slow, too late, too stupid, too … *stop*, she told herself. *Just stop.* She went back inside, lay down on the bed, closed her eyes against the tears and when she awoke it was to the sound of Eleni calling her to dinner.

Dinner was garlicky lamb and garlicky chickpeas and Kay, sitting alone at a small wooden table off the kitchen, savored every bite. Her heart was broken but the food was good and she was starving. What was it she and Charles had decided years ago to have inscribed on their respective tombstones? Charles wanted his to say *WIP* for *Work in Progress*, and hers, they'd both decided, would say *Never Missed a Meal*. She was just reaching for another piece of Eleni's homemade bread when Alkis came into the room, sat down across from her and said, in unaccented English, "Healthy eater."

So he wasn't Greek? Kay drew her hand back, shook her head no to the red wine he offered and, when he went to pour it anyway, covered her glass.

"Your loss," he shrugged. "You heard what happened to me?"

He was a sunburned, stocky man with a halo of dark hair around a large bald spot and quick hostile brown eyes. He was clearly bothered by the way the table tipped, and yanked it first to the left and then to the right. Kay watched her dinner plate shift, and waited for it to steady before attempting to answer.

"Eleni told me your ship broke," she said as he jerked the table again.

"What's 'broke' is this piece of shit. Yiannis is helpless," he muttered. He called something out in Greek to Eleni who came to the door and answered in a rush of merriment. "Her husband doesn't own a single tool," Alkis translated to Kay. "Not a hammer. Not a saw. Her son's even worse. And she's proud of both of them." He leveled his brown eyes at her. "Can you fathom that?"

"No," Kay said. "I can't fathom anything."

"Smart lady." Alkis picked up his dinner knife and ducked under the table. She could feel him fiddling with screws and bolts down there, rather too close to her bare legs, and she crossed her ankles and pulled her feet in. There was a final rough, impatient crunch and then he was back in his chair, wiping his knife off on his tee-shirt. Whatever he had done had worked, for the table was solid.

"Don't even think about it," he said. "I'm married."

Kay looked at the large copper wedding ring on his left hand and pulled a sad face. "My loss again."

"Yes," he continued, unfazed, "my wife is sarcastic too." He lit a cigarette. "She teaches a course at Cornell called *FGSS*. Do you know what that is? Feminist, Gender, Sexuality Studies."

Kay, eyes on her plate, cut a piece of lamb, said, "Sounds academic; I'd probably flunk." Then, "Did you meet my friend Charles?"

"Nope. Only been here a few days. Why? You supposed to hook up with him here?"

"Something like that."

"And he left?" Alkis leaned back and gave a long loud laugh. "He must have taken off just before my crew did."

"Mutiny?" Kay murmured.

"Now why would you think that?"

Kay shrugged.

"No, in answer to your slur, I do not know why your friend ditched you but my crew did not mutiny. One kid left because his girlfriend was having a baby and the other wanted to go back to university. I can't go home until I replace both of them."

"So until then you're stuck here?"

Alkis stubbed his cigarette out on his plate, pushed back his chair, stretched, looked her straight in the eye, said, "I'm never 'stuck,'" and left.

Kay considered the two inches of red wine left in his glass and the pack of cigarettes by his plate, realizing, with relief, that she had no interest in either of them, nor, despite his aphrodisiac blend of rudeness, arrogance, bigotry, and egotism, was she interested in Alkis. He made the horde at home seem like princes. She stabbed a piece of lamb with such force it skidded off her plate and the white cat, which had somehow gotten inside, chased it across the floor and gulped it hungrily. Eleni, coming to clear the table, yelped at the sight of the cat and her husband rose from the television in the parlor and listened as she gesticulated toward the hall where the cat had disappeared. He then lumbered toward the back of the house, said something in a deep voice, and a second later Eleni's teenage son, tall and pale, with a black mustache so new it looked penciled on, appeared and reluctantly followed Eleni's flapping fingers to look for the cat down the hall.

"Is like hugging water!" Eleni said, setting a plate of cake in front of Kay.

"Getting them to do what you ask, you mean? For me too," Kay said, "with my family."

"Is problem," Eleni agreed. She lowered her voice. "Is expensive," she added, and when her son came back, she introduced him as Christopher and gave him a coin, which he pocketed without thanks before returning to his room.

Kay watched, puzzled. "You pay your son to help you out around the house?"

Eleni shrugged. "I know. Is crazy. But Christopher super smart. He need money go college."

"College? Surely he's too young for college?"

"Fourteen already! Win all the prizes. Speaks English good as you! Look!" Eleni pulled a battered grammar book out of her apron pocket and held it up. "He teaching me too!"

If she's learning English, I should try to learn a little Greek, Kay thought, and after dinner she examined the books shelved beneath Charles's paintings. There was only one language book, an ancient tome on Ancient Greek that she knew better than to even attempt. Among the remaining jumble of novels in Farsi, French and Turkish, travelogues in German and Hebrew, and battered paperback mysteries, she found an English translation of *The Odyssey*, perhaps the same book Charles had looked at as he wrote his cards to her. Out of habit, she began to organize the books, first by language then by author. When the shelves were tidy, the way she liked them, she tucked *The Odyssey* under her arm and went up the stairs to Charles's room, to sleep, alone, in his bed.

But tired as she was, she could not fall asleep and when she finally did it was to be buffeted by one nightmare after another—Nicky pelting her with coins from the Hate Jar, Francis trapped in a cubicle of smoke-filled glass, Charles pedaling past on his bicycle, headed straight for a precipice. She woke up in a panic. Outside the hot wind tapped at the shutters. She sat up, padded to the toilet, pulled the light switch and was horrified to see the white cat perched on the windowsill outside. Seeing her, it opened its bony skull-face and uttered one meow after another, demanding to be let in. Kay covered her ears, turned off the bathroom light and went back to bed.

She slept until mid-morning and as she sipped strong coffee and watched Eleni hang laundry on the line in the courtyard later that day, she thought of all the questions she wanted to ask about Charles and his time here. Had he taken lovers? Made friends? Had he talked to Eleni about his travels? Had he talked to Eleni about her? But Eleni must have thought she was asking about Yiannis, because she started to talk about her husband instead.

Yiannis, she told Kay, was twenty years older than she and used to wait for her after school with armfuls of flowers. Eleni had laughed at him, run from him, hidden behind her girlfriends. "Yiannis keep say '*Marry me, Marry me,*'" Eleni said. "But I am fifteen years old, why marry? I want finish school, work, learn English, work in Athens. But my father say "*No, is time you marry, and Yiannis is good man, will take care of you.*" She laughed and slapped the seat of a pair of work pants she was hanging up on the line. "I cry for four, five, six months after the wedding," she said, "and then one day … " she shrugged " … is not so bad. And next day, is not bad at all. And now? Is good." She laughed again and hung up one of her son's tee-shirts. "Yiannis is heavy man. You know? In heart is heavy always. Quiet. But good, like my father say. Love me very much. But … " she gave Kay her merry smile, " … he no take care of me. I take care of him!"

"Do you mind?"

"No, why mind? He let me do whatever I want!"

"He's a lucky man," Kay said.

"I think so too!" Eleni laughed and threw a wooden clothespin at the white cat sitting on the courtyard wall watching them. The cat watched it come and, when it fell short, leapt down, sniffed it, and made several weak attempts to bat it around in the grass.

"That cat's too sick to play," Kay observed.

Eleni made a dismissive spitting noise.

"Does it have a name?"

"Christopher name it High Class," Eleni said. "Hungry all the time. But eat? No thank you very much. Always want something better." She pointed to a bowl she had set out on the patio, and Kay saw it was filled with garlic cloves and chickpeas. The cat shot Kay a private appeal and Kay thought *Okay, but if you want "something better," you'll have to wait until I find a store.*

"Go find you new home," Eleni called to it. "The painter leave this." She gestured toward a collapsed green canvas bag under the clothesline, a bag Kay remembered seeing filled with picnic supplies when she and Charles took Nicky for sunset hikes at the beach. "I think make good cat catcher."

Kay picked the bag up and looked inside. Empty. Did leaving it here mean Charles would no longer take Nicky out in his kayak or run the mountain trails with her or sit through the same movie twice or sleep beside her at the symphony? She set it down. Charles could have gone anywhere after he left here. India. He'd always wanted to go to India. Israel. Fiji. Nepal, the Netherlands, New Zealand … "It's a great big wonderful world," Francis had told her, months ago. And it was. Too big.

After Eleni went inside, Kay sat on, picking at her cuticles. She still had four days before her flight home. Four empty days with nothing to do, no one to wait on. She knew she should feel free, released, but all she felt was slightly insane and ashamed of herself for ever thinking (1) she could find Charles in a foreign country and (2) that Charles could help her if she did find him. The white cat reappeared on the wall, fixed her once again with its imperative plea, and did not look away. Kay sighed, shouldered her purse, and set off to buy the miserable beast some food.

She found a minimart at the end of the street, bought a tin of sardines, then followed a series of flagstone steps down to a massive marble church. The doors were locked but the gate to the graveyard in back was open, and she entered, bending to examine the formal black and white photographs, brass lamps, plastic flowers, icons, and tiny bottles of ouzo on the tombs. She made a bouquet of small yellow flowers she found growing on the graves and placed it on the tomb of a young soldier killed in World War II. She tried to remember the last time she had visited Ida's half-empty crypt—it must have been over two years ago—and promised herself that when she got home she would replace the bouquet in the mausoleum vase, fill it with something lavish that Ida would have liked, tall sprays of white wisteria or apple blossoms, something to make up for the six pepper plants straggling up through the remaining ashes strewn behind the castle. Still thinking of her mother, who had always wanted to visit Greece, she left the churchyard and turned back toward the town.

As she passed an open shop with *SALE* in big red English letters, she heard an American voice say, "Sweetie! Don't pout. That's perfect for you."

She glanced in to see a heavy-set woman, hands on hips, admiring a boy sullenly standing in front of a full-length mirror. "Perfect," the woman repeated, "and," as the boy plucked at the collar, "you need it, you've worn the same shirt all week." Turning to Kay, she said, "Doesn't he look adorable?" The boy shot a pleading look over his shoulder and Kay saw he wasn't a boy at all, he was probably only a few years younger than the woman.

"I swear," the American woman continued to Kay, "Greek men are impossible to please. What do you think of this blue on him? Turn around, Vasilli, you silly, and show us how hot you look. Great color with his big brown eyes or what?"

Vasilli rolled his big brown eyes and plucked the collar of the shirt again. "It's too small for him," Kay explained. Vasilli grinned and made nah-nah wings at his ears at the woman, who said, "So we'll get the next size," and, turning to the hovering salesclerk, said, "More big?" As the clerk rushed away, the woman crooned, "Mr. Immature," and hugged Vasilli, who winked at Kay over her shoulder.

She must have snatched him from some bus tour, Kay thought, or taken him from a restaurant where he waited tables. She must have *bought* him. Remembering the cash she'd slipped into Neal's pockets, the dental work she'd covered for Biff, the checks she'd written for Fenton, she flushed. Clearly this American woman felt no shame; she was as happy playing Sugar Mama—*Queen-MotherBoss—Martyr*—as Vasilli was playing Boy Toy. She left the shop uneasily and headed up the street in a direction she hoped led back to Eleni's.

Within minutes she was lost. Lane after empty lane led her sideways, crossways, backwards, around, under Byzantine arches and over paving stones painted with peace symbols. Blue-domed chapels surprised her at every turn, breaking the linked fronts of white houses and walled gardens, and every now and then a corner opened to an ancient tumbledown rubble of terra cotta bricks. The town was charming, yes—but she wanted out. As she passed the same closed ceramics shop with the same doves cooing on its roof, she started to panic. Was she to stay in this dream of dead ends forever?

"Lost?" Alkis pulled up beside her in a small black rental car. He flung open the passenger door, moved a tool case to the back, and said, "Hop in. That's an octopus on the floor but it's dead, won't bite you. Ever eaten an octopus?"

"Yes," Kay lied, stepping warily over the plastic bag of gray slime.

"Delicious," Alkis said. "You parboil it and then you grill it. A little lemon, a little oregano, lots of olive oil. You cook?"

"Sure."

"Good, because we're on our own tonight. Eleni's out until later, had to go nurse her sick mother or something. Her son Chris cooks but Christopher won't do anything unless you pay him. So now that I've told you how to do it, why don't we eat at eight?"

"You want me to cook your dinner?"

"Our dinner."

"I don't know," Kay said. "I think I want a break."

"From what?"

"Cooking dinners."

"Gotta eat."

Kay sighed.

"Good girl."

"Not so good."

"Even better." He slid into a parking place in front of Eleni's gate, which Kay saw, was right around the corner, braked to a stop and turned to her with a gap-toothed smile. His breath, a stringent mix of wine, garlic, and tobacco, hit her full on and she took it in with a cautious inhalation, liking it despite herself, as she was beginning to like his frayed black sweater and calloused palms.

"Here," he handed the sack of grey slime to her. "I'll teach you."

In the kitchen, Alkis poured a glass of red wine and kept up a steady chatter as he cleaned the octopus, which he then rinsed and dropped into a pot of boiling water. He told her about his wife, Alicia, an American scholar, smart, beautiful, twenty years younger than he, and about their two daughters, whom he missed. "I've been at sea four months now," he explained, as he quartered a lemon and handed her a bunch of wild oregano to chop. "This miserable yacht I've been skippering has been nothing but trouble. The mast broke, the rigging snapped, we ran aground, I lost my crew, and last week? A fire. The owner has gone back to his mommy's mansion in the Hamptons, where he belongs. He wants me to sell *The Pleiades* but I hate to abandon her to amateurs."

"Can she be fixed?"

"Oh sure. Everything can be fixed." He plucked the octopus out of the pot and ran it under cool water in the sink. "It just takes time. And energy. And patience. And luck. And oh yes one more thing: money."

He gave her another of his quick gap-toothed smiles. Flirting? Kay couldn't tell. It was more likely he was conning her. Thought she was a rich American who could help him as that other American woman was "helping" Vasilli. She was silent as he showed her how to chop the octopus into tentacles. "We will feast tonight," he promised, adding, as he poured more wine into his glass, "So tell me something. Why did your boyfriend lure you all the way over here if he didn't want to fuck you?"

Kay, caught off guard, the sharp smell of the red wine in her nostrils (surely getting drunk in Europe would be different, healthier somehow, better for you, than getting drunk at home?) answered sharply, "Charles didn't lure me here and he wouldn't fuck me if someone paid him. He didn't even know I was coming. I didn't know I was coming." She looked up, but Alkis's gaze was not unkind. He was simply trying to place her. She couldn't blame him. After all, where did she fit? She was not a college girl who had come to the islands looking for a good time, nor a sophisticate looking for a bad time. She was just a middle-aged divorcee on a fool's errand. "It was a last-minute decision." She paused. "I left a real mess at home."

"Husband?"

"Ex. And two ex-boyfriends. My son's furious at me. My father's dying. My brother's insane. My girlfriends are sick of me, I don't have a place to live, and I'm probably about to lose my job."

"Anything else?"

"Yes, but you don't need to hear it. Anyway, I'll fly back in a few days and get it all straightened out. You said everything can be fixed, right?"

"Almost everything." Alkis plopped a glob of octopus guts onto a saucer. "Here," he said, handing it to her. "Give this to devil cat meowing outside and when you come back would you finish dicing these potatoes? Then fire up the grill in back, you know how to do that? And throw these suckers on. Remember to baste. Takes about fifteen minutes." He looked at her and for a second, she expected him to say "Can do?" like Francis, but he only took a final gulp of his wine, set the glass down, flashed a last smile, and disappeared out the door. Watching his dark head with its bald spot jog down the back stairs toward the black car she felt a distressing jab of attraction. Then she looked at the mess in the kitchen. The jumble of half-chopped vegetables, the spill of wine, the cigarettes stubbed out in a saucer, the dismembered octopus, the half-finished marinade, the clutter of slimy knives and cutting boards. Were all men like this? Or just the ones she knew? She thought of Zabeth's husband, a loving, sweet-tempered, energetic man who ran a busy pharmacy in town, took the twins to ballet class and baseball games, and did the dishes every night, of Lois Hayes's husband, who washed her hair for her, of Dana's ex-husband, who still sent flowers every week and rushed to her aid every time she saw a spider in the bathroom sink. There are kind, generous, tender men in the world, she told herself. She repeated it once, twice, promised herself she'd call Donald Wallace as soon as she got home, then got to work, fed the cat, and cleaned the kitchen up. When she was finished, she rubbed her hands with a lemon wedge to get rid of the smell and went out to the back to see where the grill was kept.

The *kalimari*, served on the stable little table later that night, was indeed delicious, but Kay ate alone. Alkis, Eleni explained when she returned, was down at the port, hiring crew members for the trip to Turkey.

"Turkey? He's not going home to New York?" Kay cut into another tentacle, hoping Eleni wouldn't notice that she had put on lipstick for this dinner. "He has a wife and two daughters waiting for him in New York."

"Turkey is beautiful place," Eleni said firmly. "Yiannis take me there one day." She unclipped one of her sparkling barrettes and reset it in her thick hair. "Maybe Alkis take you," she added slyly.

"Bad idea," Kay said.

"Bad idea," Eleni agreed, and cleared Kay's plate. Her son sat apart, silently reading a book as he ate, Yiannis hulked in the doorway holding out a jacket with a torn sleeve, and the phone rang with a call from Eleni's brother about Eleni's father, who was recovering from a broken hip. Eleni soothed him briskly as she moved from chore to chore; she clearly hadn't lied when she said she didn't mind taking care of her family. She didn't think of herself as the waif in the cinders. She didn't see herself as abused or put-upon. She seemed content being married to a man she hadn't chosen, serving a silent son, counseling an anxious brother and tending to elderly parents. And in addition to that, she was running a guest house, learning a foreign language, baking a batch of baklava to take to a neighbor who had just had a baby, repairing her husband's jacket, fixing the drip under the kitchen sink, and sewing a sexy red dress from a pattern she had made herself. She was perfect.

Disgusted with herself, Kay said goodnight and went up to her room, not surprised to see High Class waiting outside her door. She fixed Kay with her insistent green eyes and trumpeted a loud request to enter, but Kay again pushed her back, slipped inside, and shut the door. There was nothing to feel guilty about. The cat had eaten both the octopi innards and the sardines Kay had put out for her: she could not be hungry. She was dirty, infected, injured, and unlikeable. What was Kay supposed to do? Let her in to sleep on her bed tonight, find an animal hospital somewhere tomorrow, get her defleaed, deloused, dewormed, disinfected, inoculated, microchipped, call the airlines, figure out a way to take her back home, get her spayed and keep her alive and resented for the next twenty years?

Yes.

Should she do it?

No!

But one night wouldn't hurt. Relenting, Kay let the cat in to sleep at the end of her bed, retrieved her knitting from her suitcase, and started to do her daily number of rows on Charles's scarf. Pausing to count stitches she saw she had, once again, dropped one, and she swore as she ripped back to repair it. It didn't matter, as this gift would never be given, but she was determined—perhaps wrongly—to finish the piece. What was that quote from the *Miracle* book? "*There is no need to reinvent bad relationships in an attempt to be loyal to them and their legacy.*" She had a bad relationship with this scarf. She had a bad relationship with her father, her brother, her three exes, this damn cat, and right now she had a bad relationship with Charles. And yet she could not give up on any of them. She pushed the knitting to the floor, reached for *The Odyssey* and opened to a passage she did not remember reading before: "My child, what odd complaints you let escape you. Have you not, you yourself, arranged this matter?" Now even Homer was accusing her? She pulled the covers over her head and tried not to listen to High Class purring noisily at her feet.

The next morning was hot and overcast. Eleni, scrambling fresh eggs with feta and oregano, said, "Today, I go to *monastri*, meet Mother Theonymphi. She friend of your friend, the painter. You come?" Kay nodded and followed Eleni to the old Nissan that she kept parked in back. Alkis's car, she noted, had not returned. Eleni handed her a large plastic bottle of lamp oil and a sack of oranges—gifts, she said, for the saint. They drove through the port town's market streets and followed the curve of the harbor up the mountain. As they drove, Kay asked about Mother Theonymphi, but Eleni only smiled, corrected her pronunciation, and began to tell Kay about some sort of holy arm bone that was kept at the monastery. Prayers to this bone, Eleni said, made miracles. The bone had led Eleni to convince a reluctant Yiannis to let her take driving lessons, even though no other women in the village drove, and then, when it was time to take her driver's test, prayers to the saint's bone helped her pass, and then when she saw this Nissan for sale, the bone helped her buy it. "Is great bone!" Eleni crowed.

"Must be," Kay agreed. They continued to circle up the mountain, past the caves where, Eleni told her, marble was quarried. They parked at the top, near a cluster of old buildings behind a white wall. Eleni pushed the gate open and Kay followed her into a deserted courtyard, then through another gate and down a step to the dark stone entrance room of a chapel. Breathing in, Kay smelled licorice and furniture polish and carnations. Eleni called out and two women burst through the doors, talking in rapid argumentative voices. One of the women had a torn Hermes scarf knotted under her chin; the other, younger, was in a Bob Marley tee-shirt. They fussed in a sort of private fury as they greeted Eleni and then opened the door to the chapel itself, which was lit with hanging brass lamps, light flickering from red glass candle holders.

Eleni crossed herself and began to pour oil into the lamps while Kay looked around. The inlaid black and white marble floor was piled with Turkish rugs, and tall wooden chairs, decorated with peacocks carved beak to beak, were lined single file against the walls. Gold leaf icons of somber saints unfurling scrolls of scripture covered the walls. The domed ceiling was painted with pastel angels. The glass case with a frail yellow arm bone in it was displayed on a pedestal, fresh orchid petals laid on top.

Kay pulled her jacket closer around her. This place did not speak to her, as, apparently, it had to Charles, and the arm bone was just plain creepy. But—why was she thinking about Ida again?—it was a place her mother would have adored. Ornate. Theatrical. Ida had always loved churches, their bells and candles and drifting wafts of incense. How thrilled she'd been when the Carmelites agreed to pray for her that time, how she'd clasped her hands and burst into one of her merry peals of delight. "For *me!*" she'd cried. "Imagine that! They are praying for *me!*"

Oh Mom! Kay thought, and smiled, a rare warmth filling her at the memory. It was nice to think of Ida like this, with love. She heard a light step behind her and turned to see an old woman cowled in black with friendly intelligent eyes and a full-lipped, almost sensual smile. When Eleni introduced them, Kay held her hand out and felt Mother Theonymphi's hand close around it firmly. "*Ya Su,*" Kay said, the two syllables she'd memorized that hopefully meant hello. The old woman said something to Eleni, who laughed. "Oracle is in," Eleni translated.

"Oracle?" Kay repeated, stepping back.

"Is joke. Your painter friend's joke."

"Charles had a lot of jokes," Kay agreed.

"Yes, always say Mother Theonymphi know all the answers. Mother Theonymphi say there *are* no all the answers! Only questions. What is your question?"

"My question?"

"You come with question. Right?"

The old nun smiled, and Kay, embarrassed, flushed. Did she have a question? She started to ask if Mother Theonymphi knew where Charles was, then stopped. This should be a question about herself. Her needs, her wants. Charles had taken off. She was on her own. What, after all, was the difference between asking this kind old woman the same question she'd asked all those glib and glossy self-help books? Shouldn't she ask how she could become a different person? A better person?

"Your question?" Eleni prompted.

"I guess ..." Kay shrugged. "I guess I just want to change ..."

The nun waited, smiling.

"Myself. I want to change myself."

"Ah," the old woman said, her voice rich and resonant. "You must break the string."

"Break the ... ?"

Realizing at last that Mother Theonymphi was not going to say anything more, Kay dropped her head to hide her shamed grin. She'd received the dumb answer her dumb question deserved. String? To what? Aprons? Puppets? The emergency Tampax she'd had to borrow off Eleni this morning? She started to say "Thank you" but was startled by the nun's touch once more on her hand. She looked up, met the lit gray eyes, and felt, there was no other word for it, and there was certainly no reason for it, blessed. It spilled over her, a radiance so unexpected that without thinking she stepped forward and felt the strong arms come around her and hold her tight, close and warm and safe. She could not move. No one, not even Charles, had ever held her this closely before. It was seductive and repellent and, after a minute, unbearable. Shaken, distrustful, and deeply grateful, Kay at last stepped back. She hadn't brought enough money to leave a donation but on impulse she pulled off her mother's sapphire ring and placed it in the old woman's open palm, where it sat, glowing, until the fingers closed around it. Ida would love knowing this was where her ring had ended up, Kay thought. It would have made her happy. "*Ya su,*" she said again and, feeling lighter than she had in years, bolted.

It stormed that night and then stopped so suddenly at two in the morning that Kay woke up. She heard the dripping of the eaves and a scratch at the door. White cat again? Had she been out in the weather all this time? She'd be drenched. Frowning, Kay slipped out of bed naked, grabbed a towel to dry the cat with, and went to the door.

Standing there, equally naked: Alkis.

"Oh," Kay said.

"Ah," said Alkis.

Merry eyes, glinting teeth, pulsing throat, broad shoulders, thick waist, bear hair on chest and between legs, strong legs, strong feet, about to step in.

"Wait," Kay said. She held the towel in front of her.

"I can wait." Alkis smiled. "I can do anything you want."

"I've never known what I want," Kay explained.

"So why not find out?" He took a step closer.

"Because ... "

"Because?"

Because you're married and should be home with your wife right this minute helping raise your daughters, because you left me to clean up the kitchen and cook the octopus, because you're arrogant and cold and unkind, because I mean nothing to you and yet if we have sex you will end up meaning a great deal to me and after you leave I will wonder what I did wrong and I will miss you which is pathetic but that's how I am and because that's how I am I need to take better care of myself ...

"It's not good for me," she said at last. Her voice sounded strange to her: older, steadier. Surprised, she took another breath. "It's not good for me," she repeated.

"As you wish." He stepped back, hands lifted, as she closed the door. How easy it was to get rid of a man! Why hadn't she known this before? She swaggered back to bed and lay there imagining delicious scenes in which she dismissed all the men in her life, starting with Francis and going on to Neal, Biff, Victor, and Fenton. None of you, she said in her mind, are good for me, or, for that matter, good to me, or, for that matter, good enough for me. Scat! She smiled and stretched under the covers but still the image of Alkis beautifully naked in the doorway lingered, and as the minutes passed, she felt her pride in rejecting him fade into the old uncertainty. Had she turned down a chance for connection, intimacy, romance, adventure, and the best sex of her life? Not likely, but still … The moon shone onto her cot through the shutter slats and she felt as lonely as if she were still locked in her tower.

She was almost glad when she again heard a light tap at her door. Alkis wanted her enough to be persistent? That was good, wasn't it? And what was wrong with an hour or two of impersonal passion? She had had it often enough before. Too often, actually. So why change now? Because, she thought wearily, it's *time* to change now. I need to cut that damn string, whatever it is. She sat up, pushed her hair back, covered herself again with the towel, and went to the door to tell Alkis goodbye.

But Alkis, in surfer shorts, seemed to have another idea in mind. Head turned aside, he held out the old red Speedo she had left to air on the clothesline. They were to go swimming? At this hour? Well. Okay. "Shh," he said as she took the suit, struggled into it, and followed him down the stairs to his car. Silently they drove in the dawn down to the sea, parking near a small crescent of rough sand hemmed between two rocky cliffs. Without looking at her, Alkis walked to the edge of the water and dove in and Kay, alone in the dark, hesitated only a moment before she followed. The water was warm and fresh and thick. The setting moon laid down a path she could stroke through and when she turned over on her back, she saw the bright edge of the sun just coming over the opposite horizon. She watched as the light filled the sky. It was almost autumn and the sky was cool, green gold

233

and still. There was no rosy-fingered goddess of dawn and the sea she floated in was light as limeade rather than dark as wine but it was the most beautiful place she had ever been in and she felt happier than she could remember feeling for years. She dove under and swam until her breath gave out, surfaced and swam toward the sun some more. When she finally paddled to shore, Alkis was waiting with a dry towel. She sat beside him as he smoked in silence, the sun gilding their bare legs. Then he drove her back to Eleni's. As he stopped in front of the house, she saw luggage she hadn't noticed before piled in the backseat. "Your boat's repaired," she guessed. "You're sailing to Turkey."

"Bodrum or bust," he nodded.

"Safe journey to you, then."

"And to you," he echoed as he waved and pulled away.

Rain set in later that day. Kay looked out at the storm, which was rattling the windowpanes. Downstairs Eleni worked a large press into which she smoothed sheets and towels. The steamy air smelled of soap and scorch and the parlor rang with canned laughter. Yiannis and the old father still sat in front of the television, Christopher still stayed in his room. There was no sign of High Class, which was good. She must have found another home.

Home, Kay thought. She thought of Nicky, his accusing eyes, his angry voice. She ached to get back to him. He had not answered her phone calls or picked up on her texts. She remembered leaving him with Zabeth once when she had gone away for a weekend with a man she had met in a bar; Nicky was only seven then but he had refused to look at her for a week. "Grudge carrier," Zabeth had laughed. "He'll make a great attorney!"

The weather cleared and turned hot again. She took a bottle of water and her camera and set off on a long walk that took her through the village and down a stone trail studded with wild-flowers. This is where Charles walked, she realized. She imagined him beside her, his long loping step, his quiet voice, his painter's eye pointing out things she would never have noticed on her own: the afternoon moon silvered in a dark puddle, the hoof print of a donkey in the mud. She could feel his hand on the crook of her elbow as she climbed the ancient arched bridge, could feel him challenge her to find the smoothest stone to drop into the streambed below, could hear his laugh as a bird startled from the scrub above the trail. She listened to the sheep and goat bells, took pictures of the fig trees which, old as they were, looked helplessly sexy with their smooth gray limbs and fruited branches, and ended up in another village. She found a tourist shop and bought a heavy glass necklace of a dozen colors for Eleni. She hesitated, then bought another for herself. By the time she arrived back at the house it was almost dark. Over a dinner of roast chicken with salt and lemon she asked about the cat.

Eleni smiled. "Alkis fix."

Kay, remembering how Alkis had "fixed" the table that first night with a few rough yanks, looked up. "Alkis found a home for her? She's all right?"

"Is great," Eleni assured her.

Kay nodded, unsure. Still, it was lovely having the cat gone. She could ascend the stairs to her room without being tripped, could read in bed without being stared down, could step out into the hall without being accosted or bullied. It was also, she realized, a little lonely.

It stormed again that night and in between the gusts of wind and rain Kay dreamed she heard a familiar cascade of meows outside her door, weaker now, but as imperative as ever. Reluctantly she yawned, got up, and went to the door just to make sure the devil cat had not come back. But the minute she turned the knob, there it was, a drenched white rag that flew in and leapt, triumphant, on top of her clean folded laundry. High Class, wet and filthy, with a mad gleam in its cold green eyes.

"You got away," Kay marveled. "How?" And then, noticing the dried blood on the cat's sharp claws, "Oh dear. What on earth did you do to that poor man?"

The next morning Kay zipped the cat, yowling, into the canvas carrier and took the bus down to the port of Parikia where she found a veterinary clinic that specialized in neutering strays She waited while High Class was being operated on, making sure she also got a distemper shot, had her ear sewn up, and her ringworm treated. She still did not know what she was going to do with the beast. She certainly could not take it back to the States with her. Coming back into the studio she saw Eleni's quiet son, Christopher, sitting as always alone at a corner table. A textbook on economics lay open before him. In English.

"Your mother tells me you plan to go to college in Athens," she said, stopping in front of him.

"That is correct," Christopher said, not looking up.

"And that you are saving money for tuition."

"Correct again," the boy said.

"How would you like to earn fifty dollars a month?"

"Doing what?"

"I need someone to care for this cat."

"*That* cat?" He glanced at the canvas bag in her arms. "Sixty."

"Deal. But you'll have to feed it things it likes, I'll give you a list, and you'll have to give it its medicine and keep it from bothering your mother. And I will only pay you as long as High Class stays alive. I'll want monthly texts and photos."

"No problem." The boy reached for a notebook, wrote out a frighteningly formal contract, and handed it over. Kay signed it swiftly, then gave him the cat carrier, most of the money she'd withdrawn from the ATM in town, and a promise to send more on the first of every month. Cat and Chris will make a great couple, she thought as she went back upstairs. Both are born executives.

She finished packing then sank to her knees at the window, taking in one last look at the white doves flying over the white roofs of the village below. Charles, she was sure, had found the same peace here that she had, and that, perhaps, made her whole trip worth it.

"I hate to leave," she admitted, as Eleni drove her down to the dock.

"But you can come back," and for the first time Kay heard a note of wistfulness in Eleni's voice. Eleni after all was not free to leave her life, as Kay had just left hers—but then, Eleni didn't want to. Eleni *liked* her life. Maybe that's the "secret," Kay thought, the one I haven't figured out yet.

She had an easy ride on the ferry back, leaning over the rail, watching the wake break behind the boat in ruffled white ribbons, and she had an easy taxi ride to the Athens airport. Things *could* be easy; they didn't have to be hard: why settle for chickpeas and garlic when you could hold out for sardines and cream? Life is short, brutal, nasty, as Francis liked to say, but it was also gorgeous, surprising, utterly confusing and full of magic. She dozed off but awoke with a start, Ida's voice clear and firm in her ears. *Thank you darling*, Ida was saying, *I had a wonderful time.* Had her mother been with her the whole time? Was it possible the *castle* wasn't haunted? But *she* was? She opened her eyes, blinked hard, blew a space clear on the window glass and looked down at the world far below. She would be home soon, and she needed to land on her feet.

WEEK ELEVEN

The men were waiting for her when she got back. Not at the airport, though she would have welcomed a ride in one of Victor's luxury cars, nor in the driveway as she paid the taxi with the last of her cash. They were in the Great Room, watching a game. She entered quietly and stood watching them—Francis, tapping his cigarette ash into the sugar bowl on top of his oxygen tank; Neal, in the surgical mask he wore when Francis smoked; Victor, moodily turning the pages of a large print Bible on his lap; Fenton, at the window, following a hawk with binoculars; Biff, standing too close to the television, shifting from one bare foot to another in a restless dance. No one moved to hug her or welcome her home, though Fenton smiled his slow smile and Biff blew her a kiss and Neal blinked. Francis twinkled a brief "Well whaddaya know, she made it," over the tops of his glasses, and Victor gravely waved one of Ed's bandaged paws up down. There was no sign of Nicky—the only one she wanted to see—and when she asked where he was, no one knew. Neal thought he "might be" at Tico's house, Fenton said he'd seen him earlier, "somewhere," Victor said they were out of chocolate milk again, Biff said not to worry, his new album was getting in great shape. Francis didn't say anything.

The Great Room looked different and it took Kay a minute to realize that was because there were no fast-food wrappers, gym socks, jock straps, bicycle parts, power tools, loose change, discarded newspapers, or dirty plates and glasses on the floor. The windows shone, the furniture was dusted, and Ida's portrait, which had been knocked off-kilter weeks ago by the earthquake, had been straightened at last. "What happened?" she asked. "Did you hire a housekeeper while I was gone?"

"We didn't need to," Victor said. "Your friend came over and put us to work."

"Lois Hayes?"

"Was that her name?" Neal turned to the others.

"I don't think she told us her name," Biff said.

"Odd looking," Francis said. "Walked like an ostrich."

"Hardly." Fenton put down his binoculars. "Ostriches walk on their toes."

"'The wings of the ostrich wave proudly, but are they the pinions and plumage of love?' Job 39," Victor intoned, adding, in his melancholy voice, "She was bossy."

Kay turned, went down to Nicky's room, and peeked in his door. His room was empty except for Orville, obediently coiled in his cage. A jumble of gym equipment—bar bells, ankle weights, a jump rope—lay on the floor and one of her old diet books was open on his desk. Nicky had been getting in shape all this time and she hadn't even noticed? Too self-absorbed in her own problems to pay attention to her son's? Troubled, she went back up the stairs, picked up her suitcase and climbed toward the tower. Try as she would, she could not see little Lois Hayes with her frizzy bangs and scratchy voice coming in, giving orders, and getting the men to clean house. Maybe Dana and Zabeth had chipped in to hire a dominatrix. She went on up to her tower room, stood by the window and dialed Tico's mother to see if Nicky was there, leaving a message on the answering machine. Then, exhausted, she lay down on the bed and stared at the ceiling, trying to remember what she had decided on the flight over the Atlantic. It had made perfect sense at the time—she wouldn't shout or argue or reason—she was no good at shouting or arguing or reasoning—she was not an effective fighter, never had been—she would simply leave, throw all her things and Nicky's things in the back of her car and drive off. It would probably be days before anyone would miss her. The two of them would move to the mountains, or to the seashore, or out to farm country somewhere, she would get a job as a waitress or a salesclerk, Nicky would find new friends, they would start a new life. It wouldn't matter where they went. The important thing was just to get out of the castle. She sat up. The castle cramped her, cramped them all! It was a dark, cold, cheerless prison and after the vast lit skies and seas of Greece it was intolerable. She had to cut that string! All of the strings! To everyone!

A roar rose from the television below—some star athlete from some star team must have scored either a home run or a touchdown or a basket. Rising, she emptied her suitcase onto the bed and pulled out her goodbye gifts: the oregano seeds for Neal, the heavy Orthodox cross for Victor, the CD of Balkan folk songs for Biff, the jar of honey for Fenton, the Greek fisherman's hat for Francis. The knitting she had worked on during the long flight home was in the suitcase too and when she shook the scarf out she was impressed by how good it looked—all her hard work had paid off—she had finally finished something she'd started. The scarf was perfect, long and soft and light and airy. Even if Charles never returned to wear it, she had done something right. Pleased, she folded it back, only to notice a sticky spot she had not seen before. Blood. Intermixed with short dirty white hairs. High Class.

Damn it! All the time she had put into this! All the hours she had spent knitting and ripping, knitting and ripping. Madness.

She was reaching for the scissors to chop the scarf into a million pieces when she heard a knock, and, hoping it was Nicky at last, called "Come in, honey," but it was Biff who entered, smiling, touching the back of his hair as he always did.

"Cool," Biff said, looking at the mauled wad of wool in her hands. "How was Italy?"

"Greece."

"Greece! Right! Bouzoukis! Tsabounas! Did you hear some wild music?"

Kay shook her head and waited to hear him tell her he needed five dollars for gas or a ride to the city but he surprised her with an unexpected request. Leaning forward, hands clasped, eyes liquid, Biff asked, "Can I have the harp?"

"My mother's gold harp?"

"You never play it. Nicky doesn't touch it. It's just sitting there. And now that I'm doing spirituals ... "

"But you won't be doing spirituals long. Don't look hurt. You know you'll move on to another genre next year. And then what?" She stopped, not wanting to insult him by pointing out that the harp would end up collecting road dust in the back of his Subaru along with the braguinha, bagpipes, and shofar. "I'm sorry, Biff, but I'm keeping the harp."

He continued to smile at her winningly. "Why?"

Good question. The harp was one of the many expensive enthusiasms that Ida had adopted and dropped, and Biff would no doubt put it to good use before he in turn dropped it himself. She looked at him standing before her with his expectant smile and suddenly remembered Ida, in her wheelchair, clasping the harp close to her chest as she struggled with the opening bars of "Greensleeves." This was not the merry flirt in the oil portrait downstairs, nor the raging drunk cuddling a lion skin rug, but a broken invalid in a stained bathrobe fighting to wrest something good from the wreckage of her health. This was the mother Kay had loved and this was the mother she missed.

"I told you why."

"Because it was the Dragon's? That's no reason. You can't hold onto things just because they have sentimental value."

"You can't? Why not? Find your own harp, Biff."

"Well, all right. I thought you'd be nicer about it."

"I've been nice. Anyway," she added, as he turned to leave for band practice, "I've never heard you play it either."

"Oh yeah, no I don't, harp's a girl's instrument, don't you think?"

"There's a girl in your band?"

He looked surprised. "Chiana."

"You want the harp for Chiana?"

"I didn't think you'd mind. You've always been so reasonable."

"I sure have," Kay agreed, and started to laugh.

Laughing confusedly with her, Biff waited by the door. Kay saw his hesitation, knew that in another second he'd step toward her, cup her face in his long fingers, kiss her lightly, and ask for the harp again. In a year or two she might see him at some music festival with Chiana—or some other girl—and he would be as happy to greet her as if they had never parted. "You'll be late," she said softly.

After he left, she rang Tico's house again, relieved when his mother picked up, but it seemed neither Tico nor his brothers had seen Nicky all week. Kay clicked the phone off and rang the Nordrums'. Yes, Nicky had been spending a lot of time over there, "to our delight," Hazel Nordrum added, but they hadn't seen him recently. Kay hung up. It was getting dark. She went outside and sank onto a deck chair, her fingers tapping the armrests, frowning up at the sky.

"Tired, babe?" She turned as Neal sat down beside her. "I can make you some sheep sorrel tea if you'd like."

"Yum, no, that's all right."

"Sure?"

Startled, Kay felt Neal's hand brush the worry lines off her forehead. She tried not to stiffen, tried not to break into that upbeat peppy voice she hated, tried not to judge his stained dungarees or mention the brambles caught in his ponytail. "How was Nicky while I was gone?" she asked.

"Nicky?"

"Your son?"

"Oh. Fine. Busy. You know. Soccer with Tico. Guitar with Biff, carpentry with Fenton, Bible lessons with Victor. And, of course, your dad. Video games."

"No shooting range?"

"Relax." Neal touched her forehead again. She held her breath and in a minute his hand left. Glancing up, she saw he was still wearing the surgical mask.

"I'm going to call the police."

"Why? Nicky's fine. He might be with your friend."

"My friend?"

"You know. That woman who came in the front door just as you were leaving last week."

Kay tried to remember. "The pizza delivery person?"

Neal nodded and gave a silent laugh. "We were all surprised you'd ordered pesto. You never did like basil. Too many antioxidants for you. Too healthy, too … "

Interrupting him, Kay asked, "Had you ever seen her before?"

"No."

"Have you seen her since?"

"Just that time she came over to clean up."

"Can you describe her?"

"Big neck. Dry skin. Thyroid deficiency." Neal paused, then chuckled. "Biff asked for her phone number."

"You all should have asked for her phone number! Maybe then I'd know where Nicky is tonight."

"Why don't you ask your dad?"

"I did! He didn't answer."

"Probably didn't hear you. I've noticed that sometimes Francis doesn't hear you. But your dad's smart. He knows everything."

"I do know everything," Francis agreed, when Kay went back to the Great Room.

"You do? You know where Nicky is?"

"Sure."

"Where?"

"On the roof."

Nicky was so shocked to see her he didn't even protest when Kay shimmied out her bedroom window, crawled up the slates, plucked the joint out of his fingers before he could re-light it and threw it over the edge into the redwoods. "How long has this been going on?" she asked. Nicky didn't answer. "A long time? Ever since we moved to the castle?" Still no answer. "No more," she said firmly. "That part of your life is over. Do you understand? It's history. If I ever see you with drugs again, I am grounding you for life."

"Pot isn't drugs," Nicky began. "Fenton says … "

"Shut up," Kay warned, and took his face in her hands. "You are eleven years old. Do you understand?"

"Yes."

"I doubt it. Your pupils are big as blackberries. Just promise me you will never touch this crap again. And don't lie to me. I am dead serious. I want a promise."

"I promise. Mom?"

"What?"

"Could you not call me Nicky anymore? It's a baby's name."

"What name would you like me to call you?"

"Thor."

"Forget it. Will Nick do? It will? Good. Now tell me, Nick, who gave you that joint? And don't lie. Was it Fenton? Was it Biff? Both? No, *don't* tell me. I suppose your grandfather's been slipping you sips from his scotch, and Victor's convinced you the world's coming to an end, and God knows what your father stirs into your milk. I should never have left you with them. I should never have left you at all. Didn't you get my note? I phoned every day. Didn't anyone tell you? Didn't anyone let you know where I was?"

"Grandpa said you'd gone off on a wild goose chase."

"I chased 'em," Kay agreed, "but I couldn't catch 'em."

"How do you catch a goose anyway? Like this?" Nick, clearly stoned, giggled and cupped his hands around his mouth, "Hooonnkkk?"

"Enjoy it now," Kay said grimly. "You're not going to feel this stupid again until you're grown up."

"Mom," Nick sighed, and nestled against her shoulder. She rocked him, nuzzling the top of his head, inhaling as much of his mungy mossy boy stink as she could. "I missed you, Mom."

"I missed you too, darling."

"Do you know what's going to happen to us?"

"Yes."

"What?"

"Good things. Only good things. Lots of good things. I'll tell you all about them in the morning, when you're sober. Right now, I'm getting you down from here. Come on. Carefully. Hold my hand. Tighter."

She tucked her son into bed and waited in his room until he fell asleep and then she climbed the stairs back up to the tower. She hadn't told him the truth. She did not know what was going to happen. And she had no faith that all, or even any of it, would be good. She leaned out the casement window. The summer sky was glamorous, clear, dark, and studded with stars. *Help*, she thought. She sank to her knees and bent her head. How could she figure this all out? It was too much. It was impossible. Hearing the doorbell ring, and remembering no one else ever answered it, she rose, brushed the tears out of her eyes, and went downstairs to open the door. A tall, broad-shouldered woman stood there, backlit.

"Lambkin?" the woman said.

"Oh, come here," Kay said, and held her arms out.

WEEK TWELVE

The two went straight to the kitchen table and settled down, as they used to, across from each other with a pot of ginger tea and a plate of buttered toast. Kay lit candles rather than turn on the overhead but even in the half-dark she drew her breath in in admiration. Charles's high cheekbones and long lashes and artful haircut were stunning. For a while they sat looking at each other in silence. There was so much to talk about. No place to start. "You turned out gorgeous," Kay blurted at last. "You look like I've always wanted to look." And then, childishly, unable to help herself, "What do I call you now? Are you a ... " she stopped. She couldn't say "transsexual." It sounded like an engineering term. "Trannie" was surely a slur, as derogative as "druggie" or "alkie," and "crossdresser" didn't begin to describe the fresh-faced middle-aged woman sitting across from her in black jeans and a tee-shirt. "What," she finished, flustered, "is your name?"

"That's a hard one," the woman admitted. The voice hadn't changed. The warm smile hadn't changed. "When I was a child, I wanted to be called Annabella Mirabella LaFontana. I thought that was the most beautiful name in the world. My mother went along with it for a while until my dad overheard us and beat it out of both of us. Jamie knew who I was and always called me Charlie so I kept it, for his sake. Not very imaginative of me, I guess. But a lot less paperwork."

"It's cute. Sort of jaunty. Better than Char or Charlene."

"I've regretted it. Should have stayed with Annabella Mirabella."

"Have you regre ... "

"No, lambie. Not a thing. It was the right decision for me. I'm just sorry it took me so long to actually do it. To find the courage."

"But you've always been brave," Kay pointed out. "With your art, with your life, you've always taken risks. I'll never forget how you stood up for bicycle rights at that town hall meeting and the way you coached Nicky in kickboxing after that older boy called him 'fat.' You've always stood up for your beliefs. I wish I ... " She bit her lip, then grinned. "Look at you! Totally changed! And you're the person who didn't even want me to dye my hair!"

"Your hair is a nice shade of ... "

"Brown. Rapidly graying mousy brown."

"Can't go wrong with rapidly graying mousy brown."

"You're the one who talked me out of getting Botox!"

"Botox is poison."

"You wouldn't even let me get a breast reduction!"

"Of course, I wouldn't let you get a breast reduction, you silly beast. Do you remember what else I told you?"

"Not to drink, not to smoke, not to swear, not to say yes when I want to say no, not to lose my temper, keys, wallet, mind, etc."

"And have you?"

"It's been hard," Kay admitted, and then, ashamed, for, compared to Charlie, what did she know about life being "hard"—and what were they doing talking about her life in the first place— had she always done this? Turned every conversation around to herself? "Why didn't you tell me what you were going through?"

248

"You would have been shocked."

"No I wouldn't. At least, I would have tried not to show that I was."

Charlie laughed. The laugh wasn't right yet: still too deep, and, Kay noted, it still ended in a snort. Would she have to give her friend private lessons in womanhood? How? When she herself didn't know how to be a woman! And honestly, who would want to be a woman in the first place? Women were supposed to be submissive, humble, obedient, weak, self-absorbed ... hmm, Kay thought, maybe I'd make a good tutor after all. "I just wish you'd confided in me," she finished.

"Don't take it personally," Charlie said. "I couldn't confide in anyone. I did a lot of research, contacted strangers online, prayed, journaled, painted—but for some reason I couldn't actually talk to anyone about what I wanted to do. I still don't know why. Maybe I wanted it too badly. Or maybe I hoped you'd notice on your own. Surely you saw the changes in me before I left for Bangkok? I'd been taking estrogen for months; I'd put on weight. I knew that transitioning, difficult as it was going to be—and it has been—was what I wanted to do, but I wasn't ready to talk about it, not to you, not to anyone. I know I shut you out. I had to. I'm sorry. You've always been a junkie for self-help books and I knew you wanted to change a few things about yourself—but I wanted to change everything."

Everything? It was too soon to ask, and anyway, Kay didn't want to know. Charles had always been a private person, self-sufficient, independent; he ... she ... would tell her all in time. Or not. It didn't matter. What mattered was that he ... she ... was here now.

"I never thought you needed to change one single thing about yourself. You were and are the most perfect human being I know," Kay said truthfully. Charlie's hands were strong as ever but had longer nails, shaped into ovals and softly polished, and when she squeezed them, Kay was aware of her own nibbled cuticles. "Will you still hang out with me?" she asked childishly. "Will you still … I don't know, beat me at pool, let me beat you at Scrabble, go kayaking with Nicky, I mean Nick, help me with my taxes, rub my feet, tell me off when I'm being ridiculous, ignore me when I can't stop being ridiculous … ?"

"Unfortunately," Charlie said, "yes. I'm still your friend. I'll still put up with you as long as I can stand it. After all, aren't you the reason I came back here?"

"You came back for me?" Kay felt tears begin to spill down her cheeks. "All those blank postcards … "

"Blank? I spent hours on those postcards."

"Okay, so they are beautiful, but those quotes from *The Odyssey*? Nothing personal, no *how are you, what are you up to, wish you were here* … ?"

"Well, you came anyway, didn't you?" That snorty laugh again. "You know, I actually set off to come home a few days before you flew off to leave it. Don't you remember pushing past me on your way out the front door? Stop crying, goofus. If nothing else, you got an adventure. You got out of your rut and went to Greece! Aren't you glad? You got to meet Eleni. And her lunk of a husband. I did like her son, though. We had some good conversations once I got him to talk about the things he liked."

Curious, Kay asked, "What did Christopher like?"

"Money. He'll be rich someday. Did Eleni ever take you up the mountain to see Mother Theonymphi?"

"She gave me the best advice … " Kay started.

"That old fraud. 'You want to be free? You must break the string.'"

Kay stared, astonished.

"She got that from *Zorba*," Charlie said. "She says it to everyone. It's the only English she knows."

"Oh my God," Kay giggled, "I thought it was the deepest thing I'd ever heard!"

"It's not un-deep. She changed my life. I don't know how she did it but I bet she changed yours too."

"That hug," Kay agreed. "Somehow that hug convinced me I had to get rid of all the squatters here."

"You do. I met them. Unbelievable. What are you going to do about them?"

"Me? Aren't you going to help me?"

"They're sort of your problem, aren't they, Kay?"

"Yes, but ... "

"You'll figure something out," Charlie said rising. "But you need to get to bed now. You must be jetlagged. We'll talk more in the morning."

We! That wonderful little word again. It continued to echo in Kay's heart as she walked Charlie to the door, kissed her not-so-soft cheek goodnight, staggered upstairs to the tower, got under the covers, and fell into the deepest sleep she'd had in months.

Nick woke her ten hours later. "Mom! Mrs. Hayes is here."

Lois? Had the Board made a decision? So soon? Worried, Kay pulled on her clothes and hurried downstairs. Lois Hayes was pacing back and forth in the Great Room looking uncharacter-istically upset, her hair wild and her blouse untucked. "Did the Board ... ?" Kay began, but Lois interrupted.

"Forget the Board. Their vote doesn't matter anymore. The library's ruined."

Remembering Jolene's dark threat, Kay guessed, "Fire?"

"Worse. Flood."

The story poured out in a torrent. Lois who never, "never!" she repeated, let anyone in after closing time, had opened to admit

Mrs. Holland who claimed she had left her keys on a table inside. Lois waited in front until Mrs. Holland returned and then she locked up and went home. She spent Sunday with her husband and their six Yorkies and didn't go back in again until this morning when she found the reception area flooded in two inches of water. "I should never have left her alone in there," Lois wailed. "I could tell she wasn't right. Her clothes, you know, she was wearing a bathrobe, but she sounded so normal, and she'd run the library so well, for so long, and I just didn't think."

"You came to the right place," Francis said from his chair by the empty parrot perch.

"Did you turn the water off?" Kay asked.

"I couldn't find the water valve. No one answered your phone. So I came right here! I thought you'd know what to do!"

"She does. She's calling the Fire Department right now," Francis said, not looking up from his puzzle, "and then she's taking her son, her ex-husband, her useless brother and two of her no-good boyfriends and following you down there to see how bad it is."

It was pretty bad. The four men whistled and stood in a circle outside shaking their heads and making suggestions while Kay and Nick sloshed through the sludge with Jolene, who was one of the fire captains, and who seemed, to her credit, genuinely upset. They found the faucet Mrs. Holland had not turned off, the plug clogged with rose petals. Kay was relieved to see that no books were ruined, though the volumes on the lower shelves were damp and would need to be treated, but the water had warped the worn hardwood floors, saturated the carpets, whirled around the legs of the battered desks and chairs. The music room was a shallow lake with a single tambourine floating on top of it and the children's area needed to be completely gutted and rebuilt. The library would have to be shut down for two weeks, the fire chief told her, perhaps longer. And there was a very good possibility, Kay knew, that it would not reopen at all.

Later that morning she met with Charlie for a long talk and a few phone calls and that afternoon they co-opted Nick and the three of them cooked a huge Greek meal using some of Eleni's handwritten recipes; then they gathered the men together at the dining room table for dinner. Francis took his place at the head, Nick beside him, and the others straggled in one by one—Biff, barefoot, looking amused, Neal in his overalls, looking bemused, Victor, head down, frowning, Fenton, limping only slightly now, all sitting as far apart from each other as the table allowed. "There's a few extra settings," Victor pointed out.

"Yes, we might be having guests later," Kay answered. "But before they come, I would like to make an announcement." She quickly reviewed the notes she had made that afternoon after skimming the chapter called "No Blame/No Shame" in *The Breaking Up Bible.* Be respectful, she had underlined, be kind, be honest, be firm. Don't attack. Don't defend. Just explain your position, say goodbye and good luck and get out. But what was her position? That none of them had kept their promises to her? Neal hadn't looked for work, Victor hadn't gone to counseling, Biff hadn't left when he'd said he would, none of them had contributed in any meaningful way to groceries or housecleaning. Fenton and Biff had both given illegal drugs to Nick, Victor had taught him how to shoot a gun and Neal had almost killed her with his "invention." Francis, the worst, had out and out lied. She raised a glass filled with sparkling water as Charlie went around the table offering champagne, opened her mouth for the rehearsed farewell speech, closed it, and blurted, "This has been great, guys, but it's over. You're all a bunch of free-loaders and I've been just as bad, staying on here only because I hoped Dad would pay me. We've been living badly, all of us. I am ashamed of myself and I'm volunteering to be the first to break clean and leave the castle. The rest of you can do what you want. Nick and I will be moving out tomorrow."

She gulped, set her glass down and waited, but no one said a word. Victor continued feeding Ed on his lap, Biff continued checking messages on his phone, Neal continued forking everything on his plate into separate heaps, and Fenton continued staring out the window at a hummingbird. Only Francis looked up. "Where are you going?"

"I don't know. I promised you that I would housesit until the castle sold, but you never even put the castle up for sale, did you, so there is absolutely no need for me to stay on."

"Oh, the castle sold months ago." Francis took a sip of his scotch and set his glass down. "You can run along anytime."

"What?"

Kay caught Charlie's eye and warned her, just in time, not to bop Francis on the head with the champagne bottle. "You said you never put it on the market, Dad."

"I didn't. I never had to. Glo's friends, you know. Rich folk. Paid in cash."

"One of Glo's friends bought it?"

"A couple of Glo's friends. Light-in-the-loafers lads. Like your old buddy Charles. They've wanted this place for years but they're on a world tour and can't take possession for a few more months, so in a sense, Kay, you aren't housesitting for me, you are housesitting for them. As am I."

"They bought the castle with all of us in it?"

"The rich are different from you and me."

Kay, stunned, turned to her brother. "Did you know about this?"

"When have I known about anything," Victor said sourly.

"You've tricked me into staying all these months?" Kay could barely breathe.

"Well, I had to wait for the money to clear. You do want your percentage?" Francis said.

"Percentage?" Victor repeated.

"Indeed," Francis said. "Kay, who has maintained the place all these months, more or less adequately, will be getting a large portion of the sales price to mismanage as she wishes; you, Victor, will receive a smaller portion, and I took the liberty of dividing the rest into several trust funds."

"Trust funds for who?" Victor asked.

"For whom. For the grandchildren, of course. Young Nicholas here will have to go to college eventually, unless Kay is thinking of having him play 'Heartbreak Hotel' in subways for the rest of his life, and little Victor or Victoria Junior, whichever you and Stacy produce, will doubtless have special education needs. Now if you don't mind, would someone please get the doorbell?" As Victor, dropping Ed, rose in disgust to answer it, Kay sank into her chair. Her father was helping her after all? Her entire body quivered with relief and rage. What was wrong with Francis? He could have told her this months ago! Why was it so hard for him to just plain be nice? She caught Francis's eye and bit her lip. She was damned if she was going to say thank you.

"Not at all," Francis said, and then, looking up, "Here she is!"

Kay stiffened as Glo, in tailored slacks and a cashmere twin set, her hair a dyed brown helmet above her shiny forehead, strode into the dining room and marched toward Francis who sat up straight, grinning, gripping the arms of his chair. "So!" Glo accosted him with her hands on her hips. "Dr. Deeds tells me you've changed your mind? You want to come home now?"

"Dr. Deeds says that?" Francis asked, and then, recovering himself, "Well of course I do, dear, but it will mean ... "

"I know," Glo snapped. "It will mean nurses, medicine, so what. Do you think I'm a child? I'm your wife! There's nothing I can't do for you that isn't being done here, and I can do it a hell of a lot better." Her voice rose and she turned to the others. *Playing to the audience*, Kay thought. *As theatrical as Mom. And as bad at it.*

My father's taste in women! She winced. *No worse than my choice of men.* Looking up, she saw that Glo was fully in scene now, pacing back and forth, fuming. "How could you, Frankie!" she was saying. She stamped one narrow size 11 foot. "How could you do this to me? Walk out like that? Just take off without so much as a word of farewell … "

"Isn't she marvelous?" Francis's cheeks were flushed, his eyes were glowing. "'Word of farewell.' It's the junk she watches on TV. She can't help it."

"I had to lie to my friends," Glo explained. "I had to go away myself." She wiped her dry eyes and turned to the others. "You all know what he told me? He told me he needed 'time to think things out.' He said he needed to 'find his space.'"

"One talks to the natives in the language of the natives," Francis murmured to Kay, but his eyes were shining as he looked up at Glo.

"He just needed to find out how much he missed you," Charlie said softly.

"Who are you?" Glo spun around. "The nurse?"

"Yes," Charlie said. "I'm the one who phoned you last night."

"Well," Glo snapped, "I'm glad you did."

"I am too," Francis said, his voice husky.

Kay dropped her eyes, ashamed. Calling Glo had been Charlie's idea, not hers. She hadn't wanted her father to go back to Carmel. But look at him. Francis was practically dancing in his chair. And why not? Kay had been relieved when Dr. Deeds said that, thanks to her care, Francis had "a few more months, maybe a year" and why shouldn't he spend that time with his wife?

"I just don't understand, Frankie," Glo was saying, "why you came back *here*. You could have gone anywhere on earth. Why *here?*"

Good question, Kay thought, and then the answer hit her. Her father had come back to the castle to die. *He didn't think Glo, his sheltered-child-bride-golden-girl-debutante, could handle it. But he thought I could? He trusted me enough to die on? He didn't tell me he'd sold the castle because he knew I'd leave? And he didn't want me to leave? He wanted me to be with him?* She looked at Francis, who was rising from his chair now, his eyes bright, his cheeks flushed, his lips turned up as Glo shook her finger in his face.

"Bad boy!" Glo said.

"Very bad," Francis agreed.

Glo slapped at him and received in return, to Kay's amazement, a healthy pinch on the rear. Glo yelped prettily and slapped at Francis again. Her voice moved up and down but her strangely stretched and shiny features, Kay noticed, did not. Glo had not been at any "spiritual retreat" these last few weeks. She'd been having a facelift. Not a good one either. She'd probably needed two.

"We're going to get you back where you belong," Glo said to Francis, and, turning to Fenton, purred, "I'll need some strong arms settling him in the car. Victor, dear, could you wheel out his oxygen tank? Neal, dear, would you please move your van out of the driveway so I can park closer to the front door? Nicholas, dear, would you mind walking me to the door? All this excitement has left me feeling a little faint. You sir," holding a hand out to Biff, and dropping her eyes, with interest, to his bare feet, "may keep the parrot. Kay, I suppose I should say thank you."

"Not at all," Kay said.

"She wasn't even here half the time," Francis agreed. He turned, gave a gallant bow to the group, and offered his arm to Glo, who took it. "Let's get out of this hellhole, shall we, m'dear? Oh," he added, turning to Kay, "remember to call that vet up in Oxalis, will you? He phoned several times. Seemed to want to talk to you about something, I don't know, I wasn't listening."

"Yes, you were," Kay said.

"Stay good," Francis grinned and stepped lightly away.

"Dessert anyone?" Charlie asked. She brought out the apple cake Kay had baked that afternoon and set it down on the dining room table, as Kay, exhausted, sat staring at her father's empty place. "More guests!" Charlie added brightly as Ed, in a sudden flurry of barking, leapt from Victor's arms and raced toward Stacy, who entered, demure, followed by a ruddy-faced man who must be Pastor Paulsen. Kay had talked to him for a long time last night; she had liked his matter-of-fact voice and the easy way he had agreed to intervene. Smiling, Stacy bent, gathered the delirious little dog up, and pressed him to her pregnant belly, then stood still as Victor, pale-faced, rose without a word, stepped toward her, stumbled, and fell to his knees.

It took him a long time to say it, but say it he finally did. "Forgive me," he said.

It was touching—no, Kay decided, it was scary—the way Stacy's white pink-tipped hand touched the top of Victor's bent golden head just as a ray of late summer sunlight lit both their figures. Pastor Paulsen stood behind them in benediction. They looked like three angels. Was it love of God that was prompting this reunion? Love of each other? Or, knowing he couldn't access those trust funds without claiming his baby, Victor's love of money?

"Shame on you. Don't be so cynical," Charlie whispered, then, turning to the others, "Shall we take coffee out by the pool?"

"None for me." Biff already had his duffle on his back, his banjo strapped around his shoulders, his guitar and trumpet cases in hand. "I'm outta here. Kay, walk me to my car?"

Still asking her to do things for him? Well, why not. He was leaving. She could say goodbye. "I've always cared for you, Karoony," he said as she helped him load his things into his trunk. "I wish ... well. I'll never forget what you've given me."

"What have I given you?" Kay asked, curious.

"Shelter from the storm, baby, shelter from the storm."

His gray eyes crinkled and for a second Kay remembered how she had adored him, this barefoot troubadour who had dazzled his professors and stolen every student's heart. He'd had so much promise back in the Conservatory. And yet here he was, standing by a dusty dented car, happily heading off to play church music in small town bars, doing no better with his gifts than she had, but perhaps enjoying them more. Perhaps playing his life better. "You've done a lot for me too," she admitted. They stood in silence, listening to the night sounds around them, a splash from the swimming pool as someone, Charlie probably, dove in, Nick's still-tentative guitar chords, the murmur of Pastor Paulson's steady voice as he led Stacy and Victor out the front door.

"Yep, we're a pair," Biff said at last. "We'll see each other again, you know that, don't you? We're not through."

I'm through, Kay thought but she lifted her face for his last kiss, light and sweet. As he slipped into his car, Kay saw a girl's tank top on the seat beside him. Too small to be Chiana's. Goodbye Chiana. She waved goodbye and turned, startled as always, to see Neal right behind her.

"Over him?" Neal asked, standing too close.

"Long ago."

"Good. I didn't like the way he acted around Nicky."

"How did he act around Nick?"

"Like he was Nicky's age. I don't like the way Fenton acts either, like he's Daniel Boone, and I don't like the way your father never let Nicky win a single video game."

"Dad's like that."

"At least Francis came through with your money. You're set now, aren't you, babe. I won't have to worry about you anymore."

"You worry about me ... ?"

"Why do you think I've been staying on here?"

"Because you didn't have any other place else to go?"

Neal gave his silent laugh. "I've got Padma's place."

"Who's Padma?"

"Huh. I thought I told you about her."

"Tell me now."

Lips parted, Kay listened as Neal told her that the health food store had been rebuilt and was about to reopen, that he would be managing the juice and salad bars along with a co-worker, a widowed Indian woman whom he'd been "sort of seeing" for a few months now. "The only thing I still worry about," Neal finished, frowning, "is Fenton. You're not going to marry him, are you?"

"No one is going to marry Fenton," Kay assured him.

"Good. Because he isn't right for you. You know that, don't you."

"I do."

Neal laughed indulgently. "Little Kay," he said, and with a final pat of her hair he went off toward the garden with a flashlight and a bucket to handpick slugs. Kay was about to join Charlie in the pool when she heard a familiar cough and saw Fenton limping down the driveway.

"Look who I found on my night walk," Fenton said, stepping forward with Raj on his arm. "Flew right to me."

"Ugh," Kay said, stepping back. "Can you keep him?"

"Nah. Not where I'm going."

"Where are you going?"

"Thought I'd head out up to Alaska."

"Why Alaska?"

"Why *Alaska*?" Fenton's big laugh. "Hiking, fishing, skiing, hunting, that's why Alaska. I've had a chance to do a lot of reading while I've been here and all those books you brought me from the library have made me think I might start looking for jobs in wildlife management. Might find something there. Here. Try him."

Fenton held his arm out and Raj, unperturbed, hopped off it and onto Kay's shoulders, his talons lightly gripping the same sore spot that Fenton used to massage so effectively. Kay shuddered, but the bird felt natural, sitting there, so alert and dissatisfied it was like having a second head. Something I've always needed, she thought. Maybe I can teach him some new words, she thought. Maybe I can teach him to say no.

SIX MONTHS LATER

The garden in back of the small ranch house caught the morning sun and was perfect for Kay's daily salutations. She could do six in a row now that her shoulder was healing from the operation, although her feet still scrambled for purchase on the yoga mat and she often forgot to breathe. Raj, from his perch, watched as she straightened and steadied herself. "Namaste," she prompted him, hoping today at last he'd repeat it, but the bird only coughed. Donald Wallace said the cough meant Raj missed Francis, as she did, as Nick did, as even Glo, off on another "retreat," surely did. Thinking of Donald, Kay smiled. He would drive down from Oxalis tonight to spend the weekend with her and Nick, and after her AA meeting he would help her and Zabeth and Dana set the West Valley library up for its gala reopening next week. The flood insurance—which Mrs. Holland had arranged for years ago—had paid much more than anyone expected, and that had been enough to convince the Board to keep the branch open, at least for another few years, until Kay could figure out a way to make it pay for itself. She had already started interviewing other beleaguered smalltown librarians across the country and had picked up some good ideas.

Six Months Later

The doorbell sounded and, still smiling, Kay yanked up her pajamas and went to answer it, pausing in the living room to take in the bright curtains, the refinished Chickering piano, the deep-seated comfortable chairs, the vases of flowers and walls of books. She paused before the photo Eleni had sent of a heavily mustached young man sitting in front of a computer with a sleek white cat on his lap before calling to Nick that it was time to get up. She opened the front door, glad to see Charlie so early in the day, but puzzled too. Her old friend, propping her bike against the porch railing, looked upset and tearful, her eyes red and her chin trembling.

"What is it?" Kay asked, stepping forward. "What's the matter?"

"My studio! I've lost my lease. I have to move. The landlord wants me out today. I have nowhere to go!"

Kay thought quickly. The ranch house only had two bedrooms but she could give Charlie hers. It would mean sleeping on the couch. It would mean giving up nights alone with Donald. There was room in the garage for Charlie's furniture, paints and easels. It would be inconvenient but no major hardship and it wouldn't be for long. "It's all right," she began, "you can stay here."

Suddenly Charlie laughed. "Joke," she said.

Kay, unsmiling, endured the hug. *Your friend like joke*, Eleni had said. Okay. But shouldn't jokes be funny? She stepped back inside and shut the door in Charlie's face. She could hear her still laughing as she went out to the back yard, raised her arms to the sky, took a deep breath and, once again, attempted to salute the sun.

263

THE AUTHOR

MOLLY GILES is the award-winning author of five story collections and two novels. Her last work, *Wife With Knife* won the Leapfrog Global Fiction Prize. *Rough Translations* won The Flannery O'Connor Prize, the Boston Globe Award, and The Bay Area Book Reviewers' Award; *Creek Walk* won The Small Press Best Fiction Award, the California Commonwealth Silver Medal for Fiction, and was a New York Times Notable Book; *Bothered* won the Split Oak Press Flash Fiction Award; and *All The Wrong Places* won the Spokane Prize for Fiction. Her work has also earned The O. Henry Award and the Pushcart Prize, and she has received grants from the National Endowment for the Arts, the Marin Arts Council, and the Arkansas Arts Council.

ACKNOWLEDGMENTS

This book is dedicated to Ellen Levine, who patiently guided me through countless drafts; I am very grateful for her support and wisdom. Warm thanks too to all HOME's early readers: Rosaleen Bertolino, Masie Cochran, Kristin Iversen, Emily Kaitz, Susan Keller, Terese Svoboda, Susan Trott, Debra Turner, and Stephen Winn. Rebecca Cuthbert was a dream editor and I am indebted to the entire staff at Leapfrog Press. I could not have persevered with this book without the courageous example of my late mother, Doris Murphy, and the loving support of my partner, Ralph Brott.

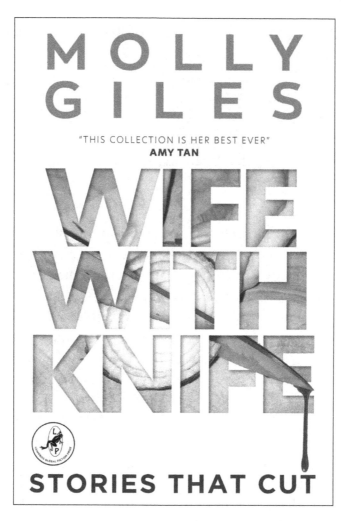

MOLLY GILES

"THIS COLLECTION IS HER BEST EVER"
AMY TAN

WIFE WITH KNIFE

STORIES THAT CUT

Wife With Knife won the 2021 Leapfrog Global Fiction Prize

Molly Giles' stories have always been among my favorites since I first read her work thirty-seven years ago. This collection is her best ever. What an irreverent original voice! I found myself gasping in shock and laughter, feeling at the end of each tale that I had garnered strange wisdom on the human heart and its unerring sense for finding trouble.

Amy Tan, author of *The Joy Luck Club*

The following short story from *Wife With Knife*, "Bad Dog" won the Pushcart Prize.

BAD DOG

Whiskery tub of muscle with flicks of spit and slime shot from spotted tongue and slick pink dick. Sly beggar eyes, wheedler's grin. The forelegs stiff in bossy supplication, the butt high, the propeller whirl of tail, the dance in place at the door, the stench of slept-in, spit-on hair and hide, the yellow sulfur farts, the bared teeth, the fetid breath, the slobber, the snuffle, the hurry up yip. Let him out! Let him in! Don't leave him here, secure in the house, warm in the car, safe in the yard! Take him with you! Let him dog you! Take the stick! Throw the stick! Take the stick again! Throw the stick again! Walk him! Not here! There! Not there! Unleash him, free him, see him circle, snarl, fight, bite, pee in six places, chase cars, attack strangers, spook horses, unseat cyclists, break the necks of sunning cats, gulp dead birds, roll in cow shit, chase squirrels up power lines, pack with Scout and Maggie and Bobo to bring down a fawn or a city child alone on the corner. Pick his dung up. Sack it. Schlep it. Pet him! Praise him! Feed him! Feed him horsemeat, cowmeat, chickenmeat, pig-meat, ratmeat, catmeat, zoomeat, roadkill, dogmeat! Gulp! Gone! Watch him gnaw the menstrual goo from your twelve-year-old's gym shorts, slop the snot off the baby's face, dig up the dahlias, bury the hiking shoe, chew the ankles of the antique bedpost, hump the limp leg of the Alzheimer patient, pull your guests' dinner off the dining room table, knock the vase down, flee as china and crystal crash to the tiles, plead guilty with hope-stricken eyes. Bad dog, good dog, come dog. Sit. Beg. Heel. Roll over. Down. Clown! you say. Comrade! Confidante! How cute he is! How clever, how comic. Look how he loves me! But how can he love you? He doesn't know you! He doesn't know you lied to your lover, stole from your mother, slapped your sister, abused your child, cheated your boss, falsified your taxes, perjured yourself in court, slashed your enemy's tires, slept with your best friend's spouse, betrayed your business partner, vandalized your neighbor, hit a pedestrian, slandered a co-worker—he does not know that you have behaved, all your life, in fact, like a dog—nor does he care. His interests are not your interests. His thoughts are not your thoughts. His dreams are of hunt, quarry, catch, and kill. His strange brain is at secret work in your house all night. Is it your house? Whose ghost startles your dog on the stair? Why does he bark at the mirror? What does he hear when the kitchen clock stills? Those claw marks high on the lintel of the locked door—where did those come from? And the flash of his moon-sharp teeth when you call? The grin of an exile, far from his kind, slavish, obedient, biding his time.

"My X" also from *Wife With Knife* will be included in *Flash Fiction America: 73 Very Short Stories*. (Norton)

MY X

My X never finishes his sentences. He'll start off with a "Did you see..." and then stop. When we first met, I thought it was charming. I'd prompt him. "Did I see what, darling?" Silence. After we were married, less charmed, I'd jump in with my own offerings: "Did I see the full moon last night, did I see the red dog, did I see the fat man in drag?" I was never right. My X would listen, correct me, and disappear. He could, literally, disappear, an act that should have made us money. "I think I'll go..." he'd say, and I'd chip in with a hopeful, "...to the store?" only to hear him say "...to India." One minute he'd be standing next to me and the next minute he'd be in a cab heading out to some seaport or in bed asleep or in the garden watering the roses he claimed I never took care of. At the end, in the lawyers' office, when I admitted that I never knew where he went, what he did, or whom he did it with, he shook his head sadly and said that was because I could not read his mind. "She's so..." he said to the lawyer.

"...exhausted," the lawyer and I said together.

"...impatient," he said.

It was true. And why not. Years had passed and I still didn't know him. In fact, that was what he often said to me: *You'll never know how much I love you* he'd say, and then, not unkindly, he'd laugh.

After the divorce there were sightings. A friend saw him in an art museum trying on silk scarves. My sister saw him pass her on the bridge in a silver Jaguar. A neighbor heard him talking Farsi with an Iranian rug dealer. We decided he either worked for the CIA or the FBI or the DEA or all three of them. Just last week, five years after our divorce, I bumped into him in a bookstore; he was standing in a corner reading the obituaries in *The New York Times* out loud to himself. He was dressed in surfer shorts and a hoodie. He had grown a mustache and had a pair of mirrored sunglasses on.

"Hi," I said.

He looked up, unsurprised. "Oh hi," he answered. "How are…"

"I'm fine," I said.

"…the roses?"

I took a deep breath. He looked thin and raggedy. It occurred to me he might be homeless.

"I'm having the Witherspoons over for lunch on Sunday," I said. "Our old neighbors. Would you like to come?"

"Do they still have their two…"

"Poodles? Yes."

"…timing son-in-law living with them?"

"Lunch is at noon," I said. "And I never slept with their son-in-law if that's what you're thinking."

"How do you know…"

"What you're thinking?"

"…whether he's still living with them or not."

"Noon," I repeated.

I was shaking when I left.

Sunday came and of course no X. The Witherspoons and I had barbecue and gin and tonics and had just settled into the living room to watch the U.S. Open when the poodles started barking and the son-in-law said, "There's a man in your back yard." I shrugged his hand off my thigh and stood up. My X was in the garden watering the roses. It was as if no time had passed. I went out to him.

"Did you see…" he said.

"No," I said. "I didn't. Hand me that hose please."

He handed me the hose and I aimed the nozzle straight at him and the blast was so strong it knocked him butt-down and his fake mustache flew off. For a second I exulted. Then because I'm an idiot I dropped the hose and went to help him up but he tripped me and I fell down hard beside him as the water spiraled fast and cold over both of us. He wrapped his arms around me and rocked us back and forth on the grass, laughing, and I felt his old male strength and smelled his sour green apple smell and for a second I was almost happy again. By the time I pushed him off and shook myself and stood, of course, nothing was left but a trail of damp footsteps in the grass, a thread from his hoodie snagged on the gate, tire marks on the curb. I ran out to the street as his bike rounded the corner, took my shoe off, threw it, missed. The last thing I heard was his voice, faint on the wind. "Don't worry dear, it's not…"

"Funny," I shouted.

"Over," he said, and disappeared.